Cassia was waiting, as he'd known she'd be.

She gave a little toss of her head, shaking the loose curls back from her face. She looked exhausted, too, with bluish circles beneath her eyes, though she'd drawn her shoulders back and straight. He wondered how her wrist felt; he wondered what she thought of him now, having come so close to gambling her away.

"Well, now, Richard," she said, as if they were standing alone and discussing the morning milk, instead of here, with a curious crowd surging around them. "I suppose you've come to claim your stake."

RAKE'S WAGER

Miranda Jarrett

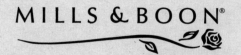

MILLS & BOON®

First published in Great Britain 2007
Harlequin Mills & Boon Limited,
Eton House, 18-24 Paradise Road, Richmond, Surrey TW9 1SR

© Miranda Jarrett 2005

ISBN-13: 978 0 263 85169 4
ISBN-10:   0 263 85169 9

Set in Times Roman 10½ on 12¼ pt.
04-0407-76389

Printed and bound in Spain
by Litografia Rosés S.A., Barcelona

Award-winning author **Miranda Jarrett** considers herself sublimely fortunate to have a career that combines history and happy endings—even if it's one that's also made her family far-too-regular patrons of the local pizzeria. Miranda is a graduate of Brown University, with a degree in art history. She and her husband, a musician, live near Philadelphia, with their two small children and two large dogs. She loves to hear from readers at PO Box 1102, Paoli, PA 19301-1145, USA, or MJarrett21@aol.com

Recent novels by the same author:

PRINCESS OF FORTUNE
THE SILVER LORD
THE GOLDEN LORD

Look for Bethany Penny's story in
THE LADY'S HAZARD
Coming soon

Chapter One

Woodbury, Sussex, England
1806

Cassia Penny sat with her spine pressed tight against the ladder-back chair, her fingers squeezing her handkerchief into a soggy linen knot in her lap. The cheap black bombazine for grieving cut into her throat and wrists, the cloth so hot and wrong on this early spring day that she could feel the sweat inside her gown trickling down her arms and between her breasts and along the backs of her knees above her garters. Though she kept her head high like her two sisters on either side of her were doing, her eyes burned from weeping, and it would take next to nothing to make her cry again.

She was only twenty, yet she felt as if part of her life had died, too. Nothing would ever be the same again, not for any of them.

Mr. Grosse, the solicitor, sat at her father's now

empty desk, using one finger to square the stacked papers of the will into tidy precision.

"I regret to say that your lives must change, ladies." He heaved a mournful sigh appropriate for the day. "Though that should come as no real surprise, considering your father's vocation."

"We know our father was a country vicar, Mr. Grosse," Amariah said, each word clipped sharp, the way they always were whenever anyone dared cross Cassia's eldest sister. "We are humbled and awed by the legacy which he has left behind on this earth, and the reward that is certainly now his in heaven."

Unimpressed, Mr. Grosse looked at her over his glasses. "Alas, Miss Amariah, such good works accumulate little interest in the bank, and your father's generosity made it impossible for him to save."

"Father was a kind, good, *fine* gentleman, Mr. Grosse," Cassia protested, rising to her feet, "and I— *we*—won't hear you say otherwise!"

At once Bethany's hand found Cassia's arm, gently pressing her back into her chair. "Mr. Grosse is only stating the truth, Cassia. Father never did worry about acquiring worldly goods, just as we never expected him to leave much of an estate."

"But we never expected him to die this soon, either." Cassia sank back into her seat, once again fighting back her tears. Father had been only forty-five; who would have guessed that so great a heart would stop so suddenly, there while he pulled the first spring weeds in the kitchen garden?

"That is why we've already begun to plan our future,

Cassia." Amariah's smile was sad, true, but also filled with a confidence that Cassia couldn't share. "Father always trusted us to find our way through life, and we shall."

"You'll have to find it away from this cottage, Miss Amariah." Mr. Grosse sighed again. "Sir Cleveland has already informed me that the new vicar will be arriving shortly. He will wish to reside here, as is due with his living. Sir Cleveland regrets the seeming haste of your eviction, but he—"

"He *says* he is most concerned for the spiritual needs of the congregation." Again Cassia sniffed back her tears. "And he is most concerned, too, for that nephew of his who's always wished to take poor Father's place, the greedy piglet!"

"Cassia." From Amariah that was warning enough. "Such talk does not honor Father's memory."

Hastily Cassia looked down to her lap, knowing that Amariah was right, the way she always was. It didn't matter that this rambling cottage with its rose garden and duck pond had been the only home that any of them had known, or that they now must part and leave it forever. She needed to be strong and brave like her sisters, and look toward the future, not the past.

Even if she'd no idea what or where that future might be.

Mr. Grosse glanced around the library, noting the crates and trunks that were already swallowing up Father's books and belongings. "Have you made provisions to remove your things and reside with another family member or friend?"

Bethany smiled serenely. "God helps those who help themselves, Mr. Grosse. Father shared his love of accomplishment and knowledge with us, and we intend to use those gifts to support ourselves."

Mr. Grosse looked relieved to be spared the guilt of shoving the dead vicar's daughters into the lane. "You have made plans, then?"

Amariah nodded, all brisk efficiency despite her new mourning. "I am considering an offer from Mr. and Mrs. Whiteside to serve as governess to their daughters at Rushington."

"And Lady Elverston has invited me to be her special companion at Elverston Hall." Bethany clasped her hands before her with becoming modesty, as if she couldn't believe her good fortune. "She most kindly recalled both my play upon the pianoforte and the little suppers I'd arrange for Father and his friends, and she believes such talents would do well at Elverston."

"How excellent," Mr. Grosse said with approval. "And you, Miss Cassia? Have you determined your future?"

Cassia's head bowed a little lower. She wasn't accomplished the way that Amariah and Bethany were. The things she did best—dressing bonnets and remaking gowns into cunning new fashions, or arranging the Yule greenery in the church to look like a magical Sherwood Forest, or telling silly stories that made the young gentlemen laugh and cluster around her and beg for dances at the Havertown Assembly each month—were not the things that could earn her way in the world, at least not as an honest young lady of good reputation, as the Penny sisters had of course been raised to be.

But it had been more than enough while Father still lived, when she'd been his little popinjay and made him laugh until the tears had streamed down his cheeks when he should have been writing his sermons....

"Cassia will find something soon enough, I am sure," Amariah said quickly, answering for her. "It is early days for us all, Mr. Grosse."

"Indeed, indeed." Mr. Grosse frowned down at the papers before him. "But I do have a certain revelation to make that might ease the immediacy of your situation. To be sure, it may not be the most welcome news, reflecting as it does upon your father's integrity. But then we can keep everything within this room, among us and no further."

Her heart beating faster at the thought of more bad news, Cassia inched forward to the edge of her chair. "A revelation, sir? About Father?"

"Yes, Miss Cassia." He turned to another sheet. "Your father wanted this kept separate from the rest of the will, but I assure you that the inheritance is perfectly legal nonetheless."

He cleared his throat, looking from one sister to the next. "Long, long ago, a grateful and repentant member of your father's flock left your father his greatest single possession...a private, ah, social club in London."

"A social club?" Cassia shook her head. "Father never cared for Society. What would he do with a social club?"

Mr. Grosse cleared his throat with a delicate, embarrassed cough. "There is little society at a London social club, Miss Cassia. That is the polite name. The other one for such a place is a—forgive me, pray—a gambling hell."

"*Father?*"

"Yes." Hastily Mr. Grosse looked back down at his papers. "But while most men would have sold such a dubious bequest, your father saw it as a gift from heaven, a way for him to make right from wrong. He allowed the house's activities to continue, contributing all the profits to the welfare of orphans and widows, particularly those who had come to sorrow from gambling."

Cassia pressed her fingers to her mouth. As worldly as Father was about some matters, he'd never countenanced any form of wagers or other games of risk and chance. Yet now it seemed that in London he'd owned an entire house devoted to exactly that. How ever had he kept such a secret for so long?

"Father owned a private gaming club, Mr. Grosse?" Amariah's brows arched with disbelief. "In London? *Our* father?"

"I am afraid so, Miss Amariah." Mr. Grosse shook his head. "I know such news much come as a great shock, after what—"

"Is this gaming club in a prosperous neighborhood?" Bethany asked. "If this is true, then Father must have viewed his involvement as being a latter-day Robin Hood—that he would take from the rich to help those less fortunate. I cannot imagine him doing it otherwise."

Mr. Grossed glanced down, shuffling through the papers. "I believe the club is in St. James Street, a thoroughly respectable address for such a, ah, such a business. Its name is Whitaker's, though who Mr. Whitaker is or was seems long forgotten. Oh, here we are—a view of the club from the street."

He pushed an engraving across the desk toward them, and Amariah took it, tipping the sheet so her sisters could see as well.

"It's quite a handsome facade, isn't it?" Cassia volunteered, not quite sure what else to say. Accustomed as she was to how the vicarage nestled into the green Sussex hills, this town house seemed as welcoming as a cold block of ice, locked tight between its neighbors. The walls appeared to be stone, three floors high, and the tall, square windows without shutters made the front seem even more severe. A solitary gentleman in an old-fashioned cocked hat pointed his walking stick at the unwelcoming entry, four shallow steps and a plain front door.

"It *is* handsome," agreed Mr. Grosse. "And from what I can gather, Whitaker's was once a favorite of gentlemen of the highest quarter of society, even peers of the realm and officers of the Crown."

Amariah looked up from the illustration. "But it is no longer?"

Mr. Grosse shrugged, hedging. "Not what it once was, no. As an absentee owner, your father let it deteriorate a bit over time. But the property itself is still sound, and finding a buyer should prove no difficulty, at a price that shall allay much of your current distress."

"But were those Father's wishes, Mr. Grosse?" Cassia asked, still looking at the grim stone house in the picture. "Did he wish us to sell this—this property of his, or were we to continue to let it do his good works?"

"Yes, Mr. Grosse, you must tell us that." Now Bethany was perched on the very edge of her chair, and Cassia wondered if she, too, was daring to think the same thing. "'Balancing the scales of our modern society' was a favorite theme of his for sermons. If he had been granted such an excellent vehicle for balancing those scales, I scarcely think he'd want us to abandon it now."

"Yes, yes," Amariah said. "And if the neighborhood is as respectable as you say, we could reside there ourselves, too, and be self-sufficient. Surely Father would wish that for us, too. Oh, yes, Mr. Grosse, we must consider this from every angle."

"I cannot say I agree." Mr. Grosse frowned and shook his head, scattering a fine dust from his gray-powdered wig. "It is unusual enough for a country vicar to pursue such an endeavor, Miss Amariah, but for three virtuous young ladies to continue in such a role, to choose to live above such a den of despair and depravity—why, such a thing is not to be done, and I should counsel you most strongly against it."

"Is it outside the law, Mr. Grosse?" Cassia asked. The town house in the picture wasn't close to being her idea of a home, but surely she and her sisters together could make it into one. "Are women forbidden ownership of such clubs?"

"There is no legal reason against it, no, but for the sake of propriety, such an arrangement would be most irregular, most—"

"Is there more you are not telling us, Mr. Grosse?" Amariah ran her fingers lightly across the illustration, as if touching it would make it more real. "Is the house being used for other, more disreputable activities?"

"Good gracious, no, Miss Amariah!" The solicitor's

face flushed a shocked purple at her suggestion. "Gaming is all—and disreputable enough for a lady such as yourself!"

"The world can *be* disreputable, Mr. Grosse, even for ladies." Amariah rose, shaking out her black skirts, and Cassia and Bethany quickly followed. "Would you please excuse us for a few minutes, Mr. Grosse?"

Grumbling to himself, Mr. Grosse had no choice but to leave them, turning his eyes toward the heavens with a hearty sigh as he shut the door.

"Well, now." Amariah sat in a muted rush of bombazine. "I cannot tell if Father has left us a prize, or only a puzzle."

"A prize—a *great* prize!" Cassia paced back and forth across the carpet, unable to keep the enthusiasm from her voice. "He has given us not only a way to support ourselves, but also a way to continue his work! And think of living in London, the greatest city in the world!"

"What I'm thinking, Cassia, is how very much we must learn." Amariah held up her hand, ticking off each ignorance on a new finger. "We have only visited London a few times, and know nothing of the city or its workings. We have no friends there, no one to turn to for advice or answers. We wouldn't even know where to find a butcher or mantua maker. And we haven't the faintest notion of how a gaming club such as this Whitaker's operates, or how it generates its money."

"We could learn, Amariah." Bethany smiled eagerly. "We are not fools."

Amariah glared at her for interrupting. "But we could turn into the greatest fools imaginable with this, Bethany. We don't know the managers of this club, or whether Father's trust in their abilities is well-founded. Even Mr. Grosse admitted that the club was no longer as profitable as it had been."

Cassia swept her hand through the air as if to sweep away her sister's objections, too. "Then we shall hire people who can improve it!"

"Where would we find such people, Cassia?" Amariah raised her hands. "Why, we don't even know how to play the wicked games that would be supporting us and Father's charities!"

"We can learn," Cassia insisted. "Think of all the things that Father taught us, Latin and Greek and geography and mathematics and all the rest that girls weren't supposed to be able to understand. We thought he was teasing when he'd said that knowledge would be our dowries, but perhaps he wasn't teasing at all."

Amariah looked back at the paper in her hands and frowned. "This would be vastly different from translating *The Iliad* for Father."

"It would, and it wouldn't," Cassia said. "Consider how quick you are at ciphering and figuring numbers in your head. I'm certain you could learn the games and oversee the accounts."

Bethany nodded, tapping her fingers on the arm of the chair with excitement. "From what I have read in the London papers, much of the success of catering to gentlemen is to give them a grand and comfortable place for their mischief. They can gamble anywhere, but they would return to our club if the food and drink are better than anywhere else."

"Which it would be, Bethany, if you were overseeing the kitchen," Cassia said, giving an excited little clap of her hands. "None of those fou-fou Frenchmen in Elverston's kitchen can hold a candle to your cooking, and you know it."

Amariah sighed—not exactly with resignation, not yet, but close. "And what role have you cut out for yourself, Cassia?"

Cassia raised her chin and smiled. She wasn't nearly as useless as she'd feared at first. She'd only had to find her place.

"I would make the club *beyond* fashion," she declared. "I would make it so original a place that everyone who wasn't there would give their eyeteeth to be able to say they were. It wouldn't be a hell once we'd done with it. "

"Cassia." Amariah groaned. "And who knows more about setting the London fashion than three vicars' daughters from Woodbury?"

"Three *handsome* daughters," Cassia said, and as if on cue the three of them glanced across the room to the round looking glass over the fireplace. Even in mourning, with their eyes red from weeping and their copper-colored hair drawn severely back from their faces, they were a striking trio: Amariah the eldest and tallest, with the bearing of a duchess; sweet-faced Bethany in the middle; and Cassia herself, Father's little popinjay, with her round cheeks and startled blue eyes.

"You can't pretend we're not handsome," Cassia continued, "because we are, or at least handsome enough, thanks to us all having Father's red hair with Mama's face. Everyone says so. Wouldn't we make you curious if you were a bored London beau?"

"Flirting with the squire's sons at the Havertown Assembly isn't the same as matching wits with London rakes," Amariah said. "We could be terribly at sea, Cassia, and not in a good way, either."

"Then the more proper we are, Amariah," Cassia said, dipping her skirts in an excruciatingly correct curtsey, "the more mysterious and exotic we'll seem to them, on account of being proper in a wicked world. And we could change the name, too, to make it our own. We could call it Penny House."

"Penny House!" Bethany exclaimed with relish. "Oh, Cassia, I do like that!"

Amariah set the picture of the club back down on the desk, and pressed her palms to her cheeks.

"I cannot believe we are having such a conversation with poor Father scarcely gone," she said softly. "London, and a gaming house named after ourselves, and whether to flirt or not with wicked men—oh, what would Father say to that?"

"He—he would call us his flock of silly geese," Cassia said, her voice squeaking with a fresh rush of emotion. "And then he would tell us to go do what we believed was right and just, the way he would do for himself. The way he always did."

Bethany came and stood between them, slipping her hands into theirs. Together they stared solemnly down at the picture of Whitaker's, sitting on Father's desk.

"We would be together in London," Cassia said. "We

wouldn't have to go different ways. Father would have liked that, too."

Bethany nodded. "If we go there and find that London doesn't suit us, then we can still sell, as Mr. Grosse wishes."

"But it *will* suit us," Cassia said quickly. "And if it doesn't, we'll *make* it suit us."

"Of course we will, Cassia, just like that. All London will bow at the feet of the Penny sisters." Amariah sighed. "You know, I never did want to look after those dreadful Whiteside girls."

Bethany looked up, her eyes bright with triumph. "And I do believe Lady Elverson will survive without hearing me play for her each night."

Cassia gasped, not quite believing her sisters had agreed. "Then we will go? We'll take Father's legacy, and make it our own?"

"To London." Finally Amariah smiled, and nodded. "It seems that, in his way, that is what Father wished us to do."

"To London!" Cassia crowed, and raised their joined hands together. "To London, and to Penny House!"

Chapter Two

Four months later
London

Richard Blackley leaned closer to the painting, inspecting the surface for cracks to better judge its age. He didn't give a fig whether the painting was two hundred years old, or two weeks, nor would he recognize the difference, except for how high the auctioneer might try to run the bidding. He glanced back at the listing in the exhibition catalog: *The Fortune Teller,* Italian, Sixteenth Century.

That made him smile. The smirking old woman was a bawd if ever he'd seen one, taking the last coin that poor sot in the foreground had in his pocket, while he was busy gaping at the strumpet in the scarlet turban at the window. It was the strumpet he liked best, with her sloe-eyed, sleepy glance and creamy bare breasts. He knew just the place for her, in his dressing room at

Greenwood, where she'd amuse him while he was shaved.

He drew a small star before the picture's number in the catalog. Generally he didn't care one way or the other about pictures, but this was one he didn't want to let slip away. What was the use of being a rich man if he couldn't buy himself a painting that made him smile?

"Excuse me, sir." A young woman had eased her way through the crowd of other viewers here for the exhibition before the auction, and she now stood squeezed between Richard and the painting—his painting. "I didn't mean to bump you."

"Forgiven," he said, lifting his hat to her as he smiled. It was easy to smile at her: she was a pretty little creature, with bright blue eyes and golden-red hair that her plain dark mourning bonnet seemed to highlight rather than mask. Whom did she grieve for, he wondered idly: a husband, parent, sibling? "Though to be honest, I hadn't noticed that you'd bumped me at all."

"Well, sir, I did," she said, "so of course I had to apologize, to make things right. It would be rude of me not to."

She stated it as simple fact, a fact that he wasn't sure how to answer, but because she was such a pretty little creature, he wanted to. She wasn't being forward, the way a demirep might be to attract his notice; in fact, if Richard was honest, she didn't really seem interested in him at all. Instead her whole attention seemed focused on the painting before him, and to his dismay she was marking a circle around the same number in her catalog as he had in his.

"You are bidding on this picture, miss?" he asked. "You like it that much?"

"That is the reason one usually comes here to Christie's Auction Rooms, isn't it? To bid on the pictures one likes?" She darkened the circle around the listing for emphasis. "Last week I sold three dreary paintings of peasants with cows, and now I plan to reward myself by buying this one."

"For yourself?" he asked, surprised. It didn't seem like the kind of painting a young lady—she couldn't be more than twenty—would choose for herself.

"It's my choice, yes, though I'm sure my sisters will find it amusing as well." She leaned closer, studying the surface just as Richard himself had done. "I don't believe it's as old as they're claiming—it's likely a copy, and not even an Italian one—but the fortune teller in particular is very nicely done, I think."

"They got that wrong in the catalog, too," he said. "If that old crone's a fortune teller, why, then I'll— then I'll—"

His words trailed off as he realized his mistake, the kind of mistake that true English gentlemen weren't supposed to make when addressing English ladies.

"Then what else could she be?" The young woman's eyes were as blue as the Caribbean itself, and just as ready to swallow him up. "The smiling soldier had just given her his payment, and now she's holding his hand as she reads his palm, while the other woman watches. His future must be improving, for him to look so jolly. Good fortune overcoming bad. That, sir, is why I wish to buy this particular picture."

She turned away from him and toward the next picture, and he joined her, unwilling to lose her yet.

"You speak as if from experience," he said, happy to let her think what she wished about the old procuress in the painting. "About good luck and bad, that is."

"There's not a person on earth that's not had experience with luck of both kinds." She glanced at him sideways, up through her lashes, and without turning her head. "Unless, sir, you are among those who don't believe in it?"

"If you mean sitting idle beside a stream and waiting for my luck to change, then, no, I do not," he said. "But I do believe in seizing the opportunities that fate offers, and making them my own."

She raised one arched brow, and laughed, a merry, bubbling sound that he instantly wished to hear again.

"That's bold talk, sir," she said, "quite worthy of Bonaparte himself."

"It's not empty talk," he insisted, "nor was it meant to show sympathy to the French. It's how I live my life."

"I didn't say your words were empty. I said they were bold, which is a very different thing altogether." She moved to stand before the next painting, and Richard followed. Clever women like this one hadn't existed on Barbados, or at least none in the society that had allowed him, too. "You must enjoy gambling."

He frowned a little, not following her logic.

"I've become good at spotting gentleman gamesters, you see," she explained with an inexplicable triumph in her voice, as if spotting gamesters were a required skill for young ladies, like singing and fine needlework. "If you're as bold as you say, then you must be the sort of sporting gentleman who enjoys his games of chance."

He shook his head, sorry to see her face fall. "Not dice, not pasteboard cards, and I've no wish to empty my pockets on account of some overrated nag, either."

"Truly?" she said, disappointed. "You are not pretending otherwise?"

"I did when I was younger," he said, to make her feel better, "but not for years. Now I'd rather find pleasure in playing for higher stakes than a handful of coins."

"Indeed, sir." Her voice turned frosty, her cheeks flushing. "How fine for you."

He barely bit back an oath, realizing too late that she'd misunderstood him again. He'd meant the dangerous investments and other merchant ventures with high-risk profits that had become his specialty, while she'd thought the stakes were her and her charming little person—her virtue, as ladies liked to call it.

"Oh, blast, I didn't intend it that way," he said, taking her by the arm so she'd have to look at him, so she'd understand he meant her no harm "Here now, miss, listen to me. I've never had to rely on a wager for a woman's company, and I'm not about to begin now."

"No," she said curtly, staring down at his fingers around her upper arm as if his touch had scalded her. "But then I don't imagine any woman willingly shares your company, not for the sake of love or money."

He sighed with impatience, wondering why in blazes she'd suddenly turned so priggish and prim. "Now that's not what I—"

"Isn't it, sir?" she said, the curving brim of her bon-

net quivering with indignation. "I may be from the country, but I am not completely ignorant of the wickedness
to be found in this city!"

Other people around them were beginning to turn
with curiosity, and Richard lowered his voice to give
them less to hear. "Listen to me, sweetheart, and stop
speaking of things you know nothing of. You wouldn't
recognize wickedness if it tripped you in the street."

"I am not your sweetheart, and I will thank you not
to fancy I am." She jerked her arm free of his hand.
"Now leave me, sir, before I demonstrate exactly how
much I know of *your* wickedness, and summon one
of Mr. Christie's guards to have you removed. Good
day, sir."

She gave an angry final twitch of her black skirts as
she cut her way through the crowd, as fast and as far
from him as she could get herself.

And that was fine with Richard. If ever he'd needed
another reminder that London ladies would be difficult,
then this red-haired chit had given it to him. He'd
thought at first she'd be different, and speak plain, but
without warning she'd become just as self-righteous
and sharp-tongued as all the rest in this city. Finding one
who wasn't would be his greatest challenge so far.

But he was willing to take his time. He'd decided
that, even before his ship had rounded Needham Point
and left the last of Barbados behind him. He had made
his fortune, and he had bought his fine bespoke clothes
and his carriage and horses and an ancient, grand country house awaited him. Now all he needed was a high-
bred lady-bride to complete the transformation, and

make the world see that Dick Blackley, collier's boy, had become Richard Blackley, gentleman.

He glanced one last time toward where the young woman in mourning had disappeared. He was sorry she hadn't turned out to be his match; he'd liked her looks and her spirit, before she'd gone and turned so sour over nothing.

And he'd be damned before he'd let her steal his painting away from him.

The auctioneer had made his way to the podium and stood testing his gavel against the palm of his hand, while his assistant was ringing the bell to signal the beginning of the auction. Most people hurried to find seats on the long benches, while a few others lingered for a final glimpse of the paintings hung and stacked along the walls. A footman carried the first painting, a murky landscape, to the front of the room, taking care to balance the ornate gold frame on the tall easel for all to see.

Richard didn't sit, choosing instead to stand along the wall where he could keep one eye on his old bawd. He crossed his arms over his chest and tipped his hat over one eye, leaning against the wall as he prepared for a long wait before his painting would be called. He glanced across the benches, but saw no sign of the redhaired woman in mourning. Perhaps he'd chased her off; perhaps she'd never had a real interest in the painting.

Slowly the sun slid across the skylights overhead as the auctioneer droned on, cracking his gavel to seal each transaction as the footman switched paintings. At last the footman lifted *The Fortune Teller* onto the easel, and Richard stood away from the wall and straightened his hat.

"Next is an Italian painting in oils from the sixteenth century entitled *The Fortune Teller*," the auctioneer announced. "Opening with a reserve of five pounds for this very fine work by an old master whose name is lost to time, but not the product of his genius. Five pounds to start, then, who'll give five pounds?"

Richard raised his hand just enough for the auctioneer to notice. He could see it hung in his dressing room at Greenwood already.

"Five pounds to the tall gentleman at the wall, a pittance for a work of this quality, of this sensibility, of this—"

"Seven pounds!"

"Seven pounds to the lady in mourning!" the auctioneer called. "The lady knows her art, gentlemen, benefit from her knowledge and—"

"Nine pounds." Richard had spotted her now, sitting on the far end of one of the benches, with all but the brim of her black bonnet hidden by a fat man in a gray coat.

"Nine to the tall gentleman at the wall, will anyone give me—"

"Fifteen!" The young woman hopped to her feet, her program rolled into a tight scroll in her black-gloved hands.

Excitement rippled through the crowd; no one had expected any serious bidding for this particular lot of paintings, especially not between a gentleman and a lady.

"Fifteen to the lady with a connoisseur's eye for an old master, fifteen to—"

"Twenty."

The woman turned and glared at Richard. When he nodded and smiled, she twitched her head back toward the front, refusing to acknowledge him.

"Twenty-five," she said, her voice ringing clear and loud in the auction room. She wasn't afraid to make a spectacle of herself, and Richard liked that. What a pity she'd learn soon enough that his pockets were deeper than she'd ever dreamed.

"Twenty-five to the lady!" the auctioneer crowed with near delirious fervor. "Twenty-five for—"

"Fifty," Richard said, and the audience gasped.

"Fifty-five!" the woman cried, tossing her head for good measure.

Richard smiled. She did have spirit, he'd grant her that.

"Fifty-five to the lady!" His round face flushed with excitement, the auctioneer peered expectantly at Richard over his spectacles. The room was nearly silent, the audience holding its breath together. "Fifty-five for this most excellent work, fifty-five for—"

"One hundred," Richard said. "Even."

The crowd exploded, whistling, swearing, applauding, cheering. The auctioneer turned back to the girl.

"One hundred for *The Fortune Teller*," he thundered, his voice fair glowing with the importance of such a bid. "One hundred from the tall, dark gentleman for this magnificent work. Do I hear one hundred five? One hundred five?"

But the young woman only shook her head and sank back down onto the bench, behind the fat man.

Obviously disappointed, the auctioneer continued. "Once at one hundred, twice at one hundred." His gavel cracked down on his desk. "Sold to the tall gentleman for one hundred pounds."

Another spattering of applause came from the audience, but the contest was done and their interest with it. Few even bothered to turn as Richard made his way to the front to pay for the painting and make arrangements for its delivery to Greenwood. With the picture now leaning against the back wall, the old fortune teller seemed to be laughing at his expense now, too—as well she should, considering how much more than her worth she'd finally cost him.

"So this is how you seize opportunities to make your own luck, sir?" The redhead was standing beside him, her cheek flushed and her eyes flashing with anger. "I told you I wanted that painting, sir, and you stole it away from me from sheer spite. You swoop down and plunder like a—like a pirate, sir!"

"I didn't plunder anything," he protested. "I bid for the painting honestly, and now I must pay through the nose for the privilege, too. Show me a pirate who'll do that."

Her eyes narrowed, shaking the scrolled program in her hand as if it were a dagger. "You are no better than a pirate, sir. A thieving, incorrigible, rascally pirate, with no sense of propriety or decency!"

"And if you had outbid me, would that have made you the pirate?" he asked. "I come from a place where piracy's taken seriously. Would the painting have become your righteous plunder instead of mine, hung alongside your skull and crossbones?"

She gasped, sputtering so incoherently as she struggled for words that he almost—almost—laughed. Instead, against his better judgment, he took pity on her.

"If you promise to surrender your sword, lass," he said, "then I'm willing to make peace over a dish of tea or chocolate."

"Go with you, sir?" Tiny wisps of red-gold hair had come free from her bonnet and now quivered around her face, echoing her outrage. "Sit with you, drink tea with you? After what you have done to me?"

"That was my intention, yes," he said, his patience shredding fast, "though you are making it damned difficult to be agreeable."

"That is because I do not intend to be agreeable to you, sir." She took one last look at the painting. "Drink tea with you, hah. Even if you were to suddenly play the gallant and give the picture to me, I would not accept it."

"But I'm not some blasted foppish gallant any more than you're agreeable," he said irritably. "The painting's mine, fair and square, and it's going to stay that way."

"I didn't need a fortune teller to know you'd say that." She retied the bonnet's ribbons beneath her chin with short, quick jerks, the black silk cutting against her white throat. "You can try to bend your luck all you want, but someday, Captain Pirate, you'll find that luck will bend you back."

He frowned as she turned away toward the door. "Is that meant to be a curse," he called after her, "or are you telling my fortune?"

She paused just long enough to look back over her shoulder, her blue-eyed gaze so startlingly intense that

he almost recoiled. "You'll have to decide that for yourself, won't you?"

She disappeared through the door, and slowly Richard turned back to the painting. Likely he'd never see
the redhead again, not in a city this large. But he'd
been in London less than a week, and already it had
come to this.

A fortune, or a curse.

"Good afternoon, Pratt." Cassia smiled at the old
man as he held the door to Penny House open for her.
"I hope my sisters haven't been making your life too
miserable today?"

"Like hell itself it's been, Miss Cassia," he grumbled,
looking down sorrowfully at his leather apron, covered
with silver polish, sawdust and general household grime.
"Fussing about like an Irish parlor maid, ordered up an'
down those infernal stairs like it was nothing—that's not
why I agreed to stay on, Miss Cassia, not at all."

"I know, Pratt, I know," she said, "but after tonight
everything will be ready, and we'll be busy running
Penny House instead of just cleaning it."

She smiled and patted his sleeve. They needed Pratt
to be happy. Pratt was the club's manager, one of the few
members of the staff they'd kept on from Whitaker's.
Once valet to the Duke of Conover, his limitless knowledge of who was who in the aristocracy had already
proved invaluable to the sisters. He had suggested which
noblemen they should invite to form their new membership committee and who should receive their engraved
invitations to join, and he'd even known that twenty

guineas should be the precise—if shocking—entrance fee to keep the club exclusive.

"I trust you're right, Miss Cassia." His sigh was more of a groan as he dabbed his forehead at the edge of his wig with a linen handkerchief. "Your sister may have been born a preacher's daughter, but she gives orders like she's lived all her life in a palace."

"Pratt, there you are!" called Amariah from the staircase, and he groaned again. "You're needed in the pantry to help move a table, and— Ah, Cassia, at last you're home!"

"Good day, Amariah," she said, wishing she could be heading off with Pratt. "You make it sound as if I've been away to China and back."

"Well, you have been gone for hours and hours, and so much has happened since you've been gone." She leaned over the railing, searching the entryway. "Where is the painting you went to fetch? Is it coming later in a cart?"

"It's not coming at all." Cassia untied her bonnet as she glanced into the refurbished dining room. "I didn't buy it. I see the painters have finally taken down their scaffolding, so I suppose the ceilings are done at last."

"But you told us the fortune telling painting was perfect!" Amariah hurried down the steps to join her, her white linen apron billowing around her. "You left the space on the wall bare specifically for it—a great, gaping, empty hole, with our first night all but upon us!"

"Then I'll find something else to put in its place." Cassia pushed open the tall double doors, eager to avoid answering any more of Amariah's questions about the auction. This was her own fault, really, for gushing on so much about the painting after she'd seen it in the preview, about how cheaply it would be had. It would have been, too, if not for that dreadful man stealing it away from her. "And I know we open tonight. However could I forget?"

"If you decided against that painting, then you should have been here, working with us." Amariah followed her through the doors. "How things look at Penny House, Cassia—that's your responsibility, just as Bethany's is in the kitchen and mine is—"

"To greet our guests, to oversee the gaming staff and to keep the books." Cassia sighed, exhausted. All three of them were, from working so hard and with so little sleep to be ready for the first night. That was probably the reason that man had irritated her so over the auction; if she hadn't been so tired, she wouldn't have paid him any heed at all. "I'm sorry I took so long, Amariah, but it couldn't be— Oh, don't the chairs look fine!"

With the protective cloths finally removed and the painters gone, she wandered through the room, running her hands lightly over the tops of the tables and chairs. The old tables had been sturdy enough to keep, but the few original chairs that remained from Whitaker's had been so rickety they'd needed replacing before some corpulent gentleman plunged through to the carpet.

Cassia herself had scoured secondhand stores along the river to find the replacements, then scrubbed and polished away the old grime from the chairs in the yard out back. None of the chairs matched, but Cassia's eye for proportion had made her choices cousins, if not

brothers, and the overall effect was lighthearted and imaginative and inviting.

But that was how she'd decorated all of Penny
House, from the private card rooms to the bedchambers
the sisters kept for themselves on the top floor. Everything was a curious jumble, from the fresh, bright paint
and well-used furniture, to the latest political cartoons
pinned beside an ancient carving from the East Indies.
Yet somehow Cassia had put it all together to make the
rooms seem more exotic and fashionable than what the
most expensive London architects were creating for
their wealthiest clients.

The Fortune Teller was going to have been one of her
few indulgences, a costly painting for her and one to be
given a special place of honor. Cassia glanced up to the
empty spot over the fireplace where the picture would
have gone, and muttered furiously to herself.

"So why didn't you buy the painting, Cassia, if you
wanted it so badly?" Amariah was watching her, arms
folded over the front of her apron. "You had money
from the old paintings you'd sold last week, and this
morning you seemed to feel sure it could be had
cheaply."

Cassia gave a dismissive sweep of her hand. "It
should have come cheaply, yes. But there was a dreadful, selfish, rude man at Christie's who stole it away
from me, as boldly as any thieving pirate might!"

Amariah listened, her expression not changing. "You
mean he was willing to bid higher than you?"

"I mean he drove the bidding so high that I could not
compete with him." Cassia stalked back and forth be-

fore the fireplace, unable to keep still. "Before the auction, he saw that I wanted the picture, and then from purest spite he let me bid as if I had a chance."

She held her hand up, palm open, over the mantelpiece. "He let me bid, Amariah, let me bid in my innocence before he finally squelched me flat as a gnat!"

She smacked her palm down on painted wood for emphasis, showing exactly what the man had done to her hopes.

But Amariah didn't blink. "How high did he run the bidding?"

Cassia let her hand slip from the mantel, not wanting her sister to realize how her fingers stung after that thoughtless, emphatic little gesture. "The reserve was five pounds, which was fair. His final bid was one hundred, which was not."

"So evidently he was either a very rich pirate, or a very indulgent one," Amariah said. "I trust you offered him an invitation to our opening?"

Cassia gasped. "I most certainly did not!"

"Why?" Amariah pulled out one of the chairs and sat. "He is gentleman enough to be at Christie's bidding on paintings, he is rich and he is impulsive. He sounds ideal for Penny House."

"But I thought we were only inviting gentlemen recommended by the membership committee!" Cassia protested. "True gentlemen, with breeding and manners, and not boorish and ill-tempered and—"

"Was he handsome, too?"

"Handsome?" Cassia paused, surprised that Amariah would ask such a question. The man *was* handsome;

she couldn't pretend she hadn't noticed as soon as she'd bumped into him. His features were sharp and regular, his pale eyes intelligent, and he was so tall she'd had to look up to his face. His dark hair had seemed too thick and heavy to stay in place, and as they'd spoken, he'd had to toss it back impatiently from his forehead. His skin was browned by the sun, as if he were a sailor or farmer, and his hands and the breadth of his shoulders seemed to belong more to a man who worked for his living rather than a gentleman. He'd certainly stood out among the crowd at Christie's.

Not, of course, that any of that would matter to Cassia now.

"He was handsome enough, in his way," she admitted with a dismissive little shrug. "In a *common* way."

"Indeed." Amariah sat back in her chair, watching Cassia closely. "Was he young, too?"

"Older than we are," Cassia said. "Thirty?"

"Young for a gentleman." Amariah sighed, smoothing her apron over her knee. "Thus the man was young and handsome and rich and impulsive. For all we know, he may already have one of our invitations. Yet because you imagined he'd slighted you somehow, you were every bit as ill-mannered as he was to you."

"I did not say that!"

"You didn't have to, Cassia." Amariah pressed her palm to her forehead and sighed. "You're saying it now, as clear as day. It's how you've always been with gentlemen."

"Only when they behave ill toward me first!" Cassia cried. "Don't you recall how Father said we were to stand up for ourselves with gentlemen, and never let them take advantage?"

"There is a world of difference between taking advantage and behaving like a spoiled, petulant child," Amariah said. "London isn't the Havertown Assembly, and you can't treat the gentlemen here the way you did with the ones at home. There will always be another lady who is prettier or more amusing, and London gentlemen won't be nearly as indulgent with you if you lose your temper."

"I wasn't *trying* to be amusing," Cassia protested. That wasn't what had happened with the gentleman at Christie's, and it didn't deserve this kind of talk from her sister. "I was trying to buy a painting."

"Yet I can imagine all too well what that gentleman must have thought." Amariah reached out and took Cassia's hand. "I know you are still our baby, Cassia, and that you've worked as hard as Bethany and I these last months—maybe even harder. And I know how set you can be on having your own way."

Cassia shook her head, even as she thought again about the dark-haired gentleman. If she hadn't turned so—so tart with him, then maybe they'd be in this room hanging *The Fortune Teller* now instead of staring at that empty space. "But I didn't—"

"Hush, and listen to me," Amariah said with a gentle shush. "We've come to London to honor Father's memory by making Penny House a success, and his charities with it. That must always come first. Neither imagined slights, nor gentlemen who haven't paid us as much attention as we'd wish. If you let your temper run away tonight, why, then the talk will begin about those disagreeable women at Penny House, and everything will be lost."

"Not *the women*. Me." Cassia sighed, her agitation slipping away. "You should have been with me at Christie's today, Amariah. It's simple for you. You are always so calm."

"I hide the rest, that is all." Her sister smiled, gently squeezing Cassia's fingers. "You'll have a fresh start this evening. Before you act or speak, think, then think again, and you'll do fine."

"I'll try, Amariah," she said, and she meant it. "For all our sakes, and for Father's, too, I'll try."

A fresh start, thought Cassia. That was what they'd all needed, and why they'd come to London in the first place. Likely she would never see the dark gentleman—the thieving pirate—ever again, anyway. Likely all he'd ever be to her would be a warning, a reminder of how she must not behave.

And she swore to push aside forever that guilty twinge of supreme satisfaction for having gotten the last word.

Chapter Three

Richard sat sprawled in a plush-covered chair, his legs stretched out before him and a glass of claret from dinner in his hands, and his temper simmering at a disagreeable, disgruntled point. He should have no grounds for complaint: his rooms here at the Clarendon were the most lavish to be had in the hotel, the fire in the fireplace was burning at a pace to match any Caribbean afternoon, and the dinner sent upstairs to him on a tray had been prepared by one of the best kitchens in the city. He had spent the day getting exactly what he'd wanted, and the proof of it was sitting opposite from him, propped awkwardly across two sidechairs like an unwelcome relative.

But the expensive rooms seemed as crowded and overwrought as the ones in an expensive brothel, the fire had made the room so close that he'd thrown open the windows, and the dinner lay ravished but abandoned on its tray, largely uneaten. Even the claret didn't seem to help, which considering the extra guinea the bottle had added to the cost of the dinner, it damned well should have.

He emptied his glass and refilled it, staring at the painting opposite him. A gentleman was supposed to collect rubbish like this, and take pride in the possessing as well as the possession, filling entire picture galleries with what they'd dragged home from the Continent.

Yet the longer he studied *The Fortune Teller,* the more he thought instead of the woman he'd outbid for it. Damnation, he should have been a gallant. He should have either let her bid stand, or made her a pretty gift of it afterward. If for no other reason, he should have done it for the practice. How else would he be ready when the right high-bred lady did come along?

And he had liked the young woman. She'd been full of fire to match the color of her hair, all spark and spit, and nothing like the sultry, languid women he'd known in the islands. Perhaps if she had been, he wouldn't have made such an ass of himself.

He heard the door from the bedchamber open, then the muted gurgle of wine as the glass in his hand was refilled.

"No more, Neuf," Richard said to his manservant, still holding the claret bottle. "I'm in a piss-poor humor as it is without dumping more claret down my gullet."

"As you wish, sir." Neuf stepped back, cradling the bottle in his arms like a baby. He had taken care to stand with his back to the fire, as close as he dared without dipping the tails of his coat into the flames, and from the contented look in his heavy-lidded eyes, Richard knew he was relishing the warmth that reminded him of their old home on Barbados. "Are you done with your dinner, sir? Should I have it taken away?"

"Done enough." Richard twisted around in his chair, watching Neuf gather up the dishes he'd scattered about the room. "Tell me, Neuf. How should I entertain myself this evening, other than sitting here alone and drinking myself into oblivion?"

"The theatre, sir? The opera, the pleasure gardens near the river?" His shrugged with morose resignation. He had been with Richard for nearly eight years, through good times and some very bad ones, and he had earned the small freedom of that shrug. "For a gentleman like yourself, London must offer every diversion."

"I said I wished to be entertained, Neuf, not lulled to sleep." Richard drummed his fingers on the arm of the chair. "You know I've no patience for playacting or yowling singers."

Neuf refolded Richard's napkin into precise quarters before he answered. "Then a ball, sir? A place where you'll meet young ladies?"

"Not yet, not yet." Richard rose, crossing the room to stand at the window and gaze down at the street below. There'd be no balls or grand parties yet, not for an outsider like him. He had brought with him letters of introduction from the island's royal governor to three noble families here in England, and he was determined not to squander them until the time was right. "I'm waiting until Greenwood is done and I've a grand home to offer a lady. What's the use in setting the trap before the proper bait is ready?"

He glanced back over his shoulder at the painting. He'd gone to the auction in search of old paintings to add respectable grandeur to his country house, and this was what he'd come away with—hardly the great work of fine art to impress a future father-in-law.

Would that saucy chit in mourning have liked the painting as much if she'd realized its real subject? Or had she wanted it so badly only because he'd wanted it too, bidding from spite rather than genuine interest?

"Now this, sir, this might catch your fancy." Neuf was holding out the day's news sheet, folded to highlight one article with the same precision as Neuf had shown with the napkin. "A new club for gentlemen, for dining and gaming."

Richard frowned down at the paper without taking it. "I don't believe in begging fate to find me and strike me down, Neuf. You know I'm done with cards and playing deep."

"But this house is different, sir," Neuf said. "Penny House, it's called, and it's said to be owned by the three beautiful daughters of a Sussex parson, and all the profits the bank earns will go to charity."

"What, hazard with the Methodists?" Richard laughed, the concept thoroughly preposterous. "Say a psalm, and throw the dice?"

"But the ladies would be a curiosity, sir—"

"Be reasonable, Neuf," Richard scoffed. "Have you ever known a woman to combine piety with great beauty?"

"They have the patronage of the Duke of Carlisle, sir," Neuf said, consulting the article again. "Surely the hero of the Peninsular Wars wouldn't give his endorsement lightly."

"He was a man before he was a hero," Richard said, "and it's likely more a case of what the sisters have given him first than the other way around. I'd wager a guinea that those three have been plucked from some high-priced brothel to front the house, and are no more country parson's daughters than you or I."

"As you say, sir." The manservant sighed with resignation, and turned the paper back so he could read it himself. "Besides, sir, this says that membership will be most exclusive. Unless a gentleman is already a member of Brook's, White's, or Boodles, then he will not be admitted to Penny House tonight unless he has received his invitation directly from the membership committee."

"Invitations to have your pockets emptied? Give that to me, Neuf." He grabbed the paper from his manservant's hands. "Even for London, that's carrying it too damned far."

Neuf folded his now empty hands before him. "It's true, sir. I did not invent it, nor could I."

"Who in blazes could?" Richard frowned as he scanned the page, feeling more and more as if it were a personal challenge to him rather than a simple scrap of society gossip. Not that any of these fine folk would know his past, or guess that they played at cards with a collier's son. "They say it's to ensure the 'genteel air' of the club. What's genteel about drinking so much that you're willing to toss away every last farthing to your name?"

Neuf shrugged his narrow shoulders. "This is London, sir, and these are London ways."

"I'll show them London ways." Richard tossed the paper on the table, and tugged his shirt over his head, ready to dress for the evening. Walking through the door didn't mean he'd have to play deep, or even play at all. "I'd like to see those three merry sisters try to keep me out of their precious gaming house because I don't have the proper scrap of pasteboard."

Neuf caught Richard's discarded shirt as it he tossed it toward a chair. "Then you are going to this Penny House, sir?"

"Yes, Neuf, I am." Richard grinned, his earlier restlessness forgotten. So far his time in London had been dull and proper. Now this evening had a purpose, an excitement. He might have stumbled at the auction house from lack of experience, saying and doing the wrong thing with the young lady in mourning, but a new gambling club run by women of dubious reputation—ah, where else would he feel more at ease?

Neuf nodded, still managing to make his unhappiness clear to Richard. If he'd known Richard long enough for a certain degree of familiarity, he'd also known him long enough to understand the combined temptation that Penny House could offer, and the futility of any warning he might give to his master.

"As you wish, sir," he said instead. "As you wish."

"As I damned well please, Neuf," Richard said cheerfully, his mood improving by the moment. "And may the devil take the man who tries to stop me."

The man's face was round and red and very shiny, and he'd had so much to drink that he didn't notice that the ends of his neckcloth were sticking out on either side of his plump neck like well-starched handles.

But Cassia noticed, and it was hard—very hard—for her not to reach out with both hands to tuck the ends back into the collar of his coat.

"And you say you arranged everything in this house in the very latest taste, Miss Penny?" he marveled, patting the front of his waistcoat. "You're such a dear young girl that I cannot believe it to be possible!"

"Thank you, Lord Russell," Cassia said, fluttering her fan as she squeezed back against the wall to let two other gentlemen pass them on the stairs. "Perhaps I did not paint every last baseboard with my own hand, but I did choose the colors, and assemble all the paintings and other little pieces to amuse the eyes of our guests."

Lord Russell tapped the side of his nose with one finger, narrowing his unfocussed eyes. "That's what a good English lass is supposed to do with her house, Miss Penny, and so I tell Lady Russell. But she'd rather have an Italian do it for her, fussing with the furnishing until a fellow can't tell where he's supposed to sit."

"Then you shall simply have to return to us, my lord." Cassia smiled, though her mouth already ached from smiling at gentlemen because she *had* to. She could not believe how many men had crowded into the house, more men—old and young and in between, handsome and homely, but most of them titled and all of them wealthy—than she'd ever seen together in her entire life in Woodbury. Amariah had been right: this wasn't like the flirtatious fun at the Havertown Assembly. It was work, hard work, and the tall clock in the hall had yet to chime ten.

Lord Russell leaned closer, swallowing as he glanced along the front of her bodice. "You know, Miss Penny, you are a fine girl, deuced fine, and a good deal easier to talk to than my wife. I'm a generous man, Miss Penny, especially to those I favor, and when you tire of this, we could make an arrangement that would benefit—"

"Have you found our hazard table yet, my lord?" Cassia said brightly, fighting the very real urge to forget her promise to Amariah and shove His Lordship back down the stairs the way he deserved. "It's in the drawing room at the top of these stairs, just to your right, and we've also tables for cribbage and whist, if those are more your pleasure."

"So you like a man who's not afraid to play deep, eh?" His Lordship leered, or at least as close to a leer as his baby-round face could manage. "You like a man who's not afraid of courting danger at the table?"

What Cassia liked was a man who'd play deep and lose badly and make their bank fatter for Father's charity, which was exactly why Lord Russell had been invited tonight.

Not, of course, that Cassia could say that to him. Instead she deftly twisted away, putting more space between them as she kept smiling over her fan. "I hear the gentlemen have already predicted it will be a lucky table, my lord."

"Have they now?" He leered again, smoothing his plump, pink hand down the front of his waistcoat. "Up these stairs, you say?"

"To the right of the landing, my lord," she said with relief. "You cannot miss it."

"Very well, Miss Penny," he said with a slight bow. "I shall— What in blazes is that racket down at the door?"

"Doubtless an overeager guest, my lord." Cassia leaned over the railing, trying to glimpse what was happening below. "I'm sure the staff will sort it out in a moment."

But Lord Russell was right: it *was* a racket. Men were shouting at each other, while the house's servants in livery were pushing and shoving and trying to keep order. Other gentlemen were crowding the doorways, determined to see the source of the excitement. In the very center, Cassia spotted the top of Amariah's head, her hair bright as a copper coin tossed in the middle of so much dark male evening clothes. For a moment, Cassia thought she glimpsed an arm, gesturing wildly in her direction, and then Amariah looked up and caught her eye.

Pratt appeared magically beside her, his face so purposefully bland that she knew things must be very bad indeed. "Excuse me, Miss Cassia, but Miss Amariah has requested you come to her directly. This way, miss, if you please."

Cassia nodded, closing her fan with a little click. She gave one last smile to Lord Russell, with what she hoped was sufficient regret, then hurried down the curving staircase after Pratt. The opening was supposed to be genteel, elegant, meant to make gentlemen want to join their club. It was not supposed to degenerate into a brawl.

"What has happened, Pratt?" she whispered. "Tell me! What's wrong?"

"Nothing that can't be set to rights in a moment,

miss," Pratt answered discreetly, no real answer at all. "Miss Amariah will explain."

He cut a path for her through the sea of gentlemen, keeping her moving through the crowd still clustered in the front hall, while newcomers at the door tried to make their way inside. "Excuse me, my lord. This way, miss, if you please, this way."

He opened the door to the small anteroom reserved for the porter, and held it ajar just long enough for Cassia to squeeze through. Two of the largest of the house orderly men were holding a gentleman tightly by the arms, keeping him from breaking free, his broad-shouldered back to her. His dark hair was mussed, and there was a rip in one sleeve of his jacket, testimony to the scuffle in the front hall that had brought him here now.

"Thank you for joining us, Cassia." Her sister stood at the end of the tiny room, another orderly man on one side and Pratt on the other. With her hands clasped over the royal-blue gown, Amariah still clung to her usual serenity, though her cheeks were flushed and the fingers of her clasped hands so tightly clenched together that the knuckles were white. "I am sorry to have disturbed you, but this gentleman here has posed quite a quandary for us, and you, it seems, are part of it."

"Cassia." The man being held repeated her name with relish, almost as if he could taste the word on his tongue. He tried to twist around to see her, but the two guards jerked him back to face Amariah. "So that's the young lady's name? Cassia? She would be called something rare like that."

Cassia pressed her hand over her mouth so he wouldn't hear her gasp. She recognized that voice, even without a face to it: he was the man from Christie's who'd stolen *The Fortune Teller* away from her.

But why was he here now at Penny House? How had he known where to find her? Or had he followed her here, intent on further humiliating her?

"What the lady is called is of no importance to you, sir," Pratt ordered, his eyes hooded. "You would do far better to consider your own situation, and how it will be viewed by a judge. Forced entry, trespassing, threats of violence against the people of this house—such charges will not be taken lightly by a court of law."

"But as they are all lies of your making, they shall not be considered at all." The man paused, and Cassia knew he must be smiling. "Now what would those self-same courts make of your treatment of me, I wonder? A respectable gentleman of wealth and position, treated like some sort of thieving scoundrel—but you can vouch for me, can't you, Cassia? You can tell them what kind of man I am, can't you?"

She flushed at the intimacy he implied, but before she could speak, Pratt answered for her.

"Do not reply, miss," he said. "The rascal has no right to address you, let alone to ask you to speak on his behalf."

"Very well, then," the man said. "Forgive me my rascally ways, my dear Cassia. I shall defend myself."

Cassia took a step forward, stunned that he'd dare be so presumptuous. He'd no right to say such things, or to shame her this way before the others, and she longed to tell him exactly that. But she'd promised Amariah she'd behave, and as hard as it was to keep quiet, Cassia did, biting back the rebuttal the man deserved.

"Sir, you still do not seem to understand." Amariah's smile was tightly polite. "Penny House is a club for the first gentlemen of this country, where they can amuse themselves among their peers. Admission tonight is by invitation only, sir, and regardless of what my sister says of you, you were not invited."

"But I should have been." With his arms still restrained, he tossed his dark hair back from his forehead with an impatience that Cassia also recognized all too well. "You should all be on your knees to beg me to stay, instead of tossing me out in St. James Street like yesterday's rubbish."

That was more than enough for Pratt. "What is your name, sir?" he demanded. "Your home?"

"I am Richard Blackley, of Greenwood Hall in Hampshire," the man answered, the pride in his voice unmistakable. "Recently returned from my plantations in the royal colony of Barbados, and presently residing at the Clarendon."

"You lie, sir." Pratt's words were clipped with contempt. "The true owner of Greenwood Hall is not you, but Sir Henry Green. The estate has been in his family for centuries."

"But no longer." Again Cassia guessed the man—he had a name now, Mr. Richard Blackley—must be smiling, despite the edge that had crept into his voice. "Shortly before I sailed, Sir Henry and I engaged in an evening of cards in a tavern in Bridgetown. He was drunk, and he lost. I wasn't, and I won, and now own Greenwood."

Pratt's expression didn't change. "Is there anyone here who can vouch for what you claim, sir?"

Blackley shrugged, or would have, if the other two hadn't held his arms. "I doubt it, not in this crowd. Best to ask poor Sir Henry himself. If you can find him, that is. Ruin can make a man damned near invisible."

Cassia listened, shocked. Since coming to London, she'd heard many stories of men who'd played deep and had lost everything, but the stories had always been remote, as distant as a nursery tale. Rich gentlemen lost money they could spare, and Penny House's bank would profit for the sake of the poor.

But this careless, offhanded description by one man who'd stripped another of his patrimony had such a grim ring of reality that Cassia couldn't look at Mr. Blackley the same way. At the auction she had called him a pirate and a thief. How could she have known how true that was?

"Cassia." Her sister's inflection dragged Cassia back to the little room. "Is this the gentleman you met today at Christie's?"

She nodded, and the two guards released him. He shook himself free, squaring his shoulders and shooting the cuffs of his black coat. He took another second to smooth back his hair, and then, ready at last, he turned around.

"Miss Cassia Penny," he said, his bow more an athlete's than a courtier's. "How happy I am to make your formal acquaintance. But will you now say the same of me, I wonder? Can I trust you to speak the truth?"

Cassia lifted her chin, determined to meet his eye without flinching. He was even more handsome in his evening clothes than she remembered from this afternoon, and the advantage it gave him was decidedly unfair.

"You can trust me to be truthful, Mr. Blackley," she said, her voice slow and deliberate, "because this is a square house in every way, you know."

"So you do know him, Cassia?" Amariah asked. "This is the man?"

"The man who outbid me fairly for the painting?" Cassia forced herself to smile, opening her fan before her in a graceful arc. He was daring her to blush, daring her to look away or stammer, and she would not do it. She would treat him like every other gentleman here tonight, no better nor no worse. "Yes, Amariah, it was Mr. Blackley."

He bowed again, though not as low, so he could keep watching her. "Your servant, Miss Penny," he said softly. "But you knew that already, didn't you?"

Swiftly she looked away, back to her sister. "But that is all, Amariah. Beyond Mr. Blackley's paying a preposterous amount for a very average painting, I cannot speak for his family, his estate or his honor, and that is the truth."

Cassia smiled at her sister, hoping she'd just damned Mr. Blackley with the faintest praise possible.

But she hadn't, not at all.

"I cannot ask you for anything more than the truth, Cassia," Amariah said. "And I thank you for it."

While she thought, she patted her palms gently together, the sound muted by her gloves, and Cassia's heart sank. From the way her sister's brows had lowered, just short of a frown, Cassia knew she was calculating exactly how much of Mr. Blackley's money could be pried from his pockets and into their charities. His family and his honor—or their lack—didn't amount to a pile of garden dirt next to that. Amariah was going to let Mr. Blackley stay, and nothing that Cassia could say now was going to change her mind.

Pratt cleared his throat. "Forgive me, Miss Penny, but we should all be returning to the—"

"And so we shall, Mr. Pratt." Amariah's face was once again serene. "Mr. Blackley, you may stay. Dine with us, play at our tables, amuse yourself however you please. But please recall, sir, that Penny House is a respite for gentlemen, and not a Caribbean tavern made for brawling. Even a breath of trouble from you, sir, and you will be banned from here for the rest of your life."

"Hah," Blackley said. "There's nothing like a threat to make for a damned cheerful welcome."

"As my sister said, Mr. Blackley, you will find only the truth in this house." Amariah glided past him to return to the others, Pratt and the guards behind her, and Cassia hurried to join them. "Now unless there is anything more you might wish from—"

"Your sister," he said. "I want her."

Cassia stopped abruptly. "Mr. Blackley, I am not—"

"As my guide, that is." His smile was wicked, teasing, knowing she'd misinterpreted exactly as he'd planned. "Since I'm new here tonight."

"We are all new here tonight, Mr. Blackley." Amariah nodded back at him, striving now to put him at his ease, as if he were behaving with perfect decorum.

"Miss Cassia will be honored to show you the features of Penny House. Won't you, Cassia?"

Cassia took a deep breath. "I…shall…be…*delighted.*"

"I'm honored, Miss Cassia." Even in the tiny room, he was too close to her, too sure of himself, the way he had been when they were examining the painting. He crooked his arm for her to take.

She ignored it, sailing ahead of him and across the black-and-white marble floor of the front hall.

"This is our drawing room, Mr. Blackley," she said with a perfunctory sweep of her hand when he joined her. "Where gentlemen may gather for conversation, or to read the latest news."

"You've no right to be angry with me," he said. "They made the scene, not I. None of it was my doing."

"Oh, no, how could you ever be at fault?" She kept her eyes straight ahead, fighting her own temper. "As you see, Mr. Blackley, we have furnished the drawing room for both comfort and fashion, wishing our gentlemen to feel at their ease."

"Is this still about the damned painting?" he asked, his voice low so the others around him wouldn't overhear, though the irritation in his words was unmistakable. "You still believe somehow that I cheated you?"

Cassia stared pointedly at the empty place over the fireplace where the painting should have gone. "You were not honest with me, Mr. Blackley. At the showing before the auction, you let me babble on like a ninny over that picture, not even hinting that you were interested in it for yourself!"

"You weren't exactly honest with me, either," he said. "Was the mourning supposed to buy my sympathy?"

"The mourning was in honor of my *father*."

"And now that you've grieved, you put it aside to bare as much skin as any other actress."

"We put it aside because it would have seemed too grim for tonight," she explained defensively, wondering why he should care so much. "Father would have understood."

He chuckled, scornful. "That may be what you told the gossip sheets, but I ask you, what kind of father would leave his daughters a place like this?"

"A father who wished his daughters to do good in an evil world, no matter what the avenue." She swallowed back the emotion that knotted in her throat. "My father was a good man, Mr. Blackley, and honorable and kind in ways someone like you could never understand."

"You don't know that, lass," he said in a hoarse whisper. "You don't know anything of me at all."

"I know enough," she said quickly, her heart racing for no reason. "And I know more than enough not to trust you."

She hurried ahead, her expression so fixed that she scarcely noticed how the other gentlemen were stepping aside for her to pass.

"I'm sorry about your father." His long legs easily kept pace with her. "And I like your gown, much better than I did the mourning. But I didn't mean that—"

"Of course you did, Mr. Blackley," she said, her careful facade of gentility slipping. "Why else would you have said it in the first place if you didn't?"

"Then you have changed my mind," he said. "Or am I not permitted to apologize?"

"This—this is our dining room, sir," she said. She did not believe a single letter of his apology, nor could she let herself slip into that kind of trap. She must keep formal and remote; she must not let herself say what she wanted, especially not to this man. "There is my second sister near the table with the cold offerings. She oversees the kitchen, and you will find her offerings rival anything served in London tonight. Do you wish to dine, Mr. Blackley? Shall I summon a waiter to take your request?"

"I'm not hungry," he whispered over her shoulder, his words coming unsettlingly close to her ear.

With her fan fluttering in her hand like an anxious butterfly, she twisted around to try to put more distance between them. But turning around only made it worse: now they stood face-to-face, her eyes level with his throat and his perfectly knotted dark-crimson neckcloth, his dark hair mussed and curling over his collar.

"Are you thirsty, then? The evening is—is *warm,* sir." But it wasn't the evening that was warm, not with him standing so close, and she worked to keep her words even. "Perhaps you *would* wish a selection from our excellent cellar? A glass of port, or—or canary?"

He shook his head, just a fraction. "That's not why I came here, lass."

"Miss Penny, sir." She corrected him unthinkingly with the explanation that Amariah had prepared for them all, concentrating instead on the slight sheen of a dark beard along his jaw. A pirate, a pirate from Barbados. "I am sorry, sir, but for the sake of the house's decorum, I must ask you to call me that, and nothing else."

"Very well," he said. "Then that's not why I came here, Miss Penny, *lass.*"

"That's wrong, sir, and no better." She sighed, a small, breathy exhale, and glanced down at the blades of her fan. How strange to be standing here with him like this, surrounded by an ever shifting crowd of black-clad gentlemen, laughing, calling, swearing, jostling, like a noisy tide around them. "For the decorum of the house, I must ask—"

"Damn the decorum of the house. That's not the same woman who crossed me today." He closed his fingers over the top of her fan, stilling its restless motion. "You can do better than that."

She thought of all the answers she could make, and how not one of them was either decorous or appropriate. "So you did follow me here?"

"I wish that I'd been that clever," he said. His gaze had shifted from her face to the fashionably low neckline of her gown, lingering there. "I'd no notion you'd be here tonight. But when I saw you, there at the top of the railing—ah, you seemed like an angel high over my head. Can you fault me for wanting to stay?"

She had to stop this *now,* before anyone noticed. She tugged her fan free of his hand, and turned toward the stairs.

"Of course you must wish to see the gaming rooms, Mr. Blackley." She raised her voice so others would hear her. "Up these stairs, sir, and you shall find the hazard table. If you wish to play, I shall introduce you myself to Mr. Walthrip, the table's director, and he can introduce you to the—"

"I'm not playing." He stopped on the step below her, making her stop as well. "Not tonight."

"But what of that story you told my sister, about how you'd stolen some poor gentleman's house away from him?"

"I didn't steal it, Miss Penny. I won it." Standing on the stairs, their eyes were nearly level. He wasn't smiling now, and with a shiver Cassia thought again of a pirate. "Luck has been very good to me, and like every good mistress, I don't treat her lightly."

"Then surely you would wish to play tonight of all others, Mr. Blackley." She tried to smile, but what had worked so effortlessly with Lord Russell seemed forced and false with Richard Blackley. "In honor of Penny House's opening, that is."

"Or else I will not be welcomed back?" His gray eyes seemed cold, almost ruthless. "If I do not play and promise to lose, like every other good little titled gentlemen of breeding and no brains here tonight, then you won't speak on my behalf again, will you?"

"I didn't say that!" she protested, but he hadn't waited for her answer, and had already passed her on the stairs. "Mr. Blackley, please!"

She grabbed her skirts to one side and hurried after him, dodging between other men gathered on the stairs. By the time she reached the top, he had disappeared into the noisiest and most crowded of the gaming rooms, the one with the hazard table. Although the gentlemen in the doorway stepped aside for her, she hung back.

Pratt had advised all three of the sisters never to enter this room, at least not when a game was at play. It was, he'd warned, not a fit place for ladies: with such substantial sums being won and lost each time the dice tumbled from their box, the players often could not contain their emotions, or their tempers.

And from what she could glimpse from the doorway, Pratt had been right. The gentlemen stood two and three deep around the oval mahogany table, covered with green cloth marked in yellow. The low-hanging fixtures cast a bright light on the top of the table, and strange shadows that distorted the faces of the players. Mr. Walthrip presided behind a tall desk to one side, the only man who kept his silence. Everyone seemed to freeze and hold their breath as one while the dice clicked and rattled in the box in the caster's hand. But as soon as the dice tumbled onto the green cloth, the men erupted, shouting and cheering and swearing and striking their fists on the top of the table so that even Cassia, who did not know the exact rules of the game, could tell who had won, and who had lost.

Then she saw Richard Blackley, leaning into the circle of light to toss a handful of pearly markers onto the table. All around him men exclaimed and pointed, making Cassia realize the wager must be sizable indeed. The dice danced from the box to the table, and two other piles of markers were pushed to join Blackley's. Another roll, and the pile became a small, pearly mountain before him, while the other men applauded, or simply stared in uneasy awe.

The caster was losing, his luck as sour as Blackley's

was golden. The man's face gleamed shiny with sweat, his collar tugged open, and this time he was holding the box in his hand so long that others began to protest. At last he tossed the dice, and as soon as they stopped, the long-handled rakes again shoved the markers toward Blackley's mountain. He looked down at it and frowned, then turned toward Walthrip.

"I withdraw," he said, loudly enough that everyone heard. "I am done for this night."

"But you can't!" cried the caster with obvious panic. "You've only begun! You must let luck turn, and give us try to win back what we've lost!"

"True, true," another man beside him said, glaring at Blackley. "No gentlemen leaves the table when he has won so deep."

"Hear, hear!" called the heavy-set man standing beside Cassia at the doorway. "It's not honorable this way! A gentleman doesn't quit when he's ahead!"

But Blackley didn't care. He bowed toward Walthrip, ignoring the others. "I believe the bank here gives its winnings to the poor, at the ladies' request. You may add my winnings to that gift for the night."

He stepped back from the table and away from the furor he'd just created, and sauntered through the crowd to the door as if every eye in the room and the hall outside weren't watching him. He came through the door, and stopped before Cassia.

"You said you wouldn't play," she said, her chin high, challenging him back. "You said—"

"I lied," he said. "But that was what you wanted of me, wasn't it?"

Her fingers tightened around the blades of her fan. "You said you wouldn't take luck for granted."

"I like to think I soothed whatever feathers I ruffled with my offering to *Bona Fortuna*. Sufficiently generous, don't you think?" From his pocket he drew one of the markers, a flat, narrow fish carved from mother-of-pearl, and pressed it lightly to his lips. "Good night, Miss Penny, until we meet again tomorrow evening."

He smiled, and before she could stop him, he tucked the fish-shaped marker into the front of her gown, the mother-of-pearl cool and shockingly sleek against the skin of her breasts.

Then he turned, and was gone.

Chapter Four

Bethany poured more breakfast tea into Cassia's cup as she read the newspaper over Amariah's shoulder.

"That part about the decorations of the club is very fine, Cassia," she said. "'The club's furnishings, arranged by Miss Cassia Penny, are most original and witty, and are sure to inspire much imitation in homes that pretend to set the fashion for the *ton.*' That should make you proud, shouldn't it? Imagine setting the fashion for the *ton!*"

But Cassia only sighed, her shoulders hunched with misery inside her calico wrapper, and dropped another spoonful of sugar into her tea with a glum *plop*. "Oh, yes, please find *something* to make poor dear Cassia proud about last night. Distract her from the discussion of that wretched pirate's antics."

"Overall, I think we did rather well nonetheless." Amariah turned the page, scanning the columns for more news of the club's opening. "To be sure, it seems to have been an uninspiring night for gossip and scandal, but we have made everyone *talk* of us."

"Listen to this part," Bethany said eagerly. "'For the first gentlemen of London who are weary of the older refuges of amusement to be found in this city, the refinement of Penny House will offer a gracious new destination after an evening's perambulations.' I wish we could have that copied out and posted on the front door, the way they do at the theaters!"

Amariah frowned over her teacup. "We do not wish to be compared to the theaters, Bethany. White's and Brook's, and perhaps Almack's—those should be our proper rivals."

"Not our rivals, Amariah, but our *inferiors*. We mean to conquer, not rival." Bethany set the teapot down in the center of the table, dropped back into her chair, and folded her arms over her chest. "Father always expected the best from us, and I do not see any reason for us to settle for less now."

Amariah made a huffy, noncommittal sound in her throat, and turned back to the paper.

But Cassia felt too tired to be so feisty. It had been close to dawn before the last of the club's guests had been ushered unsteadily out the door, and later still before she and her sisters had found their own beds. Even then she hadn't slept, tossing and turning as she played over every word she'd exchanged with Richard Blackley.

Now it was nearly noon, with the sun streaming in through the windows of this third-floor parlor that was their sanctuary. Below them, the scullery maids were already busy tidying the public rooms, the kitchen staff was preparing the meats and pastries for the evening's guests, and Pratt was meeting with Walthrip and the others to review last night's gaming. Even the sisters' gowns were being made ready, brushed clean and hanging to air so they'd be ready for another night of curtseying and smiling and charming with a determined purpose—something that only Cassia had been unable to do last night.

Now she sat back in her chair and braced her hands on the edge of the table, tired of waiting for the reprimand that she knew was coming.

"I've seen the story in the paper, Amariah," she began, "about me and Mr. Blackley and the hazard room and his—his *attentions.* I know how I very nearly ruined everything last night. You don't have to pretend you're keeping it from me."

"Your evening, Cassia—" Amariah folded the paper and set it beside her plate, smiling with grim purpose. "I wish I could pretend it away. I did wish to make Penny House the talk of all London, but not precisely in this way."

Bethany shoved back the drooping cuffs on her dressing gown, and leaned closer across the table. "Inspiring a rascally Caribbean planter to make outrageous wagers is one thing, Cassia. But then letting him stuff a marker down the front of your bodice, for all the polite world to see—oh, that was not well done."

"He surprised me!" Cassia protested. "I never expected he'd venture such a thing!"

"We must not be surprised by anything the gentlemen do," Amariah said, running her fingers along the creases of the newspaper. "That was what Pratt told us, and now we have seen the proof. Though I suppose much of this is my fault, Cassia, for letting the man stay."

Cassia poked at the toast, working a hole through the crust. "At least he gave all his winnings to the bank."

"Which of course we cannot keep," Amariah said. "I had Pratt return Mr. Blackley's money to him at the Clarendon early this morning."

"You *did?*" Cassia rose, clutching her napkin in one hand. "You sent all that money *back?* Why, he must have won hundreds—nay, thousands of pounds!"

"He was very lucky." Amariah took up her cup again, sipping delicately from one side. "There was no question of keeping it, Cassia. If we did, the man would think he had a right to you, as if he'd bought your services and your person like a common trollop."

Cassia turned away, going across the room to stand at the window so that her sisters wouldn't see her flush. As boldly as Richard Blackley had behaved toward her last night, as improper as his conversation had been, Cassia didn't feel he'd intended her to be his—his trollop.

She couldn't exactly explain why or how, and she certainly couldn't tell it to Amariah and Bethany, but there'd been something more between her and Richard, something she'd sensed rather than understood. He'd already proved himself to be a ruthless man, perhaps even a dangerous man, and even without Pratt's judgment she was certain that Richard had not been born a gentleman. Yet he hadn't made her a blatant offer, as Lord Russell had. He hadn't tried to put his arm around her waist or steal a kiss like some of the other gentlemen.

All he'd done was try to get her attention and keep it, whether by outbidding her for the painting or playing hazard because she'd wished him to. He had smiled at her, teased her, challenged her so she wouldn't forget him. He had looked at her in a way that none of the others had, a way that had made her feel on edge with low excitement, almost as if she had a fever. Even when he'd given back his winnings, it had been to ensure that he could return to Penny House and see her again.

She slipped her hand in her pocket, finding the fish-shaped marker that she'd hidden there. She should have tossed it down the stairs after him to show her scorn and outrage, but instead she'd kept it as a souvenir, a memento. He had risked a small fortune to be able to see her again, and now, with her sisters, she'd soon learn the price that she must pay for wanting to see him.

"Surely we will not admit Mr. Blackley again," Bethany said behind her, the muffled clank of silverware showing she and Amariah could go on eating their breakfast. "Not after the trouble he caused last night."

"No, no, Bethany," Amariah said. "We *must* admit him, and even consider him for possible membership. The other gentlemen will expect to see him there, to have another chance to win back their losses."

Cassia listened, and held her breath. So he would be back. She would see him again. Inside her pocket, she turned the little fish over and over again between her fingers.

"But what of his behavior toward Cassia?" Bethany asked indignantly. "I know that profit is the goal of

Penny House, but surely you don't intend to let his attention go unchecked?"

Amariah tapped the folded newspaper. "I have already sent letters to the editors of these papers, telling them that while we appreciated Mr. Blackley's generosity, we have returned his winnings to him, and advised him of the propriety that Penny House expects from its guests. There was also a pretty bit about us three being as virtuous as Caesar's wife that I'm sure they'll print."

At last Cassia turned to face her sisters. "And what of me, then?" she asked with gloomy resignation. "Shall I be banished to the garret to keep from shaming us all again?"

"That's stuff and nonsense, Cassia, which you know perfectly well." Amariah twisted around in her chair to see her. "It was hardly your fault. I told you before this wouldn't be the same as the Havertown Assembly, and I doubt there is a man like Mr. Blackley to be found in all of Sussex, nor one so dashingly handsome. He was far outside of your experience."

Cassia hung back, feeling both contrite and rebellious at once. "So I will be put in the garret, to keep from Mr. Blackley's experienced path."

"Oh, hush, you little goose," Amariah scolded gently. "You did exactly the right thing with such a man, not shrieking at him or slapping him like a fishwife. You were the model of restraint, when I know you'd prefer to flay him with the lash end of your temper."

Cassia didn't answer. There wasn't really a need to, considering.

"But next time, you won't be taken by surprise, will

you?" Amariah was smiling, but she was also watching Cassia so closely, making sure there was only one response. "Whether with Mr. Blackley or some other gentleman, you *will* make certain matters do not progress quite so far, won't you?"

"No, Amariah, I won't be taken by surprise again," Cassia said, as meekly as she could.

"I didn't think so." Amariah's smile returned to its customary serenity. "Which is good. There will be plenty of new gentlemen tonight who will expect you to bring them the same kind of extraordinary luck."

Cassia smiled, and for the first time since Richard had come toward her from the hazard room, she felt her shoulders unknot and the anxiety begin to slip away.

She hadn't spoiled everything. She hadn't shamed her sisters.

And the odds were excellent that she'd see Richard Blackley again tonight.

Bethany nodded, flipping her braid over her shoulder. "I am not quite sure why, but these gentlemen do seem to love us the more for being virtuous in an unvirtuous business. La, how many times last night did I have to tell of how we traded the vicarage for St. James Street!"

Amariah sighed, spreading another glistening blob of jam on her toast. "One old gentleman told me that we'd have twice the number clamoring for admission if only we could have our portraits taken and shown, the three of us together. Can you fancy such a thing?"

"Not yet, perhaps," Cassia said, pacing slowly back and forth as she thought aloud. "But what if we hired an open carriage and went riding in Hyde Park? That is where all the ladies go to take the air, and to be admired. We might as well do so, too."

"But not today," Bethany said quickly. "I have so many things still to do in the kitchen that I can't—"

"Yes, today!" Amariah smiled, and struck her open palm on the edge of the table for emphasis. "This is the perfect day to show that we are calm and at ease, as un-ruffled as can be by last night."

Cassia glanced at the window again, at the sunshine and watery blue sky over the slate roofs and chimney pots. It wasn't the sweet-smelling green fields of their old home in Sussex, but to put on her best hat and ride in an open carriage, to be perfectly idle and do nothing but admire the passing scenery—that would be a rare, wondrous treat.

"Might I come, too, Amariah?" she asked, her voice rising with hope, almost pleading. "Even after last night?"

"Must you ask?" Amariah's blue eyes were bright with determination, and amusement as well. "After last night, Cassia, I'd be a fool—a wicked fool—to leave you behind."

Three copper-haired visions shouldn't be hard to find, even in London.

Richard kept his horse at an easy pace as he rode through the park, weaving among other riders and carriages. He paid little attention to the trees or the newly blooming flowers, and even less to the women who smiled at him from beneath their broad-brimmed hats.

He was hunting for quarry much more specific than that, and for a few coins the footman at Penny House had told him exactly where to begin his search. A flame-haired beauty, riding with her sisters in an open carriage, should not be so difficult a needle to find in this haystack, even if Hyde Park was larger than many sugar plantations he'd known.

But in the end it wasn't her hair that led him to her, but the sound of her laughter coming from the other side of a stand of yews, merry and bubbling and unmistakably hers. Quickly he guided his horse through the trees to the next graveled path, and there she was.

"Miss Penny," he said, drawing his horse close to the carriage. "I've found you."

She smiled at him, the remnants of her merriment still showing on her face. "Gracious, Mr. Blackley. And here I'd no notion I'd been lost!"

"Lost to me," he said. "I need to speak to you."

"Then speak away, Mr. Blackley." She sat back against the dark leather seat, lightly twirling the handle of her parasol so it spun behind her. She was dressed plainly, even demurely, in a plain white muslin gown with a matching short redingote buttoned over it, more like the country parson's daughter she claimed to be than the proprietor of a gambling club. "I am found, and listening."

He didn't waste any time getting to what had bothered him all day. "Why in blazes did you return that money to me?"

"Because it was yours, Mr. Blackley." The smile remained, but the last trace of her earlier laughter had vanished. "You won it fairly, and it was yours to keep."

"But I meant it as a gift," he said. "For that infernal charity of yours, the paupers, or widows, or stray dogs from the riverbed."

He'd hoped she'd laugh again, this time for him, but she didn't. "You are perfectly free to give away every last farthing to whatever charity you please, Mr. Blackley, but you cannot do it through the Penny House bank. Unless, of course, you lose properly."

"That doesn't make a bit of sense," he said. "And I still don't see what in blazes—"

"Because your generosity appeared to expect in return a favor from my sister, Mr. Blackley." Cassia's older sister—Anne? Alice? Annabelle?—said, the other one nodding in agreement beside her. "Because you put her in an untenable situation for a lady."

"A favor?" How the devil had he overlooked the other two sisters there in the same carriage, sitting on the seat across from Cassia? "I did it because you'd made it clear as day that I wouldn't be let in again if I didn't make a profit for your blasted charity scheme. I can't help it if I won. If I wanted to see your sister again, I'd have to pay up."

"That's not what Amariah intended, as I tried to explain to you last night," Cassia said, leaning forward on the seat. "She wished to remind you that we are a gentleman's club, and nothing more. She meant that it's not proper for you to be so—so familiar with me there among so many gentlemen."

"That's ridiculous," Richard said. He hadn't done anything worthy of this damned lecture. And he didn't see Cassia herself complaining. "I didn't—"

"None of us wish to be compromised, Mr. Blackley," Amariah said. "As the owners of Penny House, we must be most careful of that, or risk ruining the club's reputation before we've really begun."

"Well, we're not at Penny House now, are we?" Richard swung down from his horse, holding the reins as he walked beside the carriage. He lifted his hat to Cassia. "Come stroll with me, lass, and we'll talk alone."

Her eyes widened as she looked down at him. "Here? Along this path?"

"It's easier than climbing up the elm trees, but I'll do that instead if you wish," he said. "Your sisters can follow in the carriage, ready to drive over me if I become too familiar."

"You won't," Cassia said, sliding her parasol shut and gathering her skirts to one side before she climbed out. "I won't allow it."

He liked watching her move, purposeful and direct and without any fussiness. The soft muslin was blowing close against her body and legs, not nearly as demure as he'd first thought.

"Cassia, I'm not sure this is wise." Bethany's face was tight with worry as she laid a gloved hand on Cassia's knee to stop her. "To be seen with this gentleman so soon after last night might be—"

"How am I supposed to apologize if I can't speak to her?" He didn't really believe he owed Cassia an apology, at least not for anything that had happened last night, but if an apology would coax her away from the others, he'd offer her a dozen. He held his hand out to help her down from the carriage. "Isn't that true, lass?"

"I don't think it's true at all, Mr. Blackley," she said without hesitation. "But I shall let you try regardless. Driver, stop here."

"Only for a few minutes, Cassia," Amariah cautioned. "Only for him to apologize. And mind, we'll be directly behind you."

Ignoring Richard's offered hand, Cassia hopped down from the carriage and once again opened her parasol, tipping it back against her shoulder. Without looking at him, she began walking briskly away, ahead of the carriage's horses. Her light cotton skirts swung back and forth with each quick step of her low-heeled shoes, accentuating her hips and bottom in a way that made him almost sorry to catch up with her.

"You didn't come find me to apologize, Mr. Blackley, did you?" she asked without turning.

He figured he'd probably do better telling the truth, especially since she'd already figured it out for herself. "No," he said. "I didn't."

Her mouth twitched at the corners, though he couldn't tell whether it was with satisfaction that she'd guessed correctly, or from some private amusement. The afternoon sun was filtering through the openwork in the brim of her straw hat, casting tiny pinpricks of light across her nose and cheeks.

"Is that because you'd hoped I wouldn't expect an apology?" she asked. "Or because you felt you didn't owe me one?"

He sighed mightily, and decided to stick with the truth. "I didn't believe I owed you anything. I didn't think I'd done anything."

"No?" At last she turned toward him, her expression incredulous. "Most gentlemen would regard placing a gaming marker where and how you did as having done quite a bit."

Richard drew himself up straighter, unconsciously squaring his shoulders as if preparing for an actual blow. London *was* different. None of the women he'd known on Barbados would have been shocked. They would have found such a gesture flirtatious, yes, and suggestive, but they also would have regarded it as a sign of admiration. They would have been flattered. It wasn't as if he'd pushed her against the wall and shoved up her skirts. He did have sense a of right and wrong, after all.

"So there's the proof you wanted that I'm not a gentleman. You've been looking for it ever since you saw me at the auction, haven't you?"

"Hardly." She blinked, surprised. "Whatever would make you think that?"

Too late he realized he'd volunteered more than he'd wanted. "You sent back my winnings this morning. You wouldn't have done that if I'd been a duke."

"Oh, yes, we would have," she said firmly. "Mr. Pratt was very convinced about that"

"Who in blazes is Mr. Pratt?"

"Mr. Pratt is our advisor about everything to do with gaming at Penny House," she said, as if it were perfectly obvious to anyone with half a thinking brain. "We could not *exist* without Mr. Pratt. He is guiding us to follow our father's wishes, you see, and help us make the money lost by wealthy gentlemen at the gambling tables do good for poor women and their children."

"But not the money I won?"

The look she flashed him beneath the curving brim of her hat showed that she clearly thought that that question had been addressed, and answered. "Charity is our goal, Mr. Blackley, not to become the mistresses of those same wealthy gentlemen."

"My *mistress?*" He stopped abruptly, letting the carriage roll past them. "You thought that was what I wanted?"

"Yes." She stopped, too, both hands gripping the parasol's handle, and two bright patches of embarrassment glowed on her cheeks. "You are not the first gentleman to ask me, you know."

"But I didn't, lass, and I won't." He had enjoyed her company and from the moment he'd met her, he'd wanted more of it, but he'd never considered anything so formal as putting her into keeping. He didn't have time for a mistress, not when he was hunting for a wife. "I've other plans, you may be sure."

Her blush deepened and she fidgeted with the parasol, twisting the tassel on the handle around and around one finger. "I'm very glad, Mr. Blackley, because I have other plans, too."

"You mean Penny House."

She nodded, a quick dip of her chin. He'd been intrigued by her chin from the start, a small, plump chin centered by a dimple, and he was sorry now—quite sorry—that he'd never have the chance to kiss it. "And what are your plans, sir?"

"To marry a lady," he said, with both pride and determination in his voice. "Preferably the daughter of a peer, though I'll consider lesser ranks if she's particularly beautiful. A wife is the final acquistion I need to complete my life."

"How vastly tidy of you, to have everything so arranged," she murmured, looking away as she began walking again. "Forgive me my ignorance, Mr. Blackley, but where does one go to obtain—or acquire—such a wife? Surely such ladies are not to be found on the block at Christie's?"

"It would be far easier if they were," he admitted. "Instead I must rely on several letters of introduction that I brought with me, and hope to proceed from there. That, and the usual lure of a sizable income."

"Oh, and your own charm, too." She glanced back at him, through her lashes, half teasing and half irritated with him. "You are very sure of yourself as a suitor, Mr. Blackley."

"I have reason to be." He considered taking her arm to demonstrate his hard-learned manners, then thought better of it before her watchdog sisters. "I have much to offer a prospective wife."

"But no title of your own," she said. "That will matter to the fathers of those daughters you seek."

"I do not hide my past, Miss Penny," he said. "I don't pretend to have been born a great gentleman. I came into this world as the youngest son of a Lancaster collier, and I'm not ashamed to say so."

Her gaze flicked over him, from the toes of his well-polished riding boots to the crown of his beaver hat, appraising him with fresh eyes. "You have prospered, Mr. Blackley. I am impressed."

"You should be," he said. "I've never believed pride to be a sin, not when it's earned. Nothing was given to me. Nothing was handed to me. Everything I have came from my own hard work."

"And dear Lady Luck." She smiled over her shoulder. "Isn't that how you said you won your house here in England?"

"Luck and skill and a good deal of Jamaican rum," he said, smiling back. "And to be honest, Sir Henry had let the house nearly tumble down around his ears."

She arched one brow, pretending to be shocked. "I thought it was the poor gentleman's patrimony!"

"A sad, sorry wager is what it was." Richard sighed, remembering how stunned he'd been by his first glimpse of Greenwood Hall, and that had been before he'd learned about the gaping holes beneath the slates in the roof and the chimneys full of swallows' nests and the plaster that had slipped clean away from the walls in the ballroom. "But I'll set Greenwood to rights. I'll make more improvements than Sir Henry ever could. It will become the best house in the county."

"I've no doubt, Mr. Blackley, that you can accomplish anything you set your mind to." She glanced ahead to the carriage before them, waving her fingers at her sisters—to reassure them, he guessed, that he wasn't in the process of debauching her right there among the crowds in Hyde Park. "All you must do to remedy Greenwood Hall is to take some of your great fortune and pay John Nash or some other fashionable architect to make everything as it should."

"That is true." Richard frowned, thinking. He'd already had to learn which tailor was considered best for bespoke coats and which bootmaker fitted calfskin to the most ducal feet, so it made sense that he'd have to discover who did the same sort of outfitting for houses. "Is this man Nash the best at his craft?"

"He is quite the favorite of the Prince," she said, "so I suppose he might be good enough for you as well."

He suspected she was teasing him again, but this was so important that he let it pass. "Did you use him for Penny House? Is that why you recommend him so highly now?"

"John Nash for Penny House? Gracious, no." She tipped back her chin and laughed, that merry, throaty sound he liked so well. "Hardly, Mr. Blackley, though you flatter me. All of our refurbishing was done at my direction, or even by my own hands."

"You?" She didn't seem like the sort of woman who'd tie on an apron and muddy herself.

"Most certainly." She held one hand out, her fingers spread before him, as if he could see through her gloves. "They're clean now, but there have been times these last weeks when my fingers were stained as black as a sweep's with paint and old varnish. "You aren't the only one who has worked hard to turn a sow's ear into a silk purse, you know."

"Then the newspaper was right to credit you?" he asked, still amazed. He'd liked the look of Penny House, stylish and opulent, but not so fancy that a man couldn't feel comfortable putting his feet up on the grate. "You did it yourself?"

"What don't you believe?" she asked, narrowing her

blue eyes at him. "That a parson's daughter could have taste and artistic sensibilities, or that as a mere woman, I could do any of it?"

But that wasn't what he'd been thinking at all. "Hang Mr. Nash. I'll hire you instead. You can have free rein to do whatever you think needs doing, and whatever funds you need to do so. I want Greenwood Hall fit for my bride, and who else would know better what another woman would want?"

"Most likely the woman herself." She raised her brows, clearly not taking his offer seriously. "I'd venture your phantom bride would have definite notions for her new home."

"But I don't know those notions, do I?" he said, enthusiasm warming his voice. "At present the place is a hellhole. I don't know how else to describe it. Green sold off what he could inside and let the rest go to rot. I couldn't even ask a lady or her father into the front hall, it's that bad. But you could make it good again. You could make it *right*."

She didn't answer at first, pausing. "You are serious? You would ask me to do this?"

"I am always serious." He smiled, confident she'd agree. "When I settle my mind on something, I don't change it. And I've settled my mind on you, Miss Penny."

She made a disparaging little puff. "To go to your house, to live under your roof—I could never do such a thing, Mr. Blackley."

"You wouldn't be alone with me. I've already begun taking on staff. The place has room for an entire regiment of footmen."

He saw the shift in her expression, the proof that she was actually considering his offer. "But Penny House has only just opened, and to leave now would—"

"I told you, I'll make it worth your while. I'll pay whatever you ask, or pay it to your charity, if you'd rather."

"I couldn't." She shook her head, the bow beneath her chin fluttering in the breeze. "Taking money from you—it would be like your winnings last night again. And though you may not care if my reputation is fodder for the morning gossips, I assure you that I care very much indeed."

He swept his arm through the air as if to sweep away her objections. "But it's business, lass! You have my word, if you'll take it. I'll be as chaste as a monk."

She rolled her eyes, back to disbelieving him again.

He decided he'd try another tack. "Very well, Greenwood Hall is a hellhole, but the grounds around it are heaven. At night I go lie in the grass and look up at the sky, just look. You can see every star imaginable, and the apple blossoms are so sweet in the air you can almost taste them. Not at all like gray old London. You'd like it there, I'm sure."

But the look she was giving him now had nothing to do with stars. "Apple blossoms and grass! I know you've sworn otherwise, Mr. Blackley, but it rather sounds as if you're inviting me to Greenwood for an assignation, not to work."

"I want to persuade you to come." He grinned. He had been imagining her there on the hill with him, not that he'd confess it, or apologize for it, either. "To give you something to consider each day when your work is done. I've always found lying in the grass to be a damned fine way to pass a spring or summer evening."

"It is." She smiled back, almost in spite of herself. "I am a country girl, you know, Mr. Blackley, from Sussex. I know all about new grass and apple blossoms, and the nightingale's song, too."

He stopped. "Then you will come to Greenwood with me?"

She stopped, too, her skirts still drifting around her legs. "For what purpose, Mr. Blackley? To lie in the grass with you, or to tell you what color to paint your drawing room?"

"Damnation, the paint must come first," he said, already sensing he'd lost her. "But I thought you'd enjoy the apple blossoms and the rest, too."

"I would." Her smile turned wistful and fleeting. "But you cannot have life both ways, sir, no matter how much you wish it, and you can't have me either way. Ahh, I see my sisters are calling for me. Good day, Mr. Blackley."

Luke stood before the captain's desk, his cap wadded tightly in his hand and his eyes locked straight ahead. He'd never been on board so grand a ship as the *Three Sisters,* and he'd never been in the presence of so formidable a gentleman as Captain Rogers, sitting grim-faced and unwelcoming on the other side of the desk.

"You wish to sign on as ship's boy?" the captain asked, his teeth clenched around the stem of his pipe. "You believe you've the makings of a sailor?"

"Yes, sir," Luke said, then realized the captain had asked him two questions. "Yes, sir."

Rogers narrowed one eye, gauging Luke's fitness. "You're a puny bit of snuff. How old are you?"

"Twelve, sir." Luke stood as straight as he could, trying to make the lie a truth and himself look taller and older than he was so the captain would take him.

Rogers grunted. "You look more like eight or nine. Does your mam know you're here?"

"My mother's dead," Luke said. He would not cry now, not even for Mama's sake. One tear, and he knew Captain Rogers would send him away.

"Convenient." Rogers nodded with approval. "She won't come yapping after me for taking away her pup. What of your father?"

"Lost at sea, sir." That was what Mama had always told him, and what Luke had never believed, which was why he was here now, praying for a place on this ship.

"Orphan, then?"

"Yes, sir." No mother or father, no brothers or sisters or aunts or uncles. Luke had been the only mourner to stand by his mother's grave while the priest had rushed through her last farewell, mumbling the Latin words together so he could leave Luke to stand alone in the steaming rain.

"Can you read and write and cipher, or only make your mark?"

"All three, sir," Luke said proudly. Mama had made sure of that, wanting him to better himself, just as she'd insisted he learn English without her Creole patois.

The captain leaned forward, drumming his fingers on

the edge of the desk. "You're not French, are you? I won't have any damned frogs in my company."

"My father's English, sir." He was glad now that he'd changed the spelling of his name from Luc to Luke, even though he'd had to betray his poor mother's memory to do it. "From Lancaster, sir."

"They breed good seamen in Lancaster." Rogers gave one final puff on his pipe. "You'll do. Bring your dunnage on board, boy. We clear Martinique for London on the morning tide."

"Thank you, sir," Luke said, and for the first time in weeks he smiled. London. At last he was bound for London.

And ready to find the father he'd never met.

Chapter Five

Cassia sat on the bench in the back of St. Andrew's parish hall, the Reverend Mrs. Barney at her side and the bored footman who'd accompanied her from Penny House standing near the door. The bare floors were swept clean, the bench so ancient that the seat was worn smooth, but Cassia knew that just outside the narrow leaded window the church's brawling, squabbling neighbors—an alehouse and a tavern, a fishmonger and a butcher—were constantly threatening to invade St. Andrew's fragile peace.

One by one the row of small charity girls, open-mouthed, wide-eyed, and snuffling and sniffling, dipped Cassia their curtseys before they presented their samplers of plain stitching for Cassia's approval. Though the girls were as scrubbed and neat as Mrs. Barney could make them, every one of them was too thin, too pale and already blighted with the blank resignation of poverty that seemed to Cassia so much worse than their rotting brown teeth or the sores on their bare feet.

"Very nicely done, my dear." Cassia smiled as she handed the crumpled linen square back to the last girl in line. But the child was too intimidated to smile back, and when Cassia reached out to pat her on the shoulder, she scurried away like a frightened little animal, back to the end of the line to cower behind the others.

"'Tis not your fault, Miss Penny," Mrs. Barney said softly. "You're a stranger to them, even if you are a grand lady, and they've learned to be wary of strangers to survive."

"I know, Mrs. Barney." Cassia sighed, wishing there was some way to coax the girls toward her. In Woodbury, she'd enjoyed teaching at the parish school, but the St. Andrew's girls were nothing like her old students. Coaxed from the most desperate neighborhoods in the city, these girls had never known any real security, and trust was as unfamiliar a luxury as fresh fruit or new clothes.

"I only wish I could be more useful to them," she said, "and not just sit here once a week as if I were Her Majesty herself."

"But you are useful, Miss Penny, you and your sisters both." Mrs. Barney clapped her hands, and the girls curtseyed again before they filed from the room, still clutching their needlework samplers before them like the rarest treasures. "You are continuing your late father's work in the most admirable way imaginable, and in a way that few other young women would dare do. Though others might have been shocked by a gentleman of faith owning a gaming club, he understood how, in this way, he could truly help God's poor."

Cassia looked longingly toward the doorway where the girls had gone. "But I feel as though I should be here with you, teaching them, too."

"What, those pretty scraps they display so proudly?" Mrs. Barney sighed with resignation. "I know that by teaching them to sew I hope that they can someday be apprenticed to mantua maker or milliner, a trade that will help them support themselves honorably. But the sad truth is that, given the chance, too many of them will slip back to their old ways in the alleys and streets."

Cassia thought of the gaudily painted young girls she'd seen around taverns or under street lamps, their languid poses and flashy cheap clothing meant to entice. No doubt her father, with three daughters of his own, had been particularly touched by their plight.

"Then how can you say my sisters and I are useful to these girls," she asked, "when we don't even do a fraction as much as you?"

"Because of the money that comes from Penny House, miss." Mrs. Barney's smile glowed with an almost unearthly fervor. "The school here is only the most humble beginning. With your contributions, I can go to Covent Garden and buy food and fresh milk to feed children and women who would otherwise go hungry. I can send babies and girls like these to live with families in the country, away from the streets and those who would prey upon them. I can arrange apprenticeships for willing boys with masters far from Tyburn and Newgate. And I can keep them all alive for another day."

She placed one work-rough hand over Cassia's. "You've a good soul, Miss Penny, and a good heart," she said, "but you also have an opportunity to contribute that the rest of us never will. It's money that can make the greatest difference, miss, and money that we need the most."

"Money," repeated Cassia softly. Everything came down to that, didn't it?

Mrs. Barney nodded. "What you and your sisters collect at Penny House in a single night can change—no, save!—more lives in the balance than ever you can imagine. How proud your father would be of you three now!"

Changing and saving lives in the balance: Mrs. Barney's words echoed through Cassia's head as the hired chaise threaded its way back from the squalid neighborhood surrounding St. Andrew's to the elegance of St. James Street.

Wasn't that why she had wanted to make this extra visit to Mrs. Barney and her girls after her altercation with Richard Blackley? She had wanted to remind herself again of the reasons behind Penny House, and how it was—how it *must* be—so much more than simply a playground for the likes of Mr. Blackley. She had needed to have her own purpose in this world reaffirmed, and she had needed to forget the heady temptation that Richard Blackley seemed determined to offer her.

She sighed, resting one hand on the chaise window's sill as the neighborhoods and passersby changed before her. He was temptation, too, every tall, infuriating part of him, and she couldn't begin to explain exactly why she was so susceptible. She'd known other men who were more handsome, more charming, more witty and certainly better mannered. She was twenty, after all. She wasn't a complete ninny about men, and she was learning more every night at Penny House.

Yet somehow Richard Blackley could walk beside her in a public park at midday, speaking of the mythical lady he wished to marry and the run-down house he needed to repair for her, and still make Cassia feel more attracted to him than she had to any other man.

It made no sense whatsoever. He'd smile, and she felt herself blush. He'd say her name in his rough, low growl of a voice, and she wanted to purr in return. He'd held his hand out to help her from the carriage, and just the proximity of his hand had sent a delicious shiver racing down her spine. He'd described lying in the new-mown grass to gaze up at the stars, and she'd imagined lying beside him so vividly she'd half expected to find twigs and blades of grass on her petticoats.

She sighed again, tapping restlessly on the seat cushion with her gloves. He'd tried so hard to convince her to come with him to Greenwood Hall, and she could not imagine a more dangerous place for her to be. Not because she feared him—if ever there was a man in control of his emotions, it was Richard Blackley—but because she feared herself.

The chaise rolled to a stop before Penny House, and she unlatched the door and clambered out herself, not waiting for the footman to help her. Briskly she marched through the door and the hallway, her heels clicking across the marble floor. Mrs. Barney had said her place was here, making sure the club turned a sizable profit. Well, so be it. She'd make sure that tonight—

"Miss Cassia!" Pratt hurried toward her, his broad face wreathed with a happy smile. "We've just now finished the hanging!"

"The hanging?" She paused, and frowned, tugging at the fingers on her gloves. "Whatever are you saying, Pratt? Or have you become Jack Ketch, and now carry out executions in your free mornings?"

He laughed, rubbing his thick-knuckled hands together with something close to glee. "You had us fooled, didn't you, Miss Cassia? Pretending you'd lost the painting at the auction, when Christie's was just mending the frame before it was delivered!"

"Pratt, you make no sense." But Cassia already could guess what had happened, even before she hurried across the hall and threw open the double doors to the drawing room.

There over the fireplace, in the place of honor reserved for it, hung *The Fortune Teller,* exactly where Cassia had both expected and dreaded.

"It does look fine there, Miss Cassia," Pratt said beside her. "The gentlemen will be amused. You do have an eye for the proper picture to grace a room, and—"

"Was there a note with the painting, Pratt?" She knew there wouldn't be, but she wanted to be certain. Oh, *how* could that wretched Mr. Blackley do this to her? Had he understood nothing of what she'd told him in the park? Did he truly believe he could change her mind with such ease, and for such a price? "A receipt from Mr. Christie?"

"No, miss." Pratt looked both wary and worried. "But the man who delivered it said—"

"Oh, a pox on the man who delivered it, and a pox on the man who sent it, too!" She pointed up at the painting, her eyes narrowing. "Please have it taken down, Pratt. Have it taken down at once!"

"Very well, Miss Cassia." Pratt nodded to the nervous footman who'd appeared instantly at the doorway. "Where would you like it placed instead?"

She knew exactly where the painting should be placed in relation to its owner, not that she'd ever say so to poor Pratt. "I'm—that is, we—we won't be keeping the picture, Pratt, because it's not mine—ours to keep. Return it to its owner directly."

"But you are the owner, miss," Pratt said, for once being particularly plaintive and dense, "and I don't see how—"

"Return the painting to Mr. Blackley," she said, watching the footman climb on a chair and wrestle the offending picture from the wall. "It's his, no matter what nonsense his servant told you."

"Very well, miss." Pratt bowed, having enough experience and sense not to show his surprise, and took the painting from the footman. "I'll have it sent to the Clarendon at—"

"On second thought, Pratt, I believe I shall deliver it myself, so I might see his face when it reappears on his doorstep." She seized the painting from the startled Pratt, holding it out before her with both hands as if the canvas carried an unpleasant stench. "Please send to the stable for another chaise for me."

Pratt hesitated. "Perhaps you might take a few mo-

ments to reflect, miss, to consider. Miss Amariah
might have—"

"The decoration of these rooms is my responsibility,
not my sister's," she answered. "Which includes deciding to return this wretched painting to Mr. Blackley as
soon as I possibly can."

Pratt cleared his throat. "I do not know if that is, ah,
the wisest course where Mr. Blackley is concerned,
Miss Cassia."

"No, Pratt," she said firmly. "Where Mr. Blackley is
concerned, this is the *only* course."

But no matter what Pratt had cautioned, Cassia felt
her temper simmering hotter with each jolt and jostle
of the hired chaise. Scowling down at the picture
propped across her lap, it seemed to her that even the
old painted fortune teller eyed her with amusement,
mocking Cassia for how easily Richard Blackley could
upset her.

She wasn't sure if he'd sent it back to her to tease her
or taunt her or bribe her into coming to his country house
with him. Whatever the reason, the result would still be
too much talk at her expense, and the more she thought
of what the gossips would say, the more her anger grew,
propelling her straight into the front hall of the Clarendon, the painting tucked awkwardly beneath one arm.
The ornate gilt gesso frame made it heavier than she'd
thought, thumping against her side as she walked.

"I am here to see one of your guests," she told the
porter who greeted her, setting the painting down on the
floor beside her. "Mr. Blackley. Mr. Richard Blackley."

The porter nodded, appraising her appearance just as

Pratt did with the guests to Penny House. "And your name, miss?"

"Miss Penny." Cassia drew herself up a little straighter. Now she wished she'd changed from the purposefully subdued clothes she wore to St. Andrew's into something a bit more stylish. From the entry alone, she could see that the Clarendon was a far cry from the country inns along the stage routes that were her only experience, and the other guests who were coming and going, with small armies of servants in attendance and mountains of trunks and boxes, were a higher class of traveler, too.

"Miss Cassia Penny, of Penny House," she said again when the porter didn't reply. "And I assure you that Mr. Blackley will recognize the name at once."

But the porter recognized it, too, a flicker of awareness darting across his eyes. He would have read the scandal sheets to learn about his guests, just like Pratt did, and he would know all about Penny House's grand opening.

And he would also know what those same papers had said about her and Richard Blackley.

No wonder he now bowed with the absolute minimum bend to his waist, and summoned a footman. "Thank you, Miss Penny. I shall see if Mr. Blackley is in. You may have a seat there, if you please."

Cassia sat on the very edge of one of the stiff little chairs, her back straight and her expression as impassive as she could make it. She hated being made to wait for Richard like this, relegated to a hall chair near the door like some dunning tradesman, and she hated the way people were looking both at her and the picture propped against her legs, their glances curious and disapproving and disdainful.

Too late to be of any use, she thought now of Pratt's concern for her welfare, and flushed at how she must look, a single woman summoning a gentleman in a hotel.

She muttered to herself, and willed her toe to stop its unladylike tapping. Self-consciously she turned the painting's face toward her, leaving the plain canvas back turned out and giving the passersby one less thing to gawk at. Once she had liked the picture enough to bid beyond her limit for it, but now she couldn't wait to be rid of the painting forever.

A pox on Richard Blackley for shaming her like this, and for keeping her waiting, and for—

"So it *is* you." Richard sauntered down the stairs toward her, as if keeping her waiting was perfectly within his rights. "The fair Miss Penny, come to call on the likes of me!"

She popped up from her chair, clutching the painting like a shield before her. "Well, it is I," she said, "but this is hardly a social call, Mr. Blackley."

"No?" His smile came slow, and he studied her with such lingering, obvious interest that she felt her face grow hot with shame. "And here I've gone and made myself fine, just for you."

He did look fine, too, in light-colored breeches, tall boots, a dark blue coat and a sky-blue waistcoat. His dark hair was combed back from his forehead and his jaw was newly shaved, and if he felt any of the effects of his late night, it didn't show. Not that any of that mattered to Cassia now—or at least she didn't want it to.

She cleared her throat to settle herself, and tried to think of the charity girls at St. Andrew's instead of how closely his breeches fit across his thighs. "Then I am sorry you've wasted your time, Mr. Blackley. I have come to you about this picture, and nothing more."

She turned the painting and held it up between them.

"Do you like it, then?" he asked, his smile widening. "You must, else you wouldn't have come clear over to this side of town to thank me for it in person."

"I have always liked the picture, Mr. Blackley," she said. "But as a gift between us, it is absolutely unacceptable."

She raised the painting higher between them, wanting to make a gesture as emphatic as her words. But her arms wobbled beneath the weight and the heavy frame sagged in her hands. At once Richard caught the picture, easily steadying it for her.

"Then don't think of it as a gift," he said, looking down at her over the edge of the frame. "Think of it as returned property. You said I stole it from you. So now I'm just giving it back to its rightful owner."

"But it's not mine because I didn't pay for it." Their hands grazed against one another, a touch she did not want, and she inched her fingers farther down the curving side of the frame and away from his. "It's yours, Mr. Blackley, and it's still yours, because I won't accept it."

"Then accept it as the first payment for your work at Greenwood," he said. "I haven't abandoned that, you know, nor am I ready to do so."

"Then you are sure to be disappointed." She felt as if she were wrestling with him through the painting. "I told you before, Mr. Blackley, that I cannot and will not accept this painting from you."

"I suppose you'll just have to earn it, sweetheart," he said, nodding pleasantly at two elderly ladies, pursing their lips with disapproval as they waited for their carriage near the door. "It shouldn't take you too long, should it?"

Bracing her feet as best she could on the polished floor, she shoved the painting back toward him. "You will take it back!"

Of course he didn't budge. "I'm driving to Greenwood later this week. Come with me, in my coach. I'll show you the house, and you can begin the changes as soon as you wish."

"Mr. Blackley," she said, her voice rising with frustration. "Mr. Blackley, sir, I told you, this is not the—"

"Please, Mr. Blackley, please, consider our other guests!" The porter hurried to them, his hands knotted together and his whole face pleading. "Might I suggest you remove your conversation with Miss Penny to the small private parlor to the right of the stairs, a place where you will not be interrupted?"

"Now that's a sorry sort of request to make of a gentleman and a lady, to go hide under the stairs." Richard sighed deeply, then plucked the painting from Cassia's hands without any extra effort at all. "Come, pet, and let us remove ourselves before we cause any more confusion and misery."

Cassia folded her now empty hands over her chest. "What if I don't wish to? You've taken the painting

back. I've no reason to stay. Why should I remove anywhere with you?"

"Because you do wish to," he said, his smile lazy and
knowing, and very close to insolent. "Because you've
still things to say to me."

"I should say there are!" she said, her voice growing louder in spite of her best intentions. "When I consider what—"

"Mr. Blackley, please," the porter beseeched again,
his face purplish red. "For the peace of this house and
for the sake of our other guests, I really must ask you
and Miss Penny to refrain—"

"Oh, we'll refrain and restrain and remove." He
tucked the painting beneath one arm, and hooked his
other through the crook of Cassia's elbow. "Come
along, sweet, before this poor fellow expires of apoplexy at our feet."

"No!" She tugged her arm free and glared. "I'm not
going anywhere with you!"

His smile vanished, and he leaned forward, his hoarse
whisper loud enough for everyone to hear. "Coward."

"I am not!" She gasped, and swept away ahead of
him, past the porter who was eagerly showing her the
way. The parlor was tiny, a room carved from beneath
the stairs that was likely used only for guests wishing
special privacy while they waited for their carriage to
be called—or for the troublesome ones, like her and Mr.
Blackley.

"Leave the door open," she ordered as he joined her.
"I don't intend to be here with you any longer than
necessary."

"How damned cordial." He dropped the painting on one of the two chairs and turned toward her. "But then that's always the way with you, isn't it? You're just like the painting, hiding behind your prim little title of clergyman's daughter."

"That's because I *am* a clergyman's daughter." There had to be some logic in what he was saying, but she was too angry herself to sort it out. "I'm not hiding at all. And I don't see what that has to do with the painting."

"Use your eyes, lass!" He waved one hand toward the painting on the chair, not bothering to hide his own temper. "That old woman's a bawd, selling the services of the yellow-haired trollop behind her. There's not one blasted bit of fortune-telling going on in that picture, except for the auction house that pinned that milk-white label on it to please the lady-buyers like you."

"Don't be preposterous!" she snapped, but now as she looked at the painting, she realized his interpretation was correct.

The sly expression on the old woman's face, the seductive half smile of her younger associate, even the overeager ardor of the soldier—the exact same ardor she'd seen last night on Lord Russell's round face—all of it now made appalling sense, especially in light of its Italian provenance, a country known for its decadence. And to think that she'd almost bought such a disreputable picture for Penny House!

He smiled, full of infuriating male triumph. "See now, you've smoked it for yourself, haven't you? I can tell by your face."

She whipped around, determined to control whatever

expression had betrayed her. "That painting has nothing to do with me!"

"Doesn't it?" He raked his hand back through his dark hair, and took a step closer to her. "Aren't you pretending to be otherwise, too, babbling on about your high holy good works when all you're doing is running a gaming house?"

"Oh, you don't know *anything!*" Cassia tossed back her head, refusing to back away from him. The door was still open, and she told herself she'd be safe enough with the hall full of other guests. "This very morning I visited the class of charity girls at St. Andrew's that my sisters and I help support."

"Aye, Lady Bountiful, scattering her blessings over the poor." He used his height to look down at her. "I know your kind, Miss Penny. Poor folk are your pets, made to sit and beg and wait upon your fancy, whenever you wish to make yourself feel generous and noble."

"That's not true!" she cried, even as her conscience reminded her of how she'd felt with the girls this morning. "That's not how it is! Those people rely on me and my sisters!"

"What they rely upon is the money," he said, so relentless that she wondered if the truth had shown in her face again. "Not that you give a damn about that. No, else you'd take whatever money came your way. You'd take the winnings I offered, and you wouldn't give two thoughts before you'd accept my offer to refurbish Greenwood. But you're being so overnice about how and why it got to you."

"To be respectable is not the same as being overnice, and I do not—"

"And I still say you're pretending you're something you're not." He took another step closer, so close she could see the tiny gray flecks in his blue eyes. "You're doing it now, acting like a fine lady with more manners than sense."

She shook her head with disbelief, her curls bobbing against her cheeks. "You're a fine one to talk, the collier's son who wants to wed the daughter of a peer!"

"I've never denied who I am, or where I want to be," he said, "and I've never pretended otherwise. But you— take you away from your sisters and that father you're still trying to please, and you can't say who or where you belong, or even what you want from life."

"Of course I know!" Her fingers were curled into tight fists at her sides. "How could I not?"

His voice dropped to a hoarse whisper, just between them, and the tiny room seemed to shrink smaller still.

"Then tell me, lass," he said. "If you're so damned sure of yourself, tell me."

She couldn't explain the shake to her voice, or why her lips had turned so dry she had to lick them, just to be able to speak. "What I want is to make a success of Penny House, and to—"

"Not that," he said, pulling her into his arms and against his chest. *"This."*

His mouth swept down on hers, kissing her before she'd realized what was happening, so fast that at first all she did was freeze, her hands still clenched at her sides. She had been kissed before, of course, but those shy, respectful kisses from boys after dances were nothing like what was happening now.

Richard Blackley was kissing her like a man, the same man who'd tucked that marker between her breasts, sure and purposeful and without any respect at all. His mouth on hers was demanding, expecting her to follow wherever he led, and the heat of it seared her, melting her limbs—and her pitifully small resistance—like butter in the sun. She kissed him back with the same fierce intensity, her hands moving restlessly against the superfine-covered wall of his chest. Her eyes fluttered shut, her head reeling with his taste. It was like bidding for the painting all over again, trying to match, then better him, as together their excitement grew.

And when he finally broke his mouth away from hers, she could only stare up at him, searching his face for the reason he'd stopped.

"You understand now, sweetheart, don't you?" His eyes were half-closed, fathomless, watching her beneath heavy lids. "Of course you do. You're a clever creature, aren't you?"

But she didn't feel clever, not about this. "Because you kissed me?"

"Because you kissed me back." His smile was slow and knowing. With his forefinger he traced the bow of her upper lip. "Because you liked it. Because despite being your father's daughter, you're a wanton little pagan at heart, where it matters."

She gasped, shocked back to her senses, and raised her hand to strike him. "I am not! How dare you say—"

He easily caught her wrist before she hit him, holding her, pulling her back toward him. "I say it because it's true. We're too much alike, Miss Cassia. If we ever came together, it would be as hot as if we'd invented sin."

She gasped again, struggling to break his hold on her wrist. "I cannot believe you would—"

"But you should," he said, his face once again close to hers, "because it's true. That kiss proved it."

"All it proved is that you are no gentleman!"

"What it proves," he said, "is that I *am.* Leastwise, I'm trying very hard to be one. I'm not going to let you dazzle me, sweetheart, no matter that you're the most passionate parson's daughter I've ever known. But I intend to marry my lady-bride, and I won't let you throw me off course, as much as we both would enjoy it."

"Speak for yourself," she snapped, a weak retort if ever there was one.

"I generally do." The muscles in his jaw were taut with determination to keep his desire at bay. "But now you understand why you'd be safe with me. You're copper-haired temptation, and I'm not going to bite. Not now, not tomorrow, and especially not if you came with me to Greenwood. You have my word that I'll hold fast. You can trot through my bedchamber naked save for your bonnet, and I swear I'll not bat an eye."

She cried out with indignation, her temper at last giving her the strength to break free of his grasp. Without a pause she swung her hand down and slapped him across his cheek, slapped him so hard that her fingers stung from the impact.

But he didn't flinch. He smiled, even as the angry imprint left by her open palm began to glow on his cheek.

"You deserved that," she said, unable to keep from wincing for him. She'd never hit a man like that before—she'd never had to—but she wasn't proud of having done it, either. "You know you did."

He nodded, though not necessarily with agreement.

"You're amused," she said, her anger cooling to irritation. "You shouldn't be, not after what you said, and not after I struck you for it."

"From you, dear Cassia, I expected nothing less." He bowed, and lifted the painting from the chair as he moved toward the open door. "I'll take custody of this until you can muster more appreciation for its genius."

"You can't go, not yet." She took two quick steps after him before she realized how foolish she must look. No, it wasn't only chasing after him; it was this whole foolish meeting, resulting in the most foolish kiss she'd ever experienced.

His smile turned rakish, and she was horribly sure he considered winking. "So you don't wish me to go, sweetheart? Even after I told you I wouldn't touch a hair on your fiery head?"

"No." Her deep breath came as more of a gulp. "That is, I refuse to let you leave with the last word again."

"Then speak," he said, turning to look back at her over his shoulder as he paused at the open door. "I promise to let whatever you say stand."

He was so wickedly handsome and sure of himself that it just wasn't fair. She had been educated beyond her gender and station, and raised to be proud of her intelligence, but all he had to do was smile, and she forgot every lick of common sense she'd ever possessed. Her father and her sisters would be aghast, and rightfully so. She sighed with humiliation, and pushed past him out the door without meeting his gaze.

"Fool," she muttered. "Fool."

Chapter Six

"Blackley! Here!" Lord Carew waved his arm as if signaling clear to Dover, his plain round face glowing with enthusiasm. "Here, come join us!"

Richard didn't smile back, but he couldn't ignore such a greeting, and with a reluctant sigh he guided his horse over to where the young Marquis of Denby was still flailing his arm like a manic windmill.

"I say, Blackley," Carew called, his eyes screwed up as he squinted into the sun behind Richard's back. "This is the most marvelous coincidence, yes?"

It wasn't a coincidence. It was an ambush, and Richard grumbled wordlessly to himself as he wondered how many times Carew had ridden back and forth through this park before he'd been able to pounce. Richard was late this morning; last night had stretched into this morning, and for once he'd dozed in his chair and let Neuf fuss as long as he wanted over his shaving soap and razor.

The question, of course, was why Carew had sought him out this way. They'd both become regulars at Penny House, but because the family's fortunes had dipped— at least that was what gossips said—Carew's father kept him on the shortest possible leash. This limited the young lord's play and encouraged his drinking instead, and most nights kept him from Richard's path altogether.

But the answer came soon enough.

"Here, Blackley, I'd like to present you to my mother and sister." Carew now waved that flailing arm toward a small open carriage with the family crest painted on the door, and Richard bowed dutifully to the two women inside.

Beneath an enormous purple hat, swathed in a matching purple shawl large enough to house a regiment, the Marchioness of Denby had clearly passed along her plain, pleasant, doughy face to her son. Beside her, Carew's sister Lady Anne was prettier than she'd any right to be, which was not to say that Richard would call her a beauty: bland pink and white like a costly, too sweet confection.

The young woman lowered her chin and peeked up at him from beneath her bonnet's brim, coquetry that seemed too determined, almost desperate. Richard nodded, as he was expected to do, but the face in his thoughts belonged to Cassia Penny.

When Cassia had looked up at him from a carriage like this, he'd forgotten every other person in the entire blasted park, including her two sisters sitting inches away from her. On her the fashionable white muslin gown had seemed unbelievably provocative, making him think of all the pleasant ways he could peel it away from her lush, round—

"So you find it to your liking, Mr. Blackley?" Lady Anne was asking him.

Richard cleared his throat and straightened the reins in his hand, stalling for time while he struggled for a reply. For over a week now, he'd been a strong man, and had kept his distance from Cassia as he'd promised. Even at Penny House, he'd ventured no more than bow to her across the gaming room. It hadn't been easy, but he'd done it. So why the devil was she haunting him now?

And exactly what in blazes was he supposed to be liking instead of the creamy pale skin of Cassia's barely covered breasts? "Any gentleman, ah, any gentleman would."

He winced. He was thinking of Cassia again, which he'd absolutely no right to do, but by some miracle the answer he'd given was still the right one.

"Yes, Mr. Blackley, how wise you are." Lady Anne nodded, solemn as a hymn. She had pale lashes to match her pale hair, giving her eyes an unfortunately blank look. "What gentleman wouldn't like London? I know myself that though I've been in town twice now, I still haven't begun to tire of it."

Lady Carew made a delicate, meaningful cough as she rested her hand on the girl's arm. "What Lady Anne means to say, Mr. Blackley, is that London is such a grand and edifying city that one could come down for a thousand Seasons without beginning to see everything."

At that Lady Anne seemed to wilt, scowling as she dropped back against the back of the seat, and now

Richard understood the disaster behind what she'd un-wittingly disclosed. The girl was in her second Season of hunting for a husband, and this year she'd lowered her sights. She'd had no choice, or else risk spending the rest of her life as a genteel spinster. Not even her father's rank and power had helped overcome a smallish dowry or those pale eyelashes, and the failures of last year hovered darkly between mother and daughter, and even over poor Carew as well.

"I've told Mama and Anne all about you, Blackley," he said, the young man's cheerfulness now thoroughly strained. "About how you'd had to sail all the way across the ocean to reach London, while we only had to come down the stage road."

"My son says you have holdings in the West Indies, Mr. Blackley." The countess leaned forward, eagerness making her clutch her shawl more tightly around her plump shoulders. "They say great fortunes can be made there by gentlemen with the right enterprising spirit."

So he was in the running, thought Richard. Interesting.

"A successful plantation takes hard work and a good deal of luck, my lady, same as anywhere else," he said. Carew had been most thorough in his investigations, a favor Richard himself meant to return. He'd want to be sure of the family, sure of their bloodlines and connections. "Sugar trading's a perilous venture in the best of times."

The countess's pause was weighty with significance. "But you *are* among the lucky ones, aren't you, Mr. Blackley?"

Did she expect him to begin listing his assets and accounts, here in the middle of the park? "I've been lucky, my lady," he said instead, "and I've worked hard, same as any other successful man."

The countess smiled her satisfaction. "You are too modest, sir. If it were that simple, then every gentleman would own his own sugar plantation."

"Sugar," breathed Lady Anne. "Oh, Mr. Blackley, I do like sugar!"

Richard forced himself to smile back. So this was why he'd been ambushed. If he wished, he would be considered a suitor where all others had fallen away, his person and fortune an acceptable exchange for Lady Anne's title—the trade he'd always wanted.

"I like sugar, too, Lady Anne," he said, striving to be gallant. "It's, ah, sweet."

"Sugar, sugar." She sighed, half closing her eyes at the blissful thought of that much sweetness. "How lucky you must be to always have it in such abundance at your door, there whenever you want it."

"It doesn't exactly drop from the skies like snow, you know," he said. "There are a great many steps between planting the cane and the stuff that you sprinkle in your tea."

"But I don't have to know how, because you do. I should leave everything like that to you." She clapped her hands together, as if applauding either him or his sugar, he couldn't tell which. "But then you are *so* clever, Mr. Blackley, just the way my brother said you were."

"Ahh, it's luck, too," he said, uncomfortable with such automatic flattery. Cassia would have just laughed at him outright, and he would have laughed with her.

"One good blow from a hurricane, and your crop's lost before it's begun, your plantation tumbled into the sea, and you're as ruined as a man can be."

"How very brave of you, Mr. Blackley! I should never have the courage to live in such a perilous place." Lady Anne smiled, her thin lips pressed together in a tight little crescent. Perhaps all that lovely sugar had taken its toll, and with queasy curiosity Richard wondered if she hadn't a sound tooth left in her head.

Yet she was the daughter of a peer, an important peer who spoke often in the House of Lords. Opportunities like this didn't happen every day, and not even Richard's letters of introduction would have taken him this high. Richard cleared his throat, and plunged manfully onward.

"I'm afraid for now I've left my plantations on Barbados, Lady Anne," he said, "and moved here to England. My new home is Greenwood Hall, or rather, my old home. They say old King Hal himself was a guest, there for the hawking. We're in Hampshire, not far from the city, and as charming a country spot as ever you'll see."

That much was true. The house was charming, or would be, and his pride in it was genuine. All it needed were a few repairs and paint and furniture and paintings, and there wouldn't be a finer seat in the county.

"Oh, that sounds delightful!" Lady Stanhope gushed. "There is nothing like an ancient home, passed down through the family!"

Before Richard answered, she turned toward her son. "George, we should go. A drive through Hampshire is next to nothing, nothing at all! If Greenwood Hall is as pleasant a spot as Mr. Blackley says, then I cannot imagine a more agreeable way to pass a day."

"Mama, please." The poor marquis flushed, fussing with the reins in his hands to avoid meeting Richard's eye. "Blackley doesn't want you poking about his place without a proper invitation."

"The truth is, My Lady, that I'm having certain improvements made about the place," Richard said quickly. The last thing he needed—or wanted—was the countess spying on Greenwood Hall's collapsing chimneys and overgrown gardens. The way the house looked now, one good peek could be enough to yank him from consideration as a suitable husband. Blast Cassia for not agreeing to help him! "I'm not ready for receiving, especially not fine ladies like yourself and Lady Anne."

"Oh, Mr. Blackley!" The girl might have blushed; she was so pale, Richard wasn't sure. "You are very kind and considerate of our welfare and sensibilities!"

"As is proper, Anne, as is proper." Lady Stanhope nodded, mollified for now, and reached up to smooth one of her nodding purple plumes. "They are necessary evils, I know, but carpenters and plasterers can be the most disruptive low creatures in the world. And, oh, the dust and filth they bring into a decent home!"

"Yes, my lady." That was all Richard could think to say. His head ached abominably, as if every horse in the park were prancing between his eyes. He needed to get away to sort all this out. He needed time to think.

He needed a brandy, the faster, the better.

Lady Stanhope, however, thought he needed food. "There is nothing sadder than a rootless gentleman, Mr.

Blackley," she declared. "I would be most remiss if I did not offer you the hospitality of our house and table. You must come dine with us one evening, sir. You must."

"Oh, yes, do!" Lady Anne blinked her pale lashes, beseeching him with all the allure of a white cony. "Say you'll come, Mr. Blackley. Say you'll accept Mama's invitation, and join us."

"Of course he'll come," Carew said heartily, stopping just short of clapping. "*En famille,* Blackley, that's what the French call keeping things within the family, and as arrangements go, it's the pleasantest thing in the world."

En famille. All of Richard's limited French had been acquired in the port towns on Martinique and St. Croix, and while families had not figured into any of his vocabulary, this meaning was clear as day.

He, Richard Blackley, was being invited into the home and the family of the Marquis of Denby. He was being given permission to court their daughter, and if he behaved himself with reasonable honor and decency, he would most likely be granted her hand as well. His wife would be the high-born lady that had warmed his dreams and fueled his aspirations. He would be presented at Court, and welcomed in the grandest houses. He'd have no title of his own, true, but together they would always be Mr. Richard and Lady Anne Blackley, and their children—*his* children—would be born with the noblest of blood in their veins.

En famille. That was what he'd always wanted, wasn't it? Not a quick-tempered, copper-haired vicar's daughter who could spoil everything, but a meek, high-bred lady who'd worship his every word?

"Please say yes, Mr. Blackley." Lady Anne's nose wrinkled with anxiety as she squinted up at him, near terrified that he'd refuse. "I know a gentleman such as yourself likely has more invitations than I can imagine, but you'll make me so happy if you say yes to Mama."

It was a wondrous world indeed when the collier's son could offer happiness to an earl's daughter. He'd come too far, worked too hard, to be distracted now. The prize was waiting there before him, as neat and tempting as a ripe plum dangling from the nearest branch. All he had to do was claim it.

He smiled his most respectful smile as he bent down to take the girl's hand, holding her gloved fingers gingerly in his own. "I will be there, Lady Anne."

Because this was what he'd always wanted, wasn't it? *Wasn't* it?

Cassia stood on the chair, her hands clasped before her as she gazed out at the small crowd of gentlemen clustered around her. Recitations had always been one of her father's favorite evening entertainments, and some of her earliest memories had been of standing on a chair like this, declaiming a memorized piece of scripture, poetry or lyric in her high sing-song voice.

But as well as she'd done, she'd never had an audience in the rectory that hung on her words the way these gentlemen did here in the front room of Penny House. They stood perfectly still here beneath the candlelight of the chandeliers, glasses untouched in their hands and their mouths open with anticipation, waiting, waiting, as she held the pause before the final line of the silly poem.

At last she tipped her head to one side. "'So how did great Caesar cross the Tyber upon his horse?'" She swept her gaze across the men's faces, giving her voice an extra little crow of triumph. "'Why, swimmingly, swimmingly, they crossed, of course!'"

The applause was instantaneous, as appreciative for this doggerel verse as for Shakespeare—perhaps even more, given the amount of liquor the audience had consumed. Cassia curtsied delicately, still balanced on the chair.

"*Brava, Brava,* Miss Cassia, another!" shouted a mustachioed general near the back. "'Tis better than Drury Lane!"

"'Tis not, sir, and you know it." She took her fan from its loop on her wrist and began to flutter it before her face. The room was warm, her dark blue gown heavy, and reciting was hard work. "But I thank you all, the kindest of kind gentlemen."

More applause rippled around Cassia as she took the arm of one of the waiting footman, and climbed down from the chair. If she'd learned anything since coming to Penny House, it was that gentlemen's tastes could not be predicted. She'd only begun speaking pieces like this three nights before, on a whim when the room had seemed too quiet, but already her recitations had become so enormously popular that she'd had to limit them to three a night, partly to keep the novelty fresh, and partly because her memory couldn't handle much more.

Also waiting, Amariah handed her a tumbler of water as the two began to make their way around the room, nodding and smiling. "That rhyme was ancient when Father was in the cradle."

Cassia grinned, and sipped the water. "I cannot believe I recalled it, let alone that they laughed. I'm coming to the end of our old recitation pieces, unless I fall back upon the ones from Father's sermons."

"Don't." Amariah smiled back, her gaze gliding around the room and into the hall beyond, deciding who was new and needed greeting, and who, after the club's first two weeks, were already important friends requiring a more extended welcome. "But Father would laugh out loud to hear our old nursery poems trotted out to such a company. Faith, but it's warm in here this evening. Come outside with me for a moment, for a scrap of air."

They slipped their way through the gentlemen to the open garden door, standing just outside on the narrow patio. Only in London would their tiny square of openness be termed a garden, but it still gave them a breath of summer night and stars high above the chimney pots.

"Much better." Cassia set her empty tumbler on the iron railing, breathing deeply of the night air. They couldn't stay away long before they'd be missed, which made the break all the sweeter. "Pratt said the last piece about icicles on Hannibal's elephant's trunk was quoted yesterday morning in the *Intelligencer.*"

"If Hannibal's elephant's trunk makes people talk of Penny House, then it's all to the good." Amariah glanced back through the open door, settling on one particular face among the others. "I see your Mr. Blackley's returned to us tonight. We haven't seem much of him lately."

"He is not *my* Mr. Blackley, Amariah!"

Amariah curled her mouth into an oval of feigned surprise. "No?"

"No, as you know perfectly well." But Cassia still followed to where her sister was looking. Richard—when had he become simply *Richard* in her thoughts, anyway?—was standing just inside the front door, the light from the hall lantern overhead sending sharp shadows across his angular face.

And though Cassia tried to pretend otherwise, she couldn't help watching him. He stood out from the other gentlemen around him, not just because of his height or how his skin had been browned by the Caribbean sun. There was simply something different about him, a determined distance that made the others wary of standing too close or meeting his eye. He was as beautifully dressed and groomed as any other gentleman in the house, but he lacked the ease that the others had. Although he was confident to the point of cockiness, he also seemed always on guard, even when he smiled. Cassia wondered how he relaxed enough at night to sleep.

"If he's not yours, Cassia," Amariah teased, "then why are you watching him like a cat with a mouse?"

Cassia flushed, but didn't look away. "I should think rather that I'm the mouse and Mr. Blackley's the cat, and a large and hungry cat at that."

"A very large cat," Amariah said, "with very white teeth."

"Most certainly." Cassia narrowed her eyes with determination, her fan whipping back and forth in her hand as she tried hard—very hard—not to remember that single, glorious, wicked kiss that they'd shared.

"He's told me himself he always gets what he wants, and since I'd prefer he didn't want *me,* perhaps I'll stay out here in my mouse hole, safe and snug and away from his teeth."

Amariah laughed softly. "You're wise to take care with him, Cassia, as with all these gentlemen. We all must. But you may not have to keep to your mouse hole much longer. I heard yesterday that Mr. Blackley has taken an interest in Lord Carew's sister."

"Lord Carew's sister?" Cassia's fan stopped fluttering. When they'd last spoken—when they'd kissed— he'd sworn that she'd be safe from him. Was this what he'd meant? "Her family would let her entertain a rascal like Mr. Blackley?"

"They would because he's one rascal who's reputed to be rich as Croesus himself," Amariah said, unaware of Cassia's thoughts. "I've heard that the old earl's suffered his share of reverses in the City, and that a liberal spoonful of Mr. Blackley's sugar money would help soothe his discomforts. Quite a perfect match, I'd say."

"Mr. Blackley told me his greatest goal was to marry a peer's daughter." At the time Cassia hadn't believed him, nor had she dreamed he'd have such success so fast. "Is she vastly beautiful?"

"Not from what Pratt says, though to be sure, I wouldn't put much weight in Pratt's estimation of beauty." Amariah said. "What Pratt said was that poor Lady Anne was as dull and plain as pudding, and didn't show well for the bucks at Almack's."

Cassia gasped. "How barbarously cruel!"

"You know how Pratt can be. He was likely only stating the truth as he saw it." Amariah plucked at the blue ribbons threaded through her hair. "But if Mr. Blackley and his fortune marries Lady Anne, then all the *ton* will suddenly decide she is the greatest beauty imaginable."

"At least the greatest of this Season." Cassia glanced back through the door to the hall, but Richard was gone. *She* wasn't plain or dull as pudding, and she was sure she would have showed quite well at Almack's, if she'd ever been invited. But she didn't have *Lady* before her name, and never would, and in the end that was what mattered most.

She shivered, though not from any breeze. "We should go inside, Amariah, before we're missed."

"I know." Amariah frowned, almost scowled and looked down at her hands. "Cassia, I'm sorry I teased you about Mr. Blackley's being yours. You didn't deserve it, not at all. You're every bit as dedicated as Bethany and I are to making Penny House a success in Father's honor, and I'd no right pretending you'd toss us over for a rich planter or any other gentleman."

"You don't have to apologize," Cassia said, her voice so low it was almost a whisper. "Not to me. No apologies among us three, ever."

Amariah patted her hand. "Unless they are necessary, and that one was. Now we'd better go back—"

"Do you ever think of marrying, Amariah?" Cassia asked. "Now, I mean, with Penny House?"

Amariah paused. "I'm too busy to think of finding a husband now, Cassia. I'd think you would be, too."

"Most days I am." Wistfully Cassia looked one more time to the hallway, to the place where Richard had stood. It was his fault for turning her thoughts on this path, and his luck to have been born a man, with the freedom to wed how and whom he chose. "But doesn't this ever feel strange to you, Amariah?"

She frowned, not understanding. "Since when does helping others feel strange?"

"Not that part," Cassia said quickly, and raised her hand to encompass the house before them. "*This.* Doesn't it ever seem strange to you that we must always be charming and pleasant to all these fine, wealthy gentlemen, and try to make this place more agreeable to them than their own homes, yet never do these things for one man from love alone, the way most women do? Don't you ever wish for one man—one that you loved with all your heart—to please you in return?"

"But we've been blessed with the chance to do so much more than most women, Cassia." Amariah's frown deepened, perplexed. "Are you forgetting why we are here?"

Cassia shook her head with frustration, struggling for words to make her sister understand. "I know we're continuing Father's work, but wouldn't he have wished us to find love and marry and have children? Wouldn't he have wanted us to share the same happiness that he had with Mama?"

"Of course he would, Cassia," Amariah said firmly. "He always wanted us to be happy. But not until we've accomplished more in Father's name, not yet. You know that, too."

"I know," Cassia said softly. She was twenty now. Lady Anne Stanhope was only eighteen, and already worrying about spinsterhood. Women from more humble families would already have two or three children clinging to their petticoats, while she, Cassia Penny, was standing alone each night on a drawing room chair.

"You are not having regrets, are you?" Amariah asked with concern. "Do you question Father's intentions for us? If this life truly doesn't suit you, why then, Bethany and I will find a way to manage, and you—"

"No." Cassia couldn't trust her voice to say more. How could she be so selfish, when her sisters could only see the good? How could seeing Richard Blackley make her think of marriage, when he was practically betrothed to another?

"Father would tell you the same. A time and a season for everything, he'd say." Amariah slipped her arm around Cassia's shoulders and hugged her close, the scent of her older sister's fragrance familiar and comforting. "Whatever you wish, Cassia, if it's meant to be, then it will happen. You won't let it be otherwise."

"You've got your eye on the youngest one, haven't you?" The man that Richard didn't know leered with open appreciation. He was tall and thin, with unhealthy blotches of red on his cheeks, but his accent and his impeccable evening clothes were the sure signs of a title. "Cassia, her name is. Cassia Penny. To my mind she's the most delectable of the three."

Richard didn't answer. It had only been a week or so since he'd last been here, but the sight of Cassia struck him as hard as if he'd been away a year. And as much as he'd tried not to, he'd missed her.

She was coming in from the garden door with her older sister, their arms looped loosely together. Her lovely face was pale as the moonlight she'd left, her usual smile and spark gone, her nose pink, and her eyes so somber he wondered if she'd been weeping. What would she have to weep about? She was young and she was beautiful, and she had her life arranged exactly as she wished. What could have happened to have made her so sad?

"She's worth your time to study, Miss Cassia Penny," the man beside him continued. "Don't care if she did come from a high holy household. Look at her walk, that fine bounce to her breasts!"

"You sound deuced familiar with the lady." Richard didn't turn, his gaze still following Cassia.

"Only in my dreams, brother. That's as close as that one will ever get to my bed." The man sighed, a morose rattle of thwarted desire, and drank deeply from the glass of wine in his hand. "They're all for show, those pretty Pennys, living upstairs like vestal virgins. No man can touch them, else he'll be shown the door. This room's full of men who've made them offers—generous offers—and all refused."

Richard nodded. She'd refused him, too, but only when he'd offered her honest work, not that he'd confess that to the stranger beside him.

The kiss—that had come for free.

He watched as she kissed her sister on the cheek and they parted, effortlessly slipping through the crowds of men with a smile here and word or two there, always moving. She'd already grown much more accomplished at this than she was on Penny House's opening night, managing a polished smile even though she was, to Richard's eyes, still clearly upset. That polish, that control, was not necessarily an improvement.

Perhaps he should go ask her what was wrong. Perhaps all she needed was a friendly shoulder to shed those tears upon. He'd come here for another reason, but he'd be her confessor, too, if she needed that, the poor lass. He hated seeing her like this. Even her curls seemed to droop.

"Here now, that fat bastard's a bold one, isn't he?" the stranger noted with indignation. "Lord Bolton, isn't it? He's got no right to crowd her like that."

But Richard was already halfway across the room, dodging and shoving and not caring who he pushed aside as long as he reached Cassia. The heavyset man had grabbed her by the arm and pushed her against the wall, trapping her there behind the bulky wall of his belly in a green figured waistcoat.

Lord Bolton was drunk, his face mottled, and he was angry, too, over some invented slight or another. Cassia wasn't fighting back, but instead was trying to calm the man, while the others around them had backed away in a stunned circle. Her voice was low and meant to soothe, but as Richard reached them he could see how fear had tightened her face and filled her eyes.

"If I want another story, then by God, you'll give it to me," Bolton said, twisting Cassia's wrist so she yelped with pain. "You're no better than any other whore with a price, you little—"

"That's enough." Richard grabbed Bolton by the shoulder and jerked him around. "Let her go, I say. Let her go now."

Distracted, the man let go of Cassia, and she stumbled to one side, holding her wrist.

"Richard, don't!" she cried, her voice breathless. "Don't do this, I beg you!"

But Bolton was already focusing on Richard, his face purple with fury. "T'hell with your meddling," he growled. "T'hell with you."

He drew back his arm to strike Richard, but before he could, Richard's fist had already found the man's jaw, and the thudding impact snapped his head back. The man roared with outrage and swung wildly at Richard's face. But before he could, Richard hit him again with practiced efficiency, sending the other man sprawling backward with a crash. He went down hard, thick arms and legs flopping outward, and crashed into a small table set with trays of cold meats. Men gasped and swore and crowded this way and that as they shouted either curses or encouragement and dodged the flying slices of ham and beef.

Richard ignored it all. Breathing hard with his fists still clenched, he stood over the other man to make sure he wasn't going to fight back. He'd saved Cassia. That was all that mattered.

But not, it seemed, to Cassia.

"*What* have you *done?*" she cried furiously, still cradling her wrist in her other hand. "Oh, Richard, *look* what you've done!"

"What I've done, Cassia, is stop that—that cur from

hurting you," he said as two sturdy footmen came hurrying up to seize his arms. "That's the one you want, lads, not me."

"*They* would have stopped him," she said, her face more than animated now. "That's their duty. We don't expect our *gentlemen* to turn Penny House into some low Caribbean pirates' den!"

He frowned. He'd acted from instinct, not from any hope of reward, but it would have been pleasant to receive some sort of thanks from her.

"At least the guests in a pirates' den would be brave enough to defend a lady." He looked pointedly from one shamefaced guest to the next. "Which is more than any of these gentlemen seemed able to do. A bully's a bully, Cassia, anywhere you put him."

"You would know." She glanced back to the unconscious man on the floor, now being tended to by Pratt and two other servants. She stepped closer to Richard, lowering her voice to a fierce whisper. "Just as you likely know that that man is Lord Bolton, the son-in-law of His Grace the Duke of Somerland. Have you any notion of what kind of trouble he could cause for us? Whatever demon possessed you to—"

"He hurt you," he said, the simple truth. "Your wrist—it's hurting you still, isn't it?"

She looked down at her wrist as if surprised to see it there, then tucked it behind her back as if hiding the evidence. But he didn't miss how she kept her wrist stiff and her fingers awkwardly curled, and he knew he'd been right.

She lifted her chin. Her hair was loose around her

face, her cheeks flushed, and she looked better than she'd any right to. "That is your only explanation?"

He stared at her with disbelief. "That is not reason enough?"

He saw her wavering, the indecision in her eyes, and she opened her mouth to speak.

"Cassia." Amariah rushed into the room, instantly taking in everything from the groggy lord on the floor to Richard pinned by the two footmen. She held out her arms and smiled warmly, encompassing all the men still gathered to gawk.

"Gentlemen, gentlemen," she said, her voice ringing out to silence any last scraps of comment. "A slight misadventure, that is all, and I pray you'll forgive us the disturbance in your evening. I've asked that a specially fine port be brought about to help restore your convivial mood."

That pleased them, and with a few cheerful *huzzahs* and the excitement done, the gentlemen obediently returned to their conversations or shifted to other rooms. Like sheep, thought Richard with disgust, the whole damned black-and-white flock of them.

Her cordial smile still in place, Amariah turned to Cassia, dropping her voice to a whisper so the others wouldn't hear. "Would you please tell me what has happened here, Cassia?"

Cassia flushed, and took a deep breath. "More than should have certainly."

Amariah glanced back at Lord Bolton being half carried from the room, and shook her head with dismay. "Do you understand what this—this mischief could cost us? How it could hurt Penny House?"

Cassia nodded, visibly marshalling her resolve before her sister.

He'd lost her, thought Richard, lost any hope of her sympathy, at least for now. His knuckles stung where he'd hit the man's jaw, and for what?

She clasped her hands before her and drew back her shoulders. "Richard—Mr. Blackley—is leaving."

Amariah's gaze flicked up toward the heavens, or at least the plaster rosettes cast into the ceiling. "I should say he is."

"The hell I am!" Richard struggled against the men holding him. "I'm not about to be tossed in the street for doing what was right!"

"That is for us to judge, Mr. Blackley," Amariah said, her smile now steely, and not at all welcoming. "And you can be sure that I shall expect reimbursement for that conciliatory port."

Wasn't that just the capper, thought Richard. Not only was he being punished for being the only stout heart in the room, but now he had to pay for filling the glass of all the other mealymouthed cowards.

She nodded, and the footmen began to drag him toward the door as she and Cassia turned away.

"Cassia, wait!" he protested. "I came here to talk to you, Cassia, nothing more!"

Cassia paused, and looked back over her shoulder.

"Then talk, Richard," she said. "Talk."

Chapter Seven

"Here?" Richard shook his head, his dark hair falling forward and his face taut with anger. "For God's sake, Cassia, can't I have five minutes with you somewhere less public?"

Cassia remembered what had happened last time when she'd been alone with him at the Clarendon, and she was sure he remembered, too. She wouldn't let herself be put in that position again, especially not with Amariah beside her.

"No," she said. The pain throbbed through her wrist where Lord Bolton had twisted it, but she refused to let either Richard or her sister see how much it hurt her. It was her own fault that Bolton had reacted as he had. If she'd been more calm, more charming, then he never would have lost his temper with her, and Richard wouldn't have come charging in. "You can address me here, or not at all."

"Very well," he said. "If you don't care who hears what I say, then I do not, either."

She sniffed, an anxious little twitch of her nose. "I have nothing that would shame me."

Which, of course, was a lie, but she was betting that because he'd come to her rescue before, he wouldn't tatter her reputation now by telling her sister and the crowd at Penny House about how he'd tricked her into kissing him.

Would he?

"Then will you at least call off your guard dogs?" He gave an emphatic shake of his shoulders. "I can give you my word that you're absolutely in no danger from me."

Cassia looked to Amariah beside her. She motioned to the men to release Richard, though they stayed ready, standing behind him with their arms crossed over their chests.

"How nice to be trusted," he said, smoothing the sleeves and lapels of his dark jacket back into place. "My reward for gallantry. Not that I expected less from any of the Penny women."

That stung Cassia's pride. "In this house, gentlemen don't knock down other gentlemen, no matter what the cause."

"In my house," he said, his gaze never leaving her face, "gentlemen don't hurt ladies."

Amariah gasped. "Is this true, Cassia? Did Lord Bolton hurt you?"

Cassia hesitated, not wanting her sister to make even more of a fuss. "He—he pinched my wrist, that is all."

"Show me," demanded Amariah, reaching for Cassia's hand. "I'll send for a surgeon."

"No, no, Amariah, please." Cassia tucked her hand

behind her back, away from her sister. "It's of no real consequence, and there's already been enough—"

"He will never enter this house again," her sister declared, "not even if he were His Royal Highness himself. Mr. Blackley, you may remain, at least for this evening. Where is Pratt? Pratt!"

She hurried away, leaving Cassia to face Richard alone—or alone save for the two guards and the crowds of curious gentleman swirling around them.

"You should listen to her, and have a surgeon look at your hand," he said. "I saw how Bolton wrenched it. You're fortunate that's all he did."

She swallowed hard, knowing he was right. "That is why we have the guards."

"Who moved precious slow in your defense."

"I know." She *had* been scared; she couldn't deny it, not even to him. Bolton's fury had flared without warning, surprising her and everyone else. What if he'd twisted her wrist a little harder? He was so much larger than she, and vastly stronger. What if he'd grabbed her by the throat instead of just her hand? "I suppose I should thank you."

"You should, yes." He leaned forward to her, his voice becoming unexpectedly gentle. "Will you show me your wrist, Cassia?"

She shook her head, keeping her hand behind her back. "It's only bruised, no more."

"Then you won't mind showing it to me," he coaxed. "I'm no surgeon, but I can tell if you need to call one. Look."

He held his own hand up for her to see, gingerly

flexing the fingers and making a fist. At once the two guards stepped forward, but he held his other hand up and open to keep them back.

"Look," he said again. "I only struck him twice, and you can see the sorry state of my knuckles. Ugly to gaze upon, but nothing lasting. But your little wrist—that could be a far different story."

"It's fine." Talking about her wrist seemed to make it hurt more. Surreptitiously she waggled her fingers, Father's old test for broken bones. If she could do that, then she must be fine.

"Are you sure?" he asked with such real concern that she wished she could fall into the comforting circle of his arms. "There must be a score of tiny bones in your hand, and that bastard could have broken one or more of them without trying."

"I am sure." His matter-of-fact talk about tiny broken bones was making her feel light-headed. "Truly. Now what was it you came to tell me, Mr. Blackley?"

"I like Richard better." His smiled, his first real smile of the evening. "I like the way you say it."

"If that is what you came to say to me, Mr. Blackley, why, then, I—"

"I need you, Cassia."

Not again, she thought with dismay, and she reminded herself how he was courting the daughter of a marquis. "No. I don't care that you just saved me. I won't be any man's—"

"I didn't mean it like that, lass, I swear," he said quickly. "What I need is your talent, your expertise, your eye. It's my house that needs you, Cassia, and needs you now."

"Oh." She flushed, feeling like the greatest fool imaginable. No wonder he hadn't minded speaking so publicly, if this was all he'd wanted to say. "I hear you are to wed, Mr. Blackley. Surely your new wife—your *lady* wife—would wish to follow her own tastes and make her own changes in your home."

"But there's nothing at Greenwood to change," he said. "Sir Henry saw to that. It was a grand place once and will be again, but now—now if I took Lady Anne or her parents there, they'd never receive me again."

From purest selfishness, Cassia imagined that happening. "Then why not ask Mr. Nash or one of the other architects? London must be full of such men."

"Yes, but the best ones are too busy to accept new projects," he said, "and I can't wait. You were my first choice, Cassia, and you still are. I've only to look about this place, and know that."

She sighed wearily. "Nothing has changed, Mr. Blackley. I cannot do what you ask, for all the same reasons as before."

He nodded, as if she'd agreed. "Just name your price, lass. Whatever it is, I'll make sure the sum's delivered to you tomorrow morning. I'm trusting you, you know. You can do whatever you please, and I know it will be right."

"I still can't do it, and I won't," she said, remembering her earlier conversation with Amariah. "My place is here, not at Greenwood. And I don't understand why this is so wretchedly important to you."

"Because once I've set my mind on something, I don't give up." He rubbed the back of his bruised knuckles, his expression as determined as any bulldog's. "What if I made a gift in your name to a charity of your choosing? That little parish school you visit, say?"

"No money to me, no money in my name," she said, her conviction matching his. "We contribute the money taken in by the House's bank, and none other. If that is all, Mr. Blackley, then I must excuse myself to see to our other guests."

He bowed to her, and smiled again. "I don't give up, Cassia."

"So you've told me, Mr. Blackley." She didn't smile back as she turned away. "But this time, I believe you have met your match."

The director sat on a high chair at one end of the hazard table. Mr. Walthrip was wizened and ancient, with long wisps of white hair above his oversize ears, and an expression that never changed. No one could guess how old he was, or how long he had ruled over hazard tables with his long-handled rake, but all agreed that he had seen every risk, every possible wager, every scandal that the game could offer.

Until tonight.

He looked to Richard, the caster, with the box with the dice ready in his hand. "What main, m'lord?"

"Five," Richard said, without any hesitation. He always began with five. Most players chose seven, simply because it was reputed to be lucky, but in Richard's own experience, it was a much more difficult number to combine with others for a winning toss.

"Five it is, m'lord," repeated Walthrip. Every man

was a lord to Walthrip; it was easier than bothering to separate out the few commoners. "Main is five."

Richard flipped the box and sent the dice skipping over the green cloth. A four, and a three. Two more than the five he needed to nick it and win outright, but an excellent number nonetheless.

"Chance is seven," called Walthrip. "Five to seven."

Five to win, seven to lose. Richard couldn't have asked for better odds, three to two in his own favor, and the very best cast to be had at hazard.

Yet still the players around the table made soft murmurs and whistles of commiseration. Others eagerly pushed their markers toward him to make their own bets, counting on Richard's luck to sour.

He raised the box in his hand, motioning to Walthrip.

"You wish to increase your stake, m'lord?" He peered up at Richard with rheumy red eyes, his liverish lips barely moving. "A change, m'lord?"

"Yes," Richard said, keeping his expression purposefully flat and emotionless. He hadn't come to this room with this in mind, intending to play for diversion only, but then the idea had flashed upon him like a spark, the way all great ideas did. It was perfect; it was brilliant. All it needed to become reality was for his luck to hold, the same luck that this night had created the small gleaming hill of counters on the table before him.

"See now, Blackley," called another player indignantly. "You can't go changing your wager in the middle like this. It's not done."

Richard nodded, acknowledging the man's protest. He'd already made himself the center of talk this evening by coming to Cassia's assistance and knocking Bolton to the floor. By morning, he was sure his name— and Cassia's linked to it—would be in every newspaper and buzzing over every breakfast table.

"As caster, all established bets against me stand," he said. "What I request is to add another fresh wager against the house."

"The house shall decide." Like any good judge, Walthrip remained impassive. Special bets were uncommon, but they did occur, usually when a man was losing so badly that desperation clouded his reason, and race horses, family jewels, even entire estates, became part of the play. "What figure do you wish, m'lord?"

"Twenty thousand pounds to the house," Richard declared soundly, so there'd be no question or mistake, "if I lose."

Excitement raced through the room, the air in the closed room turning electric with it. Twenty thousand was a ridiculously high stake for hazard, and as rich as Richard had become, he couldn't deny he'd feel such a loss. He wasn't even sure the house would accept such a figure. On most nights, he doubted the bank opened with that much in its till. But he wanted a sum that Cassia couldn't ignore. If her charities came before everything else, then by God, she'd have to accept the chance to make twenty thousand pounds if he lost.

Which, of course, he'd no intention of doing. He'd always sensed when the luck was running in his favor, just as he knew when to walk away, no matter the losses. After this, he'd swear off hazard for at least a year, maybe two, if he truly didn't wish to tempt fate. But tonight—tonight he felt luck was sitting on his shoulder, ready to guide the dice to whatever combination he needed.

Tonight, for Cassia, he'd win.

"Twenty thousand pounds, m'lord." Walthrip's voice droned over the others, silencing them into breathless anticipation. "And if you win, m'lord? Shall you claim the same stake in return?"

"No." Richard chose his words with deliberate care. "What I wish from the house are the services of Miss Cassia Penny for one month, for the sole and exclusive purpose of making improvements in my property at Greenwood Hall."

Exclamations and oaths exploded around the table, until Walthrip raised his hand for quiet.

"You wish, m'lord," he said, "to have the house declare the lady as your stake?"

"Not the lady," Richard said. "There will be nothing carnal to this stake, and I will swear to that in any manner Miss Penny desires. I wish to make use only of her taste and talents, such as she has used to the betterment of Penny House itself."

"Talents!" the gentleman beside him at the table exclaimed, leering. "You're a fortunate rascal, Blackley. How I'd like a taste of the lady's talents, too!"

Richard ignored both the comment and the raucous laughter that followed.

"Most irregular, m'lord, most irregular." Walthrip flicked the end of his rake to call over a footman. "Go below, boy. Summon Mr. Pratt to come to me directly."

He then dragged his heavy-lidded gaze to Richard,

clearly disapproving of the interruption to his game. "I must halt the play, m'lord, until a decision is reached."

Richard nodded, content to wait. He could afford to be patient now.

Luck was on his side, and soon Cassia Penny would be, too.

Cassia sat on a stool in the kitchen, out of the way of the cooks and maids chopping and simmering and slicing and garnishing the dishes to be carried to the gentlemen upstairs, the liveried footmen holding the gleaming silver-covered dishes high over their heads. The air was full of wondrous smells, but it was also unbelievably hot from the open fires and bake-ovens, with every face gleaming with perspiration from the heat and tempers running short amid the clattering ladles, knives and heavy copper-bottomed pans. This was her sister Bethany's domain, the crowded kingdom that she ruled as queen of Penny House's cookery, and the single calm voice amid all the crashing and clamor.

"Here you are, Cassia." Bethany lay a dishcloth over Cassia's knees to protect her gown, then set a flat wooden trencher filled with chipped ice on her lap. "Now lay your sorry old wrist and hand in the ice, and I'll pile more on top."

Cassia did, and winced at the cold. "That—that stings too much to be helping."

Bethany heaped more of the ice on top of Cassia's hand, burying it in cold. "That's what it's supposed to do, you silly noddy. There's nothing like ice to take the pain and swelling from a bruise. You're just fortunate that we had fresh ice delivered today, and that I'm willing to put you ahead of some hungry gentleman's frozen custard."

"I would have been more fortunate still if I'd kept clear of Lord Bolton altogether." The ice was making her wrist feel better, numbing the pain with the cold. "All I did was refuse—and politely, too—when he asked me to recite another piece, and then he grabbed me by the arm. It was not—not agreeable."

"I'm sure it wasn't," Bethany said softly. She reached out and smoothed Cassia's hair from her forehead. "Poor brave goose! Pratt warned us there were always such dangers, even with gentlemen, but I never believed him."

"I'll be fine," Cassia said yet one more time. "Especially with the ice."

"Don't wiggle," Bethany ordered. She wiped her wet hands on her apron, turning away to critically survey a platter with a whole salmon before she nodded her approval and sent the fish on its way upstairs. "And you must stay there until the ice is quite melted. Either you do, or I'll have that handsome Mr. Blackley come watch over you to make sure you take your proper cure."

"You wouldn't dare." With her uninjured hand, Cassia scooped up a handful of ice and tossed it at Bethany. "Besides, I don't believe Mr. Blackley wants anything more to do with me, not this—"

"Cassia!" Amariah came rushing down the stairs and toward them through the kitchen, dodging a boy balancing a sweating pitcher of lemon water in each hand. "Cassia, I must talk to you at once."

Cassia's heart began to thump. From the grim, worried set of her sister's expression, she knew that something very bad had happened. "Oh, Amariah, is it Lord Bolton? Has he—"

"Lord Bolton is not the issue," Amariah said as Pratt joined them. "It's Mr. Blackley."

"Richard?" Cassia rose, hastily putting the sloshing bowl of melting ice on the stood. "If Lord Bolton has hurt him on my account, then I—"

"I told you, Cassia," Amariah said. "This has nothing to do with Lord Bolton, and everything to do with you."

Bethany wrapped a clean cloth around Cassia's dripping hand. "Use my little office room off the scullery if you wish to speak in privacy."

"Thank you, Miss Bethany," Pratt said, "but there isn't time. Miss Cassia, Mr. Walthrip has been confronted by a great quandary in the hazard room. Mr. Blackley has asked that the house bank agree to special stakes for him, and all play at the table has been stopped until a decision is made."

Cassia cradled her swaddled hand, all her earlier pain forgotten. "Mr. Blackley isn't an impulsive player, and because he is so wealthy, I am sure he would honor whatever increased sums he—"

"He didn't want to have his wager raised." Amariah took a deep breath. "He wanted you."

"Me!" Cassia's voice squeaked upward with outrage. "He has no right, no right at all, to make such a disgraceful, disreputable—"

"That's not what he wants, or what he says he wants," Amariah said. "He was very specific when he spoke to Mr. Walthrip. Nothing carnal, he said, nothing indecent."

"How vastly flattering," Cassia said, her outrage now colored with bitterness. "Even you'd say so, wouldn't you, Amariah?"

"Stop fussing, Cassia," her sister ordered, "and *think*. Has Mr. Blackley ever mentioned to you any nonsense about refurbishing his house in the country?"

Cassia flushed. "Well, yes, he has. Often, in fact, but I have always refused, because my place is here at Penny House."

Amariah and Pratt exchanged quick glances, proof enough that they'd discussed this already without her.

"Did he say exactly why he wished you to go to his house?" Amariah asked. "Have you any notion of why it was so important to him that you do this for him?"

Cassia sighed, determined to make her explanation as forthright as possible. "He won some great wreck of a house at cards. He liked how I made over Penny House, and he asked me to do the same for his house. He wants it done as fast as possible so he can invite his lady-love and her noble family, and he did not care what it cost."

"He has placed the value of your services at twenty thousand pounds, Miss Cassia," Pratt said, with a slight bow, as if to honor such an outrageous sum. "That is to say, if he loses, he will pay the house bank twenty thousand pounds. If he wins, then he will either expect these services from you, or the bank must pay his stake of twenty thousand."

"And we can't, Cassia," Amariah said, twisting her hands together. "There is never that much in the bank, not even half that, because I have always wished to send as much money as possible to Reverend Barney."

"Which is what Father would have wished you to do, of course." Cassia could already see where this was leading, a dwindling dark tunnel with no way out but one. "What happens if we explain this to Mr. Blackley if he should ask for the money?"

"I am sorry, Miss Cassia," Pratt said sadly, "but we must honor every gentleman's wager, even if it breaks the house's bank, and the club with it."

Blast Richard for trying so hard to get what he wanted! "Couldn't we have Mr. Walthrip simply refuse the wager? Couldn't he tell him the stake cannot be changed?"

"We are too new a club for such favors." Amariah sighed. "The gentlemen would see it as dishonorable and unforgivable, and our membership committee would be furious."

"Then I have no choice but to agree," Cassia said, and with her uninjured hand she smacked her fist with frustration hard on the stool. "Oh, a pox on him for manipulating things this way, trapping me to agree!"

"I am sorry, Cassia," Amariah said with miserable contrition. "If only I'd turned him away as I'd first wished to, and never let him into the house!"

"He would have found a way inside," Cassia said darkly. "He is hideously clever, and impossible to turn aside."

"Then perhaps this is not so very evil," Bethany said, smoothing her hands along her apron as she considered. "Mr. Blackley seems determined to protect you, so let him. It might be wise for you to leave London for a bit anyway, until this unpleasantness with Lord Bolton is forgotten and your hand is healed."

"But I belong here, with you, and—"

"For a month, Cassia, only a month," Amariah said, soothing. "Bethany and I will manage. You can't deny that you'd enjoy spending his money while you force your taste into every corner of this great house of his."

Pratt nodded in agreement, striving to make his dry voice sound reassuring, too. "There is also an excellent chance that none of this will come to pass at all, Miss Cassia. The odds at the hazard table favor the house far more than they do the players."

"That's true," Bethany said. "When Mr. Walthrip comes down for his tea, he will tell story after story of how many gentlemen have ruined themselves at hazard, and been so besotted by the game they didn't realize their loss until morning."

Amariah slipped her arm around Cassia's shoulder. "And consider, sister, consider how much Penny House stands to gain if he loses, too. Twenty thousand pounds. *Twenty thousand pounds.*"

"It would serve him as he deserves." Cassia sniffed. "And even if he wins, this time he will not have his way."

"High time you came back, you old fox," Richard muttered to himself as Pratt finally slipped through the door. Pretending that every eye in the hazard room wasn't watching him, the manager made his way to Walthrip's chair. A moment's whispered conference between the two, and the decision was done.

Walthrip looked to Richard, pausing one more moment for the speculation among the players to quiet, and for an extra dollop of drama.

"The house accepts your stake, m'lord," he said with a regal wave of his rake. "Resume the play."

Richard nodded, again ignoring the reactions of the others around him.

"Would Miss Penny care to join us as a spectator?" he asked. "I would consider her most welcome. Certainly the rules against ladies in this room could be bent this once, under the circumstances."

"No, sir," Pratt said curtly. "Miss Penny wishes no such favor."

Richard's guess was that she was done favoring him as well, at least for now, nor was she pleased with being named the stakes, either. He hadn't really expected it to be otherwise—what respectable woman would feel flattered by such a dubious honor?—but just the same, he would have liked having her here beside him for luck.

He'd also like having her there when he won. Not *if,* but *when.*

"Seven to five. Resume play, m'lord," Walthrip said again, testy. "*If* it pleases you, m'lord."

It did. Richard reached for the box with the dice, rattling them gently inside. He knew some men who whispered to the dice, singing little songs or rhymes to them, even adding a kiss or two to woo the ivory cubes into obedience. He'd stick to luck, and the odds. He drew back his arm, ready to throw.

"Not quite yet, Walthrip." A thin gentleman in an extravagantly old-fashioned wig tapped his hand on the table, the heavy emerald ring he wore catching the lanterns' light from overhead. "Enter me on the same terms, for the same wager with the house against the caster."

Walthrip turned his head like an ancient tortoise. "That is a private wager, m'lord, between a gentleman and this house."

"Except that the caster is no gentleman at all, but a base-born scoundrel from the offal heap." The thin man smiled at Richard, and the rest of the room fell as silent as death itself. "I'm surprised the house accepted his wager in the first place."

At once Richard was on his feet. "You should choose your words with more care, sir."

"And you should mind your actions with your betters, Blackley." With an exaggerated sigh, the man rubbed away a smudge on the face of his emerald. "You may have taken my nephew by surprise earlier, but you shall not do the same with me."

"My Lord Ralcyn, Mr. Blackley, please," Pratt said with a bow. Behind him two of the largest of the house's guards now stood, adding teeth and muscle to Pratt's polite request. "I must remind you that this is a gentlemen's club, and that here we abide by the rules of society."

Slowly Richard sat back down in his chair, his gaze never leaving the other man's intentionally bored face. So the man was Bolton's uncle, more sorrow to him. Lord Ralcyn: a name he hadn't heard before, but he'd remember it now. Once again he swirled and shook the dice in the box, preparing his toss.

"I've not had my answer, Pratt," interrupted Ralcyn again. "Or is my coin a shade too fine for this game?"

"In the case of a private wager with the bank, M'Lord," Walthrip said, "the decision for your wager must come from the caster."

"What, if he's willing to share his little Penny?" Ralcyn's laugh had no humor to it. "How is it to be, Blackley? I fancy winning the services of the chit, too. A gift for poor Bolton, to ease his humiliation. I'll take your main, for the same stakes."

"Done," Richard said, his voice as sharp as his temper. "I am certain the ladies will put your twenty thousand to good use."

"Seven to five for Mr. Blackley," Walthrip intoned as Ralcyn pushed his markers across the table. "Five to seven for Lord Ralcyn."

What in blazes had he done? He had broken his greatest rule of gaming, which was to be ruled by intellect, not by impulse or emotion. He'd let the other man goad him into a damned fool's wager. He'd made Cassia the stake, and because of her, he'd made himself vulnerable, too.

What in blazes had he done?

Ralcyn yawned. "Before the cock crows, Blackley."

Richard forced himself to focus on the box and the dice instead of Ralcyn. The odds still favored him. That hadn't changed. Earlier luck had been with him, too, and there was no reason to believe it would abruptly abandon him now.

He needed a seven or eleven to win. A twelve, and he lost. A five, and Ralcyn was the winner.

The dice rolled to a stop, a pair of threes.

"Six, m'lord," Walthrip said. "Seven to five."

The men around the table groaned in sympathy as Richard scooped the dice back into the box to try again.

A four, and a six. "Ten, m'lord. Seven to five."

Richard felt the sweat prickling along the back of his collar as he rolled again. He'd never sweat like this from gambling before, but then he'd never had to try to keep Cassia Penny from Bolton's hands, either.

A three, and an eight. "Eleven, m'lord. Seven to five."

Twenty-three more times he tossed the dice, and twenty-three more times they stopped at numbers that carried no weight. If it had been only a matter of the money, Richard would have laughed out loud.

"You're cursed, Blackley," Ralcyn growled. His forehead around the edges of his wig were damp, with little rivulets trickling through the white powder he'd dusted on his face. "Or is it just that your base-born hands don't have the proper touch?"

"Nine, m'lord. Seven to five."

When had a run ever gone this long? Maybe he was cursed. Maybe he'd be at this table for the rest of his mortal days, praying for the winning toss. What had happened to his deuced fine luck?

"Three, m'lord. Seven to five."

A footman opened the door to bring in another bottle of port. The motion caught Richard's eye, distracting him, and he looked up just before the door swung shut. The hall outside was full of people, faces pressing close to the door, craning to learn what was happening.

But Richard saw only one, her blue eyes wide, her face pale, her lips parted, a white cloth wrapped around her wrist. Did she know about Ralcyn's wager? Did she know how fast he'd accepted it?

Without looking back to the table, Richard let the dice fall from the box.

A four and a three, for a seven.

"Seven, m'lord," Walthrip said, his inflection exactly the same as it had been with every other toss. "Chance wins, m'lord."

The room erupted, cheers and applause and oaths and men crowding around him to clap him on the back and shake his hand and tell him he had the very devil's own luck. Yet all Richard felt was exhaustion sweeping over him as surely as an ocean wave, and if he hadn't been standing with his arms on the table, bracing himself, he doubted he could have kept from toppling face forward onto the green cloth.

But there were no congratulations from across the table, where Ralcyn was standing. With his hands clasped behind his back, the older man's face beneath his wig was so taut that it might have been carved from wood. He watched Walthrip rake away the fish-shaped counters that represented his twenty thousand, knowing he'd have to settle with the bank before he left that night. Richard might have won, but thanks to Ralcyn's side wager, so had Penny House.

"A lucky throw, Blackley," he said, biting off each word as if it had a bitter taste. "Any ape could have done it, given the time and the box in his paw."

"That is the appeal of hazard, isn't it?" Richard forced himself to stand upright, to collect his wits. His night, it seemed, wasn't done yet. "The dice could just have easily fallen your way."

"But they didn't." Ralcyn leaned over the table toward Richard, his eyes narrowed to slits. "You are not done with my family, Blackley. No one insults us as freely as you have, and walks away. Know that, and be ready."

He turned on his heel and left without waiting for Richard's reply. Richard didn't care. He had no reply, and he was far to weary to think of one. He pushed his way through the well-wishers, into the hall.

Cassia was waiting, as he'd known she'd be. She gave a little toss of her head, shaking the loose curls back from her face. She looked exhausted, too, with bluish circles beneath her eyes, though she'd drawn her shoulders back and straight. He wondered how her wrist felt; he wondered what she thought of him now, having come so close to gambling her away.

"Well, now, Richard," she said, as if they were standing alone and discussing the morning milk, instead of here with a curious crowd surging around them. "I suppose you've come to claim your stake."

"Not now," he said, his voice ragged and rough. "Not yet. For your sake, Cassia, I've made two enemies tonight. Please God there won't be any more."

Not trusting himself to say more, he turned toward the stairs, and left.

Chapter Eight

Luke stood at the taffrail, waving at the *Three Sisters'* men bound for shore-leave as the dinghy pushed off from the ship. He wished he'd been able to say more of a proper farewell, for they'd been kind to him on the long voyage. They didn't know it, of course, but this was the last he'd ever see of them.

"Don't be lookin' so long in the face, Lukey-lad," said the bosun at the rail beside him. "You don't belong with that lot and their carousin', not yet. Drinkin' and whorin' and spendin' every last scrap of tin in their pockets—you're too young for that nonsense."

"Aye, aye, sir." Luke still watched the boat heading for shore, the scrap of a bawdy song drifting over the water.

The bosun patted his shoulder with kind commiseration. "You stay here with me tonight, Luke, safe and snug. Your time will come soon enough, but for now London's no place for a little lad like you."

But Luke was looking to the river's shore, to the

stone steps from the water that led to the city streets.
Late tonight, in the middle of the last watch, he could
slip over the side and swim to land with his few belongings and his pay tied around his waist. He'd do it without rippling the water, too, the way every good
Martinique boy could do. No one on board the *Three
Sisters* would notice he was gone until tomorrow, and
Captain Rogers would judge it easier to replace him than
to hunt for him in a city as vast as London.

Luke looked higher, to the rooftops and chimneys
and church spires that seemed to go on and as far as the
ocean had been wide. He'd never dreamed any city
could be so vast, and without any friends or a place to
start, he wasn't sure exactly how he'd begin his search.

He knew so little of his father, only what Mama had
told him and what Luke had learned for himself: his
name, and that he was an Englishman, born in a town
called Lancaster. That he'd been a sailor who'd won a
sugar plantation on Barbados, and that he'd been lucky
and grown rich. That he'd left the plantation in the hands
of overseers, and sailed for London, where he wore a
coat made of silver, and diamonds on the buckles of his
shoes, and went to grand balls at the palace and danced
with the queen.

And that because of Mama's shame, he'd never
known Luke existed.

He looked higher still until he found the North Star
high and bright in the sky, the same star that had guided
them night after night across the Atlantic. He smiled,
oddly comforted. Captain Rogers had told him that as
long as a sailor could find the North Star, he would

never be lost. With the star to guide him, he'd always find his way.

And soon, very soon, Luke would find his father as well.

"You are certain you have everything you'll need, Cassia?" Amariah crouched down beside the trunk, checking the lock one more time. "This does not look like nearly enough for a month."

"It's not as if I'll need a new ball gown for every night, Amariah," Cassia said. "This is not a pleasure junket. I am going to Greenwood Hall to work."

She looked down with satisfaction at the trunk, hat box, and two smaller bags that were the sum of her luggage. With so little, not even Richard Blackley would think she was planning anything else but the toil he'd wagered on.

Amariah sighed, dusting her hands together as she rose. "I hope you will spare a few hours to forget London and enjoy yourself. It would be like being back in Woodbury, walking through the fields and beneath the trees."

"You should be the one going instead of me." Cassia took the sides of her skirts in her hands for a mock curtsey. "Lah, lah, my month in the country!"

Amariah laughed. "Isn't that a play?"

"If it is, I expect it's a farce." Cassia glanced at the tall clock. "He's already a half an hour past the time he promised, and you know how I hate to be kept waiting. I'll have to break him of that habit if we're to accomplish anything together."

"I thought you were hired to refurbish the house, not the master," Amariah said wryly. "You'll want to leave a few rough edges for his wife to polish."

"She will be perfectly welcome to all the rough edges she could ever want." Restlessly Cassia crossed the hall again to peek out one of the long side windows by the door. No coach, no Richard, with the street empty and quiet so early in the morning. She hadn't seen Richard for three days, not since the night of the infamous hazard game, and even then he'd spoken only a handful of barely civil words to her. All their traveling arrangements had been made between Pratt and Richard's manservant Neuf.

"You'd think he would have shown his face by now," she said, her irritation growing, "especially considering what he had to do to make me come with him."

"I hear horses," Amariah said, hurrying to the other window. "That must be Mr. Blackley."

"It's only a hack," Cassia said. "Mr. Blackley would want a coach to drive clear to Greenwood, and— Oh, it *is* Mr. Blackley!"

He left the hackney waiting at the curb and came bounding up the steps so fast that Cassia barely had time to duck away from the window and retreat to her pile of dunnage while she waited for a footman to come answer the door. It was one thing for Richard to see that she'd been ready and kept waiting for him, but quite another for him to think that she'd been so eager for his arrival that she'd been watching for him at the window like an anxious schoolgirl.

"Good day, ladies," he said brusquely, entering before the footman had opened the door all the way. He was dressed for travel, in a gray coat and dark breeches that wouldn't show the soil of the road. "You are ready to leave, then?"

"Not alone in a hack, I'm not," Cassia said, "not without servants to keep things proper, the way you promised, and not all the way to Greenwood."

He frowned. "I wouldn't do that. I left Neuf to oversee loading the coach at the Clarendon, and came to fetch you," he said, testy. "We won't be together long enough for you to be ruined, not even by me."

"Oh, Cassia, I'm so glad I didn't miss you!" Bethany rushed into the hall, followed by a boy carrying an enormous wicker hamper. "I know how dreadful the food can be in the stage inns, and so I've fixed you a few things for your journey."

Richard stared down at the hamper, and then to Cassia's trunk and other belongings. "You are taking all of this with you?"

"Yes," Cassia said indignantly. "And that's precious little for a lady for a month."

"Is it?" He snorted with disbelief. "I've seen women sail for a new life in America with less dunnage than this."

"If you wish me to come with you, Mr. Blackley," Cassia said, "then this comes with me."

He sighed again, and nodded for the footman to carry her belongings out to the hack. "It still seems like a great lot of foolishness to haul about the countryside."

"It's not foolishness," Cassia said. "And if you had ever traveled with a lady before, you would realize that I have been the model of restraint."

She turned back toward her sisters to say her fare-well, tears stinging her eyes. She had never in her life been separated from her sisters, and the reality of the parting struck her hard. She didn't try to speak because she didn't want to weep before Richard, and contented herself with embracing them each in turn.

"Take care, Cassia," whispered Amariah. "I know things will go well for you, but if ever you need us, you know we'll come as soon as we can."

"Don't cry, silly duck." Bethany held her close, her hair and clothes redolent with the fragrances of the meat pies she'd been baking. "You're doing a grand thing for Penny House, and then you'll be back before you know it. And if anything's amiss, Greenwood's not so far from London."

"Nothing—nothing will be amiss," Cassia said with a shaky gulp. "And I will make you proud."

She sniffed again and tried to smile one last time at her sisters. Her belongings had been carried out from the hall, including the hamper of food, and Richard was standing in the open door.

"You are ready, Miss Penny?" he asked again, as if he were the one who'd been standing here waiting for a good half an hour. "Can we go now?"

"Yes," she said, sailing past him through the door. "We can, and we will, even though you were the one who was late, not I."

She didn't wait for him, climbing into the hackney with the footman to hand her in, and squeezing herself into the far corner so that not even her skirts would touch Richard.

This wasn't easy. While most of her belongings had been strapped to the roof beside the driver, Bethany's hamper was squeezed in at her feet and another smaller bag beside her knees. It made for a very small space, and Richard was a large man who seemed to have grown larger as he settled beside her. He tapped on the roof, and the driver drew away into the street.

"No more tears?" he asked warily, watching her as if she might explode or combust or manifest some other disastrous natural occurrence. "It's not as if you're being transported, you know. The wager and these consequences were your choice."

"I know," she said, the words wavering up and down as she saw the last of Penny House. "I won't go back on my word."

"That's something, I suppose." He folded his arms across his chest, the only place left to put them. "But all that folderol with your sisters—you make me feel as if I were about to clap you in irons and haul you away."

"I couldn't help it." She sniffed again, wishing she could pull out her handkerchief without reinforcing his notion of her as a useless, blubbering ninny. "Farewells of any sort affect me."

He frowned with uncomprehending distaste. "That's sentimental rubbish, indulging your emotions that way."

"It is not!" she exclaimed. "My sisters are all the family I have, and they are most dear to me. Saying goodbye to those you care for—surely you must know how hard that can be."

He paused, and beneath the brim of his hat, his eyes seemed curiously blank.

"Not like that, no, I don't," he admitted. "When I left Lancaster, my mam was long dead and father gone with another woman, and my sisters were married with families and sorrows of their own. I've never left anyone behind me weeping, nor felt the lack of it."

"You have no one who cares what becomes of you?" she asked, incredulous. In her family, she'd always been surrounded by so much love that she could not imagine life without it. "Not in all the world?"

"Not like that, no," he said with equal disbelief. "I've never been given to dramatic demonstrations."

"How sorry I am for you," she said, and she meant it. "And that lady-wife you want so desperately."

"You can keep your pity to yourself." His expression didn't change. "I've done well enough on my own. And my wife will learn my ways, I've no doubt of that."

But Cassia doubted it very much, and hoped for Lady Anne's sake that she had a good, strong backbone to stand up to such patent male nonsense. Cassia almost felt sorry for her, too.

Richard was looking down at her hands, neatly folded in her lap. "Did you see a surgeon for your wrist?"

She tipped her head to one side. "You do not consider such a question to show too much concern for my welfare? You're not afraid I'll make some disturbing, maudlin display?"

He sighed, and leaned his head back against the worn cushion behind it. "I ask from purest practicality, sweetheart. If you are still in pain and had not seen a surgeon, then I would take you now myself. I have you for only a month at Greenwood. You would be less useful to me there if you were crippled by your hand."

"How vastly kind and thoughtful of you, Mr. Blackley." She held her gloved hand up, twisting it this way and that to demonstrate. "As you can see, my wrist is still a bit stiff, but the bruise is yellow by now, and in another few days the ache should be gone and I should be put to rights again. And no, I did not consult a surgeon, nor need you make such an expense on my behalf."

"How vastly kind and thoughtful of *you*," he repeated, his smile as angelic as he could make it, which wasn't very angelic at all.

She smiled in return—no angel there, either. "Take care, Mr. Blackley, or you'll make a dramatic display."

"Fair warning taken." He pulled the brim of his hat down a little lower, at a more rakish angle over his eyes. "So our friend Bolton didn't return to trouble you?"

Cassia's smile faded. "If he tried, he would have been turned away at the door. He is no longer welcome at Penny House."

"Be sure that Pratt and the others keep it that way," he said sharply. "I don't care how high-born that bastard is. Bolton doesn't deserve a place in decent company."

She smoothed the trailing ribbon on her bonnet between her fingertips. "That's likely what he's saying about you."

"Oh, I'm certain of it," he said, almost as if daring Bolton to again. "He wouldn't be the first, nor the last, either."

"I suppose not." She looked away, out the window, and frowned. "Where are we?"

"In London, Miss Penny." Consciously he relaxed, and smiled. "In England."

"That's not what I meant." She twisted around in the seat, craning her neck for a better view. "We're near the river, aren't we? There's London Bridge, beyond those houses. Look, Richard, look."

He didn't. "How stunningly perceptive of you."

"Then hush, and listen to me," she ordered. "Either this driver has no notion of where the Clarendon is, or he has great hopes of coaxing a bigger fare from you for a roundabout ride by way of Dover."

"Not quite Dover," he admitted, unconcerned, "only by way of Thames Street. One of my ships came into port two days ago, and I must stop by my countinghouse before I leave town. It won't take but a moment."

"Your countinghouse?" she asked, aghast. No wonder she'd thought they were far from the hotel. "That's hardly a fit place for a lady!"

"Neither is a gentlemen's gaming club, but you manage there well enough," he said. "Besides, no one that carries tales will see you among the countinghouses."

That was true. She couldn't imagine any of the well-bred Penny House gentlemen among the clerks, sailors and longshoremen. "But near docks and the ships—"

"Without the ships and their cargoes, there'd be no Greenwood Hall," he said, "and no money for you to spend refurbishing it, either."

She made a grumpy *harrumph*. "You could at least have told me. Common decency would dictate that."

"I did tell you, and decently enough for the Queen herself," he said, opening the window to lean out. "Anything more decent, and I would have had to weep. Here we are."

The streets were narrow and crowded here so close to the river, with those on foot jostling through wagons and dray horses and handcarts. Blocking the pavements were high pyramids of barrels and crates, being loaded either in or out of the rows of brick warehouses. The air was alive with men shouting and cursing and calling orders back and forth, and with the whinnies and snorts of horses feeling the flick of the drover's lash.

But what Cassia noticed first as she stepped from the cab were the smells, so different from St. James Street and striking her nose as forcefully as a blow: melting tar, fresh-cut timbers of pine and oak bound for the yards, frying onions and roasting beef from the open tavern doors, the manure from the horses and the sweat of the men, and, weighing over everything, the heavy, fetid stench of the summertime Thames.

The countinghouse was a narrow brick building, as plain as the warehouses except for the glossy black door and the signboard with the names Satter and Blackley picked out in gold. She hadn't realized he was both a merchant and a ship owner, and he'd made it clear he owned more than one. She'd guessed he was rich from how cavalier he was with his spending, but she was beginning to realize Richard might fall among those men who were very, very rich.

Richard called over two rough-looking men by name and asked them to watch the hackney with Cassia's trunks, tossing them a few coins as payment.

"Who is Satter?" she asked as Richard led her past the glossy black door. "Your partner?"

"Once he was, long ago in Bridgetown," he said, offering her his arm. "John Satter was an old Barbados rascal who taught me all he knew about trading sugar and molasses, and then took me on as his partner, too. After he died, I kept his name on the firm, out of respect."

"So there *has* been at least one person who once cared for you." She decided against taking his arm, instead walking side by side. She was probably being overcareful, but on this, the first hour of the promised month, it seemed wiser to be cautious. "It sounds as if he was your partner, your mentor and your friend."

"Satter?" Richard laughed. "The only reason Satter made me his partner was so I wouldn't take his secrets to one of his rivals. He was a clever old goat. You can sit in this chair by the door, and I'll have someone fetch you tea."

She blinked, her eyes growing accustomed to the shadowy interior after the bright morning sun. The room was plain, even severe. Maps of shipping lanes and foreign ports were pinned to the whitewashed walls, and three shelves held rows of ledgers and boxes. Four clerks sat at their tall desks beside the windows, making a great show of industry before their master even as they tried to steal a peek at her from beneath their arms, while the straight-backed chair that Richard was offering looked both uncomfortable and lonely.

"I believe I'd rather come with you, Mr. Blackley," she whispered, standing closer to him. "If you please."

"Oh, I please." He looked down at her, and smiled as

he raised a single brow with teasing surprise. "I please very much."

"Good day, Mr. Blackley, good day!" The sandy-haired manager of the counting house came hurrying to greet them from a private office in the back. "I have everything waiting for you to sign, Mr. Blackley, and—ah, good day, miss."

"Miss Penny, Mr. Barker." Without pausing for more pleasantries, Richard headed for the office, leaving Cassia to follow. "I'm bound for the country today, Barker, and I'd like this finished as soon as possible."

"Very well, sir, very well." Barker scurried to keep up, his hands clasped tightly before him. "The bills of lading are ready for your consideration, with the proper letters attached."

"Good." Richard made himself at home at Barker's desk, beginning to read the papers stacked neatly in the middle before he'd even sat in the chair.

So much for pleasing now, thought Cassia crossly, standing forgotten in the middle of the room. Richard was all business, as if she weren't even there. Not that she wanted anything more from him, but it would have been nice not to have been tossed aside quite so quickly for an old pile of papers.

"No surprises on this voyage?" he was asking as he scanned the top sheet. "None of the crew jump ship, or lost at sea?"

"No, sir. And it's all the usual cargo, sir, especially at this time of year." Barker hovered behind Richard, watching and making certain his emphatic signature slashed across the page in all the necessary places.

"Though Captain Page did bring a few baubles that might interest the lady."

"Eh? Baubles?" Richard was reading, and not really paying attention. "What the devil are you talking about, Barker?"

"I'll show her, sir." Barker bustled to the strongbox in the corner, unlocked it and brought back a small leather pouch. He tipped the contents into his palm, and held it out for Cassia to see.

"Amethysts, miss," he whispered with theatrical awe. "Gems painted the purple of royalty, carved from the jungles of Brazil!"

Cassia frowned, perplexed. She didn't see royal purple; she saw dull gray rocks streaked with faint lavender.

"You don't have to pretend to see something that's not there, Miss Penny," Richard said. "Captain Page fancies he has an eye for fine gems, which he doesn't, and Barker here encourages him."

His pride wounded, Barker curled his ink-stained hand over the stones, covering them as if they were fireflies he wished to keep from escaping. "But once these amethysts are cut and faceted, sir, then—"

"Then they will still be gray and unsalable," Richard said. "Tell Page if he wishes to speculate with such rubbish he's to do it from his own pocket, not mine."

"That's all right, Mr. Barker," Cassia said to the crestfallen manager. "Unlike most women, I've not much interest in jewels, nor could I tell good from bad. But perhaps you can tell me what that is instead."

She pointed to the large, rough slab of wood leaning against the wall, so large that it must have been a vertical slice of some enormous tree. Eagerly Barker scooped the disgraced amethysts back into their pouch and turned to the wood.

"Why, this—this could be anything, Miss Penny!" Mr. Barker ran his hand over the rough piece of wood. "This is the finest mahogany from Honduras, coveted by every cabinet maker in this city and imported by Satter and Blackley exclusively for the use of the best in the trade. When it is planed and polished and fashioned into a chest of drawers or dining table, this wood shines like a red flame."

From his desk he reached for a finished cube of the gleaming, varnished wood, passing it to her. "You can see for yourself, Miss Penny. The hands and tools of a master craftsman are all this piece needs to release the spirit of this rarest of precious woods!"

"Barker, you sound like some damned milliner," Richard said without looking up. "Stop trying to sell Miss Penny our mahogany as if it were a new pair of gloves. She's not interested."

"But I am." Cassia turned the cube of polished wood in her fingers, her thoughts racing ahead. "Would you be willing to spare some of this mahogany for Greenwood? For paneling, or a special table—I can't say exactly what just yet—but something that reflects your trade, your interests, your past."

She came to stand before the desk, thumping the block down on top of the stack of papers to make sure Richard heard her. "That's the sort of thing that will make Greenwood your home, Mr. Blackley, not just your house, and make it look as if you'd lived there all your life."

He stared at her without blinking, frozen with the pen in his hand and one lock of black hair slipping down toward his brows.

She stared back because she knew she was right, her fingers still curled around the mahogany cube.

Barker cleared his throat, not sure whether he should speak or not. "Most of Captain Page's mahogany shipment is still not spoken for yet, Mr. Blackley, and I believe we've still a few more pieces from the last cargo left in the warehouse that were determined to be too figured for use—"

"Consign the lot of it to Miss Penny, Barker," Richard interrupted as he finally came to the last paper in the stack. "She can have as much or as little of the mahogany as she needs."

She narrowed her eyes, suspicious of how he'd agreed so easily. "Just like that?"

"Like that." He signed the last letter, then rose. "You can have those wretched amethysts, too, if you can find a use for them. There, Barker, that's all of it for now."

"You agree even before I've seen the house?" She turned the cube in her fingers, remembering how she'd scrimped and made do when she'd been setting up Penny House. What a luxury it would be not to pause and question every last farthing! "You would trust me that much?"

"I already do," he said firmly. "Which is why I sought you out. You know exactly what to do and what is needed. You are working hard to prove to me that I couldn't have hired a better man for the job."

She frowned a little, wishing his praise hadn't come

with that edge. "You forget that I'm not a man, and you didn't hire me. You won me, or rather, my services."

"Oh, I haven't forgotten," he said. "I remember absolutely everything where you are concerned."

He smiled that slow, lazy smile that sent ripples down her spine. He was thinking of that kiss, and making her think of it, too, and she wished he wouldn't do that. She really wished he wouldn't.

Richard climbed the hotel's stone steps two at a time, muttering and swearing to himself. The luggage was secured on the carriage, the horses were ready, and God knows they were already leaving town hours later than he'd first planned. So where in blazes was Cassia?

She wasn't in the front hall, or the ladies' parlor, where he risked his neck to look inside among the outraged viragos and dowagers, and she wasn't in the dining room, either. His uneasiness growing, he was heading to the porter's station to demand a search of the premises when he passed by the gentlemen's parlor, and found her.

"Oh, Mr. Blackley, I am so glad you are here!" she said, as if there was nothing unusual about a young woman standing unescorted in a room reserved for men, with three of the said men attending her with the most besotted, worshiping expressions imaginable. "You can come settle a dispute for us."

"Some other time, Miss Penny." Richard reached for her arm, determined to extricate her from her worshipers as soon as possible. "Now the carriage is waiting, and it's high time we were on our way."

But she didn't budge, and instead pointed toward the mounted head of a tiger that hung fiercely over the mantel. "Something like that would be very handsome and exotic and masculine to have at Greenwood. Are there tigers on Barbados? Or perhaps lions?"

"Oh, of course there are, Miss Penny," one of her gallants answered, rocking back and forth on his heels. "Those foreign heathen places always have big cats."

"Barbados is a Christian colony of Great Britain," Richard said, "and being an island, its only cats are the tabbies keeping the rats away from the sugar cane. Miss Penny, come with me *now*."

"Good day, gentlemen," she said sweetly, then left the room at such a brisk pace that Richard had to hurry to catch her.

"I'm sorry to have plucked you from your admirers," he said, "but we're damnably late."

"And whose fault is that?" she asked. "I was merely making use of my wait for you to observe how the public rooms are done in a hotel that caters to guests of the first order."

"Then you can tell me every last thing you observed on our way," he said as they walked past the footman holding the front door open. "God only knows what time we'll finally make Greenwood."

But she'd stopped dead on the steps, gazing wide-eyed at his carriage. It was a handsome carriage, dark-blue picked out in gold, with a team of matching grays with polished brasses, but he was still secretly pleased that he'd managed to earn such a reaction. She hadn't said a word at the countinghouse, or let out even a breath of amazement over how he owned a half-dozen merchantmen, with shares in many more. For a parson's daughter born in the country, she was deucedly hard to impress.

She nodded, and smiled, as if the sight alone of the blue carriage was enough to give her pleasure. "I must confess, Mr. Blackley. I've never traveled in any conveyance as beautiful as this."

"Then wait until we're on the open road," he promised. "With the new design of these springs, you won't feel—"

"There you are, Blackley!" Lord Bolton stood on the pavement, his legs apart and his coat flipped back so his hand could rest on the hilt of his sword. His whole body was tense with furious rage, his face livid above his white neckcloth.

At once Richard stepped between Cassia and Bolton, shielding her from the other man's anger. Behind them a woman shrieked, and others strolling on the pavement outside the hotel scurried away.

"Why is he here?" she asked, her eyes round with fear. "What does he want from you?"

"Nothing he's going to get," Richard said firmly. "Here, get in the carriage, and I'll join you in a moment."

She held his hand longer than she needed to as she climbed inside, giving his fingers a little squeeze. "Take care, Richard. Please, please, don't be foolish!"

"Blackley!"

Reluctantly Richard stepped back as the footman latched the carriage door shut, and turned back toward the other man. "I've nothing to say to you, Bolton. I've made that clear enough, haven't I?"

"If that's what you call slinking away from town," answered Bolton, his voice echoing against the buildings in the narrow street. "But what else can be expected from a cowardly bastard like you?"

Richard took a deep breath, then another. He would not give in to Bolton's bullying. For the last three days, he'd been ignoring the overtures of Bolton's second, and he wasn't about to accept such an idiotic request now, before Cassia. Nothing would be gained by it, and everything could be lost.

"You can insult me all day, my lord," he said as evenly as he could. "You won't change my mind."

"Then perhaps this will, you scoundrel." Bolton drew his sword, the blade scraping against the scabbard. "I demand satisfaction from you, and I won't leave until I get it."

Chapter Nine

"No!" Cassia gasped with horror, wrestling with the latch on the carriage door. "You cannot do this, my lord!"

But Lord Bolton ignored her, concentrating instead on Richard. "You made a fool of me, Blackley, aye, and my uncle, too, and I'm not going to let that stand."

She couldn't believe how bravely Richard stood his ground, there by himself, unarmed and unprovoked. He'd been right from the beginning: Lord Bolton was a bully.

"Then don't be a damned fool again," he told Bolton. "This is London. You can't go around brandishing a sword in the street in front of the Clarendon, demanding satisfaction when at least I have the sense to be unarmed."

Finally Cassia yanked off her glove to give her fingers more dexterity, and unfastened the door. Grabbing her skirts in one hand, she hopped from the carriage and ran to Richard's side. "I'll tell you why you cannot do this, my lord, and that's because it's against the law!"

"Back in the carriage, Cassia," Richard ordered. "You don't belong here."

"But I do." She folded her arms over her chest so he wouldn't see how her hands were shaking. She'd told herself she'd never see Lord Bolton again, and now here he was, not ten feet away, with a sword in his hand. But she wouldn't back down, not for her own sake or for Richard's. "His Lordship wouldn't be angry at you in the first place if it hadn't been for me."

"You talk too much, you little slut," Bolton growled, shaking his sword at her as well. "Shut your mouth, before I shut it for you."

Cassia caught her breath, shocked as much by his language as his threats, and took two steps closer. Surely the man must have been drinking, even though it was still early in the day. What other explanation could there be for this kind of behavior?

"I don't care if you are a lord," she said with an angry little toss of her head. "I was raised to believe every person deserved simple respect and kindness from others, no matter what his rank! You've no right to address to me like that, or to Mr. Blackley, either!"

"Cassia, don't," Richard warned.

But she'd already gone too far for Bolton. "'Address you', hell! I'll talk to you any way I please, you impudent little bitch!"

He lurched forward, closing the gap between them. The blade of his sword glinted in the sunlight as it arced in the air above her. She shrieked, as much from surprise as from fear, raising her arms over her head to protect herself.

As if that will help you, you silly fool, your blue wool traveling gown against his sword! You will die because you dared be brave, you will die because you spoke for yourself, you will die because you did not want to see Richard die first.

Ah, Richard, I am sorry!

But as she bent over she glimpsed a dark blur beside her, flying forward. With Bolton distracted, Richard threw himself toward him, lunging and catching the other man in the chest beneath his raised arm. Bolton grunted as the wind knocked from his lungs and he toppled backward, as heavy as a superfine-covered sack of stones, while Richard rolled to one side.

The sword flew from Bolton's fingers, clattering harmlessly across the pavement toward Cassia's feet. Swiftly she scrambled to grab it by the hilt, holding it over Bolton with both hands. Her heart was racing so fast that she gasped for breath, and the way the hilt and the guard still carried the sweaty warmth of Bolton's palm against her own wrenched at her stomach.

Suddenly, belatedly, the street now seemed to swarm with men, the porter and footmen from the hotel, their carriage's driver, a pair of watchmen, all racing toward the red-faced nobleman flopping and gasping on the street like a trout fresh pulled into a boat.

Then Richard was there, taking her arms to steady her, holding her even as she still held the sword.

"You're not hurt, sweetheart, are you?" he demanded. His hat was gone and there was a scrape on his cheekbone, a bruise sure to follow, but all she saw was the concern in his face. "You're unharmed?"

The hotel's porter was there, too, his round, worried face crowding in beside Richard's. "Is the young lady injured? Should I call for a surgeon?"

Cassia shook her head, strangely giddy with relief. "I was brave, Richard. I didn't back down. And—and I got his sword."

"Which you must give back, you know." Richard shoved his hair back from his forehead, leaning closer to her as he searched her face. "You're certain you're all to rights?"

"We saw it all, miss," the porter said. "Like it was a play. We'll swear to it in court, too. His lordship fell upon you with his sword drawn like a common footpad, here in broad daylight, and practically on the Clarendon's very steps! It shall not be tolerated, miss, it shall not be borne!"

Gently Richard pried the sword from Cassia's fingers, and handed it to the porter. "I believe his lordship will wish to have that returned. Come now, Miss Penny, we should be on our way."

The porter held the sword gingerly in his fingertips. "You will not stay to speak to the watch, Mr. Blackley? Surely you will want to swear a complaint against Lord Bolton!"

"What I want is to leave town as soon as is possible," Richard said as he helped Cassia back into the carriage, pausing only to retrieve his hat from where it had been knocked to the pavement, "and to leave Lord Bolton behind with it, both of which I will do directly. Driver, on."

The driver snapped the reins over the horses' backs and the carriage jerked forward so quickly that Cassia tumbled back against the leather squabs. At once Richard was beside her, settling her.

"You are sure you're well?" he asked, slipping his arm over her shoulders.

"Quite, Mr. Blackley." As much as she wanted to stay sitting beside him, she eased free and moved to the other seat across from him, folding her hands in her lap. She took a deep breath to calm herself, then another. "Why didn't you want to stay? He did come after us. Why didn't you want to stay to speak to the magistrate?"

He sighed, taking his hat from his head and setting it on the seat beside him. "Is that it, then? You wished me to do that?"

"I don't know what I wished." She looked down at her hands. "When he—he treated me ill that night at Penny House, I thought it was my fault, that I'd done something to make him displeased. But this time seemed more deliberate, more planned. Different."

"Of course he planned it. He's been trying to draw me out to fight him since that night at Penny House."

"You mean a—a duel?" she asked, scandalized. Duels were against the law, much discussed at Penny House, but so far she'd never actually known of one taking place.

Richard shrugged to show how little it mattered to him. "Bolton sent some other drunken idiot as his second, but I refused to see him. I suppose by his lights that marks me as a miserable coward, but I'm not about to risk my life to appease some jackass lord's idea of wounded honor."

"But you struck him."

"With my fist the first time, and today with my shoulder, and both in defense after he'd acted first," he said firmly, the difference clearly obvious to him. "I didn't challenge him to prance about with a sword in a public street. Which is just as well, considering my nonexistent skill with a sword."

"I'm not sure I should believe that." He'd worked so hard to become a gentleman—his fortune, his clothes, his accent, soon even his wife—that she'd assumed he'd try to master the gentlemanly art of swordsmanship, too.

"You should," he said, all seriousness. "Pistols or fists are my choice. I've never had the time or the patience to master a blade."

Hearing him speak of swords and guns and fists with such directness gave her a twinge of that same sick feeling that had come when she'd held Bolton's sword. Father had condemned all violence, from the gentlemen riding their hunters after the foxes in the fields around Woodbury to the apprentices and farmers' sons boxing at the fair, and there'd never been a weapon of any sort in their home, not even a small musket for chasing away rabbits from the kitchen garden.

"How did you learn how to hit with your fists, then?" She wasn't ready to discuss pistols just yet, especially since now she suspected he had one or more stashed somewhere in the carriage.

"No one taught me, if that is what you mean." He made a fist of his right hand and frowned down at it, then thrust his fingers out. "In the streets of Lancaster where I was born, a boy was more likely to be cuffed than petted. You learned how to fight back, or you didn't survive."

"Oh." She thought again of the peaceful, peaceable cottage where she'd been raised. How vastly different their lives had been to this point! "Then I suppose it was a good thing you did learn to fight, else you wouldn't be here now, would you?"

"Here with you, you mean?" He was watching her closely, waiting for her answer.

She flushed, not sure that was what she had meant, but not certain it wasn't either, and so she said nothing, instead turning away to gaze from the window. She knew so little of him, really, yet here she was trusting herself alone with him, driving farther and farther from her sisters and her home.

They were on the outskirts of the city now, with more trees and fields than houses and shops, and the wagons and carts were becoming fewer, too, so that the horses pulling the carriage were free to increase their pace. The breeze that came through the open windows smelled of country, not town, and even the sun seemed brighter, warmer. Here and there she saw people by the side of the road who'd stopped to watch them pass, eager for a glimpse of someone so fortunate as to travel in this grand way.

"You're very quiet," he said softly, interrupting her thoughts. "You're certain you're not hurt?"

Reluctantly she turned back. "Is that why you did not wish to speak to the magistrate, Mr. Blackley? Because you would not fight a duel with Lord Bolton?"

"What, be shamed because I want no part of his idiocy?" he asked, bemused. "No, lass, my hide is tougher than that."

"But now he will be your enemy!"

"I already have my share of those who dislike me. One more or less will make no difference." He smiled. "No, lass. I did it for you."

"For me, Mr. Blackley?" She frowned. "How can you say such a thing? I didn't want to leave, to run away like a frightened rabbit with his white tail in the air. I would happily have gone before the magistrate and told him everything, Mr. Blackley. Everything."

"Oh, Cassia." He shook his head sadly. "When we're before others, you may call me Beelzebub for all I care, but while it's just us together, please, please call me Richard. You've slipped and done it before, and it hasn't killed you."

She made an impatient swipe through the air with her hand. True, she had used his given name before, but only under duress, and granting him that informal intimacy seemed like a risk so early in their journey.

"Don't try to talk circles around me, if you please, Mr. Blackley," she said. "Please answer my question. Why wouldn't you go with the watchmen and swear a complaint against Lord Bolton after he tried to kill us? And he did try. There's no use denying that he did."

He sighed, folding his arms over his chest. "I told you, sweetheart. Because of you."

"Mr. Blackley, be serious!"

"I'm being as serious as the grave," he said. "You'll face enough gossip and hard questions for coming with me to Greenwood, even if I brought an entire militia to guard your virtue."

"At Penny House, we cope with such gossip every

day," she said, striving to appear worldly. "It's part of our position in the public eye."

"But nothing like this, I'll wager." He leaned from his seat toward hers for emphasis, his elbows on his knees. "Do you really wish to make all of London, rich and poor, in print and in coffeehouses, whisper over how you are the centerpiece in a thwarted duel? You think the gossip rags plague you now? Your name will be as tossed about and worried as a mutton bone among strays. And once you've sworn to the whole story in a court of law— Why, Cassia Penny, you would become the most notoriously celebrated young woman in the kingdom."

"Not the *most*," she said, her bravado faltering before this hard truth. A pox on him, he was right, and the scandal would wash over not only her name, but her sisters' as well.

"Well, then, you might be second," he said. "I'll grant that you're not familiar with the bedchambers of the Prince of Wales. At least I don't believe you are."

"Mr. Blackley!" she exclaimed with genuine shock. "Please consider who I am!"

"Oh, I'll answer, then," he said, trying very hard not to laugh. "I didn't want to go with the watchman because of you."

Cassia ducked her chin, watching warily from beneath the brim of her hat. Exactly how was she supposed to respond to this? She may have been tired and overset from what had happened earlier, or maybe she really was as dense as she felt, but she was in no mood to be teased.

"Pray forgive me for not understanding, Mr. Blackley," she began, "but I do not—"

"Richard." His eyes were a gray so silvery as to be luminous here with the sunlight filtering through the window, so silvery she could easily forget how he spoke of guns and fighting with such ease. "It's not so very hard to say, is it?"

She took another breath, beginning again. "Forgive me, Mr. Blackley, for not understanding what it is—"

"What I do not understand is why you cannot grant my little wish regarding our given names," he said. "'Mr. Blackley' sounds as if I am your solicitor or overseer."

She sighed, closed her eyes to compose herself, and pressed her fingertips to her forehead. "Very well, *Richard.* I am giving in only because you will never answer my question until I do, *Richard,* and my question is more important than how I address you. *Richard.*"

"Thank you, Cassia." He reached one hand toward her, as if intending to take hers, or perhaps rest his palm on her knee, but at the last minute instead settled it on the seat beside her, smiling ruefully at his own cowardice. "Now ask away."

She looked down at the large, tanned hand beside her skirts, and tried not to think of how much she wished it were holding hers. She'd lost her gloves earlier and her hands were bare, and she could imagine how warm his fingers would be around hers.

"Why should you care at all about my name or my honor or whether both are tattered through the streets?" she asked. "You say yourself that you care for no one but yourself, and that in turn no one cares for you. So why, then, should you give a tinker's dam about me?"

She glanced up just in time to see a shadow cross through those silvery eyes, or maybe it was only a passing cloud outside the window that played the trick.

"That's an easy answer to give, too," he said, his voice so low over the sounds of the horses' hooves and the squeaking carriage wheels that she almost didn't hear it. "You came to my defense, so I came to yours."

"What else was I to do?" she asked, surprised. "Lord Bolton was going to hurt you, and it was my fault. I was hardly going to sit cowering in the carriage while that happened."

His smile now seemed tight, forced. "Most ladies would have done exactly that."

"But I'm not most ladies." This was logic she could understand. "Father taught the three of us to think, to follow our consciences and always to do what we believed. He didn't want us to be empty-headed noddies who cared only for new bonnets."

"No," he said slowly. "You're not that, not at all."

"No," she echoed softly, her thoughts bouncing from the past to the present. "Father would have approved of how you behaved today, too. You tried your best to reason with Lord Bolton. You kept your temper, and you only fought back when you had no choice."

"Then your father must have been a wise gentleman." He reached up and cradled her cheek in his palm, and his hand was every bit as warm as she'd imagined. "You know, you are the first person who has ever come to my defense."

"And twice now you've had to come to my rescue. Father would most definitely have approved of that." Father had been her great shining hero, the man who'd always save her whenever she needed saving—just as Richard had saved her today. Her eyes filled with tears. Richard's face blurred and swam before her, and she turned away from him to look out the window, hoping he hadn't noticed.

"There now, there now, don't cry," he said gruffly. "Oh, hell, please don't cry."

"I cannot help it," she whispered miserably. Now that she'd let those first tears squeeze free from her eyes, it felt as if a whole torrent was falling, hot and salty as they slid along her cheeks no matter how hard she tried to hold them back. She found her handkerchief, soon turning it into a soggy wad pressed into her palm.

"But—but what if you had died, too?" she asked. "What if you had died, as suddenly as Father? What—what if you'd been killed today?"

"But I wasn't, was I?" He switched seats, coming to sit beside her. "It will take more than that high-born idiot Bolton to do me in, sweetheart, I can promise you that."

He slipped his arm around her shoulders to fold her in against his chest, and she turned to him with a broken little sob. She had not wept since she and her sisters had come to London, walling in the emotions that had torn at her since Father's death. She'd had to be strong, for all their sakes. She'd had no choice. But now that she had someone else being strong for her, the careful wall around her cracked and collapsed, and her sense of loss—and near loss—was overwhelming.

"There now, Cassia," he said as he drew her close, the wool of his coat rough against her cheek and his arm a heavy ring of security around her. "It's not so bad as all that. Neither of us was harmed, were we? The sun is out, and the sky is blue, and—and—damnation, but I haven't the faintest idea what to say or do to make you stop crying."

She lifted her head from his chest, her breath breaking into shuddering sobs as she tried to regain her composure. She was shaming herself horribly, and she wiped at her tears with her fingers. He pulled his dry handkerchief from inside his coat and handed it to her without a word, and just that simple thoughtful gesture was enough to make her begin again.

"Oh, Richard, I'm—I'm sorry," she whispered as she looked up at him, crumpling the fine linen of his handkerchief into a lumpy ball. "I'm such a ninny to act like—like this, and I'm such a ninny that I don't—don't know what to say, either."

"Then maybe we should stop trying," he said, turning her face up toward his.

He kissed her then, and though she'd realized she'd been expecting it, he still managed to surprise her. His lips were soft but firm, the way she remembered, coaxing her own lips to part. This time she was prepared for the demanding heat of his tongue, and instinctively she answered, her mouth widening hungrily as he deepened the kiss. Her heart raced and her head felt as light as the breeze in the highest trees, and when he finally broke away, she was breathless with wanting more.

"Oh, Richard," she whispered. She dared to reach up

and touch her fingertips to his lips, marveling at the sensations they seemed to rouse so effortlessly within each other. "We weren't supposed to do that, were we?"

"No," he said, his mouth shifting beneath her fingers before he kissed them, too. "We're not supposed to be doing this, either."

He tipped her back against the soft leather squabs to kiss her again, and with a sigh she went with him, curving her arms around the back of his neck. His hair was surprisingly silky where it curled over her wrists, contrasting to the play of the hard, lean muscles in his back and shoulders beneath his coat and shirt.

Her hat slipped from her head, and she did not care. Hairpins were sliding free from her hair, scattering to the floor of the carriage. Her skirts would be mussed with telltale wrinkles, but she didn't pause to smooth them.

When he kissed her like this, she could forget Father's death and leaving Woodbury and everything else that was unsettled in her life. She could forget everything but this moment, and the pleasure that was swirling and simmering and building inside her. No matter how Lord Bolton threatened them, they had survived, and this—*this*—was proof of the vibrancy of life.

He shifted again, settling more closely upon her, but instead of feeling crushed, she relished his weight on her. She had never realized how vastly different a man's body would be from her own, or how much pleasure could be found in exploring those differences. She slipped her hands inside his coat and under his waistcoat, feeling the heat of his skin through the linen of his shirt. She and her sisters had always been taught to be ladies, not to be shameless or wanton, but why hadn't anyone told them that this existed, too? If she was supposed to think for herself, why couldn't she think of this as well?

"Sweet Cassia," he growled, breaking away from her lips long enough to leave a trail of kisses along her jaw and down her throat, feathery kisses that made her shiver. "You're delicious, lass."

She chuckled deep in her throat, arching up beneath him as she pulled his mouth back toward hers. "So are you, Mr. Blackley."

"Richard," he said. "Don't tease me, lass. It's Richard."

Her laugh was swallowed up between them as he kissed her again. She was only half aware of his hand shifting from her waist to the front of her redingote, easing open the row of tiny corded buttons. For a man, he did that extraordinarily well, she thought with the fragment of her brain that was still capable of thinking. She often had trouble with those buttons herself.

And then his hand found her breast, and that last bit of thinking stopped, too. She gasped as his fingers caressed her through the thin muslin of her shift, making her flesh feel warm and heavy as the sensation grew. Beneath his fingers, her nipple tightened and pushed against his hand most shamelessly, and she arched against him, greedy for more.

"Richard," she murmured, her breath coming in rapid little pants now as her eyes fluttered shut. "Ah, Richard, that is too fine!"

"It's you, lass," he said raggedly. "You'd make any mortal man—oh, damnation and hell!"

Abruptly he rose, lunging across the carriage to tug the shade over the window.

"We're stopping," he said, stuffing his shirt back into his trousers. "We must be watering the horses. Quick now, you've only a moment before we're at the inn."

Cassia didn't need to be told twice. Swiftly she rolled forward, grabbed for her hat, and raked her hair back with her fingers before she jammed the hat back onto her head.

"I am hopeless with you, Richard," she whispered fiercely, furious with herself for behaving so—so *irresponsibly*. Her fingers were fumbling with excitement as she struggled to fasten the long row of buttons on her redingote, each button fighting each little loop in turn. "Absolutely, wretchedly hopeless! We'd both agreed we wouldn't risk kissing again, and now look what has happened!"

Belatedly he found his hat, too, shoving it onto his head. "Another ten minutes, lass, and we would have given them a great deal more to see."

"Oh, a pox on you, Richard," she said, still fighting the buttons. "It's not amusing in the least!"

"I never said it was." With a sigh, he tied back the window shade as the carriage finally rolled to a stop. She could see the leg of the footman climbing down from the top, and a few seconds later he was opening the door for them.

They had arrived at a busy country inn that was the center of a small village as well as a watering stop on the road. The yard was crowded with travelers, horses and local people, and the innkeeper himself was hurry-

ing to greet them, wiping his hands on the front of his
green apron while his wife trotted along behind him.

Ten minutes, indeed: they would have had an audience worthy of Drury Lane.

Richard held out his hand to help her from the carriage. "This isn't going to work, Cassia. We both know
it. I should take you back to London directly, before we
cause any more mischief to one another."

Her gaze straight ahead, Cassia ignored his offered
hand and began to climb down from the carriage alone.

"Damnation, Cassia, you're not in this by yourself."
Richard grabbed her hand while he smiled for the ben-
efit of the grinning, bowing innkeeper. "We can't do it.
The wager's off."

"Oh, no, you won't, Richard," she said through the
gritted teeth of her smile as she forced herself to nod
pleasantly at the innkeeper. "I intend to fulfill my part
of this devil's bargain, and handsomely, too. If you call
off the wager, then Penny House must give back Lord
Ralcyn's stake, and we're not going to do it. The wager
stands."

"Would your lady like a dish of tea, Mr. Blackley?"
asked the innkeeper, beaming at Cassia. "My wife has
just brewed a fresh pot of black China."

"Thank you, no," Cassia said, answering for herself.
"All Mr. Blackley and I wish is to take a bit of exercise.
Isn't that so, Mr. Blackley?"

"*This* way, Miss Penny," he said, steering her back
toward the stables and the kitchen gardens. "What in
blazes are you doing, anyway?"

She glanced back at the innkeeper and his wife, who

was shaking her head with sad concern. Clearly the woman had decided that she and Richard were having some sort of lovers' quarrel. At least half her guess was true.

"I'm not quitting, Richard," Cassia said as soon as they were out of hearing of the others. "I'm going to refurbish your house exactly as you wished, and I'm going to do it without kissing you ever again."

He shook his head, every bit as determined as she was. "And I say it won't work. You are a beautiful woman, Cassia. *Too* beautiful. I've worked too hard to get this far in life, and I'm not about to ruin my future because of you."

She gasped as the reality of what he was saying sank in. "You mean Lady Anne. You don't want me causing a scandal that will turn her family against you. All that— that *nonsense* about caring for me because I'd come to your defense meant nothing, didn't it?"

He looked down, avoiding both her question and her gaze. "You and I each have our goals in life, Cassia. Yours is to run Penny House with your sisters. Mine is to marry Lady Anne Stanhope."

She could not recall ever being as angry as she was at this moment, not only at him, but at herself as well. It was bad enough to have given in to her baser passions with a man she scarcely knew, but when that same man was already promised to marry another woman—oh, that went beyond shame and wantonness, and straight to rank, humbling stupidity.

She inhaled sharply, making sure her voice would not shake or tremble. "I've only two things left to say to you,

Richard Blackley. First, I am still coming with you to Greenwood Hall."

He paused. "And the second?"

"You have stuffed my wet, lace-trimmed handkerchief into the front of your breeches." She smiled sweetly. "I shall be waiting in the carriage."

Chapter Ten

Richard swung down from his horse's back, letting the animal graze while he watched the sky pink with the rising sun. He'd always liked this time of day, the hour when it was barely day at all and when everything seemed possible. The air still held the chill of night, with dew heavy and wet on the grass and the last few stars sprinkled faintly around the setting moon.

He gazed out over the fields around Greenwood and breathed deeply, determined to clear his head and his thoughts with the clean, fresh air. As far as he could see, the land belonged to him. This was his home. This was where he belonged, where his children and grandchildren would be born and live out their days.

So why didn't it bring him one damned moment of peace?

He swore, long, rambling oaths that made no sense and didn't improve his mood, either. His eyes were dry and scratchy from sleeplessness, his tongue was thick from the rum he'd futilely hoped would help him to sleep, and he smelled like he belonged in the stable instead of the master's rooms.

"Damnation, but I didn't mean that," he said to the horse, patting the animal's foam-flecked side. The horse whinnied softly in return, better company than Richard deserved. He didn't ride with an English gentleman's straight-backed finesse, but instead sat low over his mount's neck the way he'd learned in the islands, letting the horse set a wild, breakneck pace across the fields to this hilltop.

But not even that had helped him this morning. The sordid truth was going to follow him wherever he went, and not even he could outride it.

He'd behaved like an ass, though he wasn't exactly sure how, and now he'd have to apologize, though he wasn't exactly sure for what.

It was as easy, and as complicated, as that.

All he'd done was tell Cassia Penny the truth. He'd told her he found her irresistibly beautiful, and that for both their sakes, they should keep apart to avoid temptation. He'd already explained to her that he wanted to marry Lady Anne, explained it ages ago. That was the reason he'd wanted her to help with Greenwood Hall in the first place, and he'd told Cassia that, too.

Kissing her had been a mistake, a bad mistake. He'd admit that, and she would, too. The spark between them burned too hot, and he'd been hard for her at once. If the kissing had been that good, that feverish, then burying himself in her warm, willing body would be heaven in this life. Not that he'd ever find out, not with the minister's daughter. Lord George had enough reasons to be leery of him as a son-in-law without adding that one.

Richard kicked his boot heel into the soft ground, trying his damnedest to think of what he'd say to Cassia. Although he had never lied, and he'd never set out to deceive her, and he'd only kissed her twice, he'd still somehow managed to upset Cassia so thoroughly that she hadn't spoken to him for the entire rest of the drive to Greenwood. She'd retreated to her room, eaten dinner alone, and announced they wouldn't meet until this morning, when they'd review the house.

With a final sigh, he climbed back on his horse and turned toward the Hall. He'd wash, shave, change his clothes and breakfast as he prepared for battle.

And pray that this time Cassia would understand.

The shape came slowly into focus over Cassia's head. A deer, she thought drowsily. No, a squirrel. That was it, a gray-brown squirrel with his tail arched over his back, and Cassia smiled, glad that the question had been resolved, and let herself begin drifting back to sleep.

But what was a gray-brown squirrel doing floating over her head, anyway? She forced her eyes open again, rubbing the sleep from them for good measure, then wrinkled her nose with distaste.

It wasn't a squirrel over her head, or even a deer. It was an ugly brown blotch of a water stain, the kind that came from a leaking roof. Jagged cracks radiated from the stain across the plaster, over the ceiling and down the wall beside Cassia's bed, close enough for her to touch, if she wanted.

Instead she groaned, and pulled the sheets up high over her face. She wasn't in a nest of floating squirrels, but at Greenwood Hall, and somewhere under this same roof lay Richard Blackley himself, doubtless sprawled naked and snoring in some enormous, lord-of-the-manor bed, his dark hair tousled and his well-muscled arms thrown careless across the—

No. Hadn't she already resolved not to squander any more of her thoughts on Richard? She'd learned her lesson, and he most definitely was not worth learning it again. She was determined to keep so busy with his house that she'd have no time left to worry over him. She'd prove to him that he hadn't misjudged her abilities, and she'd prove to herself that she was strong enough—more than strong enough—to resist his amorous charms.

It had been dark when they'd arrived last night, and she'd been so exhausted she'd barely nibbled at the cold supper brought here on a tray before she'd collapsed into bed. But now the new day's sun filled her room, and any excuses she might have had to avoid Richard were gone.

She pushed the sheets back from her face and looked up again at the squirrel-shaped stain. With daylight, she now could see that her bedchamber had splendid proportions and tall windows that looked out on what had once been the flower gardens, but the plaster walls were cracked as well as the ceiling, with bits of lathe poking out here and there, and she was sure no fresh paint had come through the door in at least half a century.

She threw off the coverlets and padded barefoot to the rickety chair that currently served as a makeshift washstand, beginning a mental list of what needed doing. The oak floorboards beneath her feet were worn and water-stained, with neither carpets nor curtains at the windows. The leading had popped free around the windowpanes. The only furniture left in the room was the plain, narrow bedstead, a cupboard missing its doors and drawers, and the two unsteady chairs.

Swiftly she splashed cold water on her face and dressed, determined not to waste another moment. Thirty days would fly by. If this room was any indication of the rest of Greenwood Hall, she would need every minute, and every miracle she could collect from the painters, plasterers, and carpenters she'd met in London while working on Penny House.

She opened her door onto a long, gloomy hallway that seemed no brighter now than it had the night before. Here, too, the house seemed lonely and neglected, the walls stripped bare of any pictures. She caught herself tiptoeing past the other closed doors, as if there'd been guests still sleeping within. More likely she was the first true guest the house had seen in years, not counting the field mice that had nibbled their way through the rotting woodwork.

"G'day, miss," the young servant girl said, a bucket of wash water in her hand. In the gloom, Cassia had nearly walked into her, and the girl's round country face was startled and wide-eyed. "Might you be needing anything, miss?"

Cassia smiled, ready to make allies wherever she could. "Has Mr. Blackley come down for breakfast yet?"

"Th' master, you're meaning?" The girl blushed so

furiously Cassia could see it even in this half light. "Nay, miss, I've not seen him this morning, though he could have taken his breakfast in his rooms. We don't know his likes and habits yet, him being here so little."

"Then I'll just have to find him myself," Cassia said. "Might I ask your name?"

The girl ducked a quick curtsey. "Bess, miss."

"I'm glad to meet you, Bess," Cassia said. Father had insisted that servants were merely doing their jobs, and had treated them as any others rather than as an inferior race. "Is Greenwood a good place for you?"

"It is now, miss." The girl grinned, and tipped her head shyly to one side. "Oh, everyone favors the new master, miss. How couldn't you, a bachelor gentleman like him, and considering how he be so young and so handsome and so pleasant?"

"Indeed." No wonder Richard enjoyed his ramshackle country house if all the sweet-faced serving girls were as agreeable to him as this one. Clearly he could have company enough in that big master's bed if he wanted it, she thought, the quick stab of jealousy surprising her.

Stop that, Cassia Penny, stop that at once! The Greenwood servants made the whole foolish arrangement respectable, and soon the house would be filled with an army of workers and craftsmen. Why should she care who Richard takes to his bed? A servant maid now, a marquis's daughter later? Why should it matter, as long as it was not her?

She made herself smile again. "How large is the staff here, Bess?"

"There be five o' us, miss, Cook and Mr. Carroll and Bob and Jemmy and me."

Cassia nodded, adding another item to the list in her head. A staff of five was far too small for a house of this size. Lady Anne and her mother would be expecting at least triple that for proper service.

"Might I fetch you tea, Miss Penny?" Bess asked, clearly hoping Cassia would free her from the bucket in her hand. "Toast, jam and butter?"

"Thank you, no, Bess," Cassia said. "Not yet. I believe I'll explore a bit more before I have breakfast."

She was supposed to have breakfast with Richard, but obviously he'd left no orders for that when he'd gone to bed. But because she was determined to be successful with the house, she was willing to make peace and wait for him to join her.

She turned down another hall where the doors stood open. These rooms, too, were empty and shabby, her footsteps echoing across the dusty floors with a ghostly sadness. Stripped bare like this, she wasn't even sure of the purpose of each room: a parlor, a room for dining or billiards or music, a library? She understood now why the established architects in London had refused to accept this project, especially given the limited time that Richard was insisting upon.

She ran her hand lightly along a carved marble mantel, its shattered corner likely all that had saved it from being pulled out and sold, too. This was the other side of the gaming at Penny House, the sorry result of Sir Henry Green's ill-chosen wagers and worse luck. How many other patrimonies had been destroyed by cards and dice, she wondered? How many other gentlemen had cast away the hard work and achievements of their ancestors for another chance at a win that never came?

And how, because of another wager, had her life twisted about so she'd be the one to bring life back to the shell of a house that remained?

Unconsciously she gave her shoulders a little shake, feeling the gloom pressing down on her, and hurried from the room. She needed to go outside, away from so much dust and ruin. The end of the hall became a kind of windowed gallery that in turn opened onto a sheltered walk, and with relief she pulled open the door and stepped outside.

The mist was rising from the grass, the sky still kitten-gray and pink. Cassia tucked her hands beneath her arms to keep them warm and smiled with pleasure at the view, feeling the house's oppression slipping away.

"A fine good morning to you, Cassia." Richard's voice came from behind her, startling her so that she whipped around.

And gulped, speechless. He hadn't come through the door after her, the way she'd thought. Instead he was already here, on this sheltered stone walk with a broad bank of dark-green yews rising behind him. But he wasn't even standing beside her, or sitting on a garden bench.

He was lolling in a stone bathing tub, chest deep in the water while he read a London newspaper. Only the steam that rose from the heated water into the chill morning air protected his modesty, and hers.

"It is a fine, good morning, too," he continued, as if there was absolutely nothing wrong with him being naked before her. "The best hour of the day, to my lights. I am glad to see you favor the mornings, too, Cassia. I was afraid you'd lie abed until noon, keeping your Penny House hours."

"I always rise early," she said, striving to concentrate only at his face. His hair was wet and shining, sleeked back, and his face sparkled with drops of water. "Even if I'm kept up late the night before, I still keep country hours."

"A wise plan," he said. He folded the newspaper into neat quarters and sailed it onto the garden bench nearby, the motion of his arm making the water crash around him like a small tidal wave. "No doubt that's how you keep yourself as fair as country cream, even in the middle of evil old London. That, and your rare air of Penny righteousness."

"Then I shall be righteous now, and not disappoint you," she said, her hand already on the latch of the door. "We'll speak when you're dressed, Richard. We can meet then, in a more seemly fashion."

"Wait, Cassia, please, wait. Wait."

Though she stopped, she didn't dare turn, not when she heard the water sloshing and splashing from the tub to the pavement.

"I'd things I'd wished to say to you before we met about the house," he began, "and now is as good a time as ever."

"A better time still would be when you're wearing your trousers."

"Ahh, so you did notice I'd left mine behind in my rooms?"

She turned the latch and opened the door to leave him.

"Wait, Cassia, I'm sorry," he said quickly. "That's what I meant to say anyway. I'm sorry. I'm sorry for whatever I did yesterday that hurt you, and I'm sorry I'm naked as a newborn babe in this tub. I'm sorry for every damned thing I've done or said or ever will do to cross you, Cassia, and I give you my word that that's the truth."

She didn't answer at first. She hadn't expected him to apologize, and she needed a moment to comprehend the importance of what he'd said. Men who declared they always got their way seldom bothered with apologies, and never ones as inclusive as this. But he believed it, too. She'd learned that always being right meant Richard didn't bother with lying or other forms of dissembling. Even yesterday, when he'd told her he'd cared for her safety, he'd likely been telling her the truth. It was her fault for reading more into his words, not the other way around. For so worldly a gentleman, Richard Blackley was remarkably truthful.

But she still knew better than to turn around to face him just yet. "Why are you bathing out of doors like that? I cannot imagine that complete immersion in the open air does not pose a grave risk to your health."

"Are you accepting my apology, sweetheart?" he asked, and without looking she could hear the grin in his voice. "Will you absolve me from my mortal sins?"

"I'm not a Romish priest, so I'll do nothing of the sort," she said as tartly as she could muster, which, under the circumstances, wasn't very tart at all. But she knew he sensed that, for now, she'd forgiven him enough. "How do you keep the serving girls from spying on you from the bushes?"

"I don't know if I do." He laughed, clearly pleased by the notion. "It's Neuf's responsibility to keep them at bay. The only reason you passed through is that he went to the kitchen for more hot water."

As if on cue, a small, dark man appeared on the other side of the windowed door, solemnly carrying a pair of steaming oak buckets in his hands. Cassia opened the door for him, and he nodded without smiling, and took the buckets past her to Richard. Still she didn't turn, but she could hear the hiss of the fresh hot water being poured into the tub, followed by a frantic muttering of words and expressions that a minister's daughter had no right to recognize.

But Cassia did, and she laughed.

"If you can laugh at my suffering, woman, then you can face me," he ordered, and at last she turned around. His face was bright red, and he was gripping the sides of the tub with both hands as the steam from the water rose in pale curls around him. "God knows I'll cause you no trouble now."

"Do you do this in London, too? Bathing out-of-doors?"

"Not in London, no," he said as Neuf bowed and left with the empty buckets. "The water would be gray and thick with coal dust, and so would I. But in Barbados, the very air can steam like this, and this is the only way to keep from melting. The effect is quite different here in England."

"This looks more like a stewing pot, I'd say." She

sat on one of the stone benches, primly crossing her hands in her lap as if posture could somehow counterbalance conversing with a man naked in his tub. "If you're wise, you won't tell Lady Anne of this before you're wed."

"Oh, there are a good many things on that list, I assure you," he said blithely. "Now you, Cassia. You I would simply invite to share the waters with me. There's plenty of room for two, even accounting for splashing."

Her face went stony. *"Richard."*

"That is, I would do so if we were kissing, which we are not," he said, leaning back in the water. "As we agreed, sweetheart. I haven't forgotten."

"Nor have I." She sighed, part of her wishing she hadn't agreed. Splashing with him in a tub of water would be quite different from the carriage seat. "Now about the improvements to the house. I scarce know where to begin, Richard, things are so dismal."

"You see why I needed you, Cassia," he said. "You and your righteousness. You'll make the workmen quake in their boots, until they'll beg to be permitted to toil night and day to finish the job."

"Not even I can do that, Richard," she said. "I haven't seen the entire house yet—"

"I'll show you about," he said. "Once I'm dressed."

"I should hope so." She sighed again. "I know I agreed to thirty days as part of the wager, but I'm not sure it can be done."

"It can," he said confidently. "You have whatever resources you'll need. In this world, money can accomplish anything, even with carpenters. I intend to invite

Lord and Lady Stanhope to Greenwood next month, and I expect everything here to be ready for their visit."

"Don't you realize how much that will entail, Richard?" she asked, stretching her hands out to show the scale of the task. "Wishing and willing alone aren't going to be enough here. Have you used your eyes? Have you truly *looked* at the state of this house?"

"You don't like it." Abruptly he sat upright, water streaming from his bare shoulders. "That's the truth, Cassia, isn't it? You think my house is as ugly as a sow's ear, and you don't like it."

"Don't put words in my mouth, Richard Blackley!" she said indignantly. "I never said your house was ugly. I said it was dismal and shabby, but not ugly. And when I'm done with it, I want Greenwood Hall to be so beautiful that it takes his lord and ladyship's noble breath away."

"It damn well better." He reached over the side of the tub for the towel that lay folded over the bench. "This is my house, Cassia. Can you understand that? *My* house."

She managed to turn around just before he stood. "Of course I understand that! I want you to be proud of your house, Richard, maybe even more than you want to yourself."

"You can't be, Cassia," he said, the water slapping out of the tub along with him. "That old place on the plantation in Barbados, the rat's nest where I was born, even those rooms at the Clarendon—they don't count, not like this house. This house is my home, lass, every last broken shingle and cracked wall. I felt it the first time I saw it. Greenwood's my home. It's mine."

"But that's why I want everything to be right, Richard, no matter if it takes thirty days or a hundred!" she cried. "I want to make it that way for you! I can't let Lady Stanhope or Lord Bolton or anyone else laugh at you behind your back, or whisper that your house is common and coarse. I want it to be perfect, for you!"

"Why?" He caught her by the upper arm, his fingers wet, as he pulled her around to face him. "Why in blazes does it matter so much to you, anyway?"

"Why?" Her gaze dropped down for a moment, only long enough to see that he'd wrapped the towel around his hips, letting it hang precariously with only his other hand to hold it in place. The rest of him was bare and glistening with water, the dark hair plastered to his broad chest in a pattern of tiny waves. She'd never been this close to a man so—unclothed, almost as Adam in the Garden, and she wasn't prepared for how beautiful he was, or how much the sight affected her. Overwhelmed, she tried to pull away, but he held her arm tight.

"I asked you first," he growled.

Distracted, she'd forgotten what it was he'd been asking. She forced herself to look up, where it was marginally safer to look, and tried to remember.

"I'm not going to kiss you again, you know," she said, the first thing in her head.

"I'm not going to try," he said, even as he leaned close over her, so close that the droplets of water fell from his jaw and hair onto her.

Furiously she brushed them away with her fingers, as if the water were somehow charged from having been on his bare skin first. "Step back, Richard. You're making me wet."

"Hell." He cocked one brow and paused, just enough to make her realize she'd said something she shouldn't have. "It's only water, lass."

Why was her heart racing so fast? "Yes, and I don't want it dripping on me."

He didn't move, his hand still clasped around her arm as the water seeped through her muslin sleeve to dampen her bare skin. "So why does it matter to you what becomes of my house?"

"Because of the wager," she said, thankful that he'd reminded her. "Because I always wish to do my best, whatever the task before me."

He turned his head slightly, watching her so closely she flushed again. "That is all?"

She sighed, deciding no harm would come of saying more. "Perhaps it's also because I'm not high-born like your Lady Anne, and perhaps I want to prove to her and her mother that my taste and my eye for beauty are still as good as anyone's in London."

His smile slowly grew. "That's the spirit, lass."

"I *am* as good as they are," she said proudly. "Better, maybe. And so are you, Richard."

"I know that." His smile had spread to a boyish grin, and he shook his head with the exuberance of a wet dog. "We'll show them, won't we, lass?"

She grinned in return, giddy with the power he was offering her. "I will have to spend a prodigious amount of your money to finish in thirty days."

"Spend away." He bowed grandly, the towel nearly

slipping from his hips. "If you are willing to do this for me, sweetheart, then how could I refuse?"

Her smile faded. Was she doing this for him? Not as part of the wager, but for him? Hadn't she promised herself she'd not tumble into that trap again, mistaking his interest, even his admiration, for true caring and love that would never be returned?

"You can't refuse me," she said at last, and gently pulled her arm free of his fingers. "Not when there's so much to be done. Make yourself decent, and you can show me about the house so I can begin my plans."

But don't care, Cassia, she warned herself. *He cares for no one but himself, and never has. Don't ever care, or you'll only be hurt.*

None of this was going the way Richard had thought it would.

An avalanche of ancient plaster and rotten beams crashed to the floor of the ballroom beneath him, shaking the entire house and even making the tea in his cup quiver. A ragged cheer rose up from the carpenters who'd caused such havoc and disaster, followed by a smattering of applause and whistles. If he listened hard enough, he'd probably be able to hear Cassia's voice in the middle of the chorus, cheering the loudest at the destruction she was causing. Likely she'd be swinging a mallet, too, eager to destroy every last semblance of peace on his country estate.

So much for the idyllic retreat he'd pictured when he'd first asked her here. He'd had only the haziest notion of how the house would be brought back to life.

He'd pictured Cassia in some sort of gauzy white dress with her hair down, choosing colors for the painters to quietly, calmly brush onto the walls, while she walked the grounds on his arm and amused him. He'd imagined a good deal more going on between them on those grounds, especially in the tall grass of the meadow behind the oaks, but he'd understood those activities would remain strict fantasies. Reality would be the furniture and paintings appearing in a van from London to be put magically into perfect places, followed by the wondering, awestruck response from the Earl of Stanhope and his family as his first guests.

But reality was proving to be noisy, dusty, dirty and destructive. In this past two weeks, entire armies of workmen had arrived to camp on his lawn, devouring everything poor Cook set before them each midday. Terrified bats flew through what remained of his house, while one surprise thunderstorm had sent torrents of water washing through the half-shingled roof.

And Cassia—the reality of Cassia was that she'd become Lord Wellington in petticoats, a leader born with a vision that only she could see, a general who oversaw and led her devoted armies with dash and courage. In the same dowdy patched pinner every day, her hair braided and hidden inside a dun-colored mob cap, she boldly made decisions and sorted out disputes among her troops.

She was unafraid to lead by example with hammer or paintbrush, and quick to send to London for reinforcements when her legions faltered. Not even Richard could deny that, in action, she was a most magnificent sight, a veritable Amazon of architectural decoration.

Yet still he longed for his original bucolic vision. He wished he could see her once in a while alone, just the two of them, with her prettily dressed and not clambering up a scaffold. He wanted to be able to make her laugh, and tease her with splashing bathwater. He wanted the old Cassia back from Penny House, lovely, amusing, and dust-free.

He groaned and shook his head as another crash rocked the house, and he reached for the neat pile of mail that Neuf had brought him. He flipped through the letters, several invitations and correspondence from Barker at the countinghouse. But he stopped at one, on rough paper and addressed in a purposefully clumsy hand. The back was closed with a common wafer, without a wax seal to betray the sender, and with a certain foreboding, Richard unfolded the letter.

The message was short, and simple enough, and much what he expected.

Blackley you Bastard Why don't You face your Betters? You Bloody Coward you will not stand for yourself but Hide away with Your Whore in the country Do You believe You will not be found There?

He turned the page over, looking for anything else that might present itself. It must be from Bolton, or Bolton's friends. No one else would try so hard to make a letter look like it wasn't from an English lord. No one else would want to, either.

"Oh, Richard, how happy I am to find you here!"

Cassia bustled into the room, holding a scrap of painted wood in each hand. "I know this is sudden, but you must make your choice now, and not keep the painters idle. Which color do you prefer for your dining room?"

She held out one painted sample. "This is called Imperial Crimson, a shade much favored by the Prince of Wales, while this—" she turned with the other scrap of wood, the pair cradled in the crooks of her arms like Moses with his Commandments "—this is Peacock Jade. Which is your choice?"

"I don't have one," he said, and he truly didn't. "You decide."

Her mouth dropped open with surprise. "This should not be for me to choose, Richard, not in a room as important as the—"

"We're going up to London tomorrow," he said, tossing the unsigned letter across the table toward her. "Someone seems to feel put out that we have retreated to the country, so I say we should oblige them, and show our faces in the city. I'm sure there's something more you'll need to buy for the house."

"It's Bolton, isn't it?" she asked before she'd even leaned forward to read the letter. "Oh, Richard, this is awful. He's threatening you outright."

"He's just rattling his sword, that's all." He leaned back in his chair, linking his fingers behind his head. "Besides, if he means to come down here, than I think we should most definitely go up to town, just to be provoking."

She was frowning down at the letter. "You will show this to the constable, won't you?"

"What constable would dare use an unsigned billet-doux such as this one as an excuse to chase after a well-connected nobleman? How seriously do you think that constable would take my grievance?"

"I don't care how well-connected the sender may be," she said. "The constable should do his job, and you should bring this letter to his attention."

"No, and for the same reasons as before." He waited for a moment, giving her time to remember how she'd figured in those same reasons. "I don't believe I have a choice, Cassia."

"But you will be careful?" she asked, her worry so genuine he wished he could kiss her then and there. "You won't take any foolish, masculine risks?"

"Not at all," he lied. "You don't have to come to London with me, Cassia. If you wish to stay here, I'll understand."

"There must be rules." She twisted her mouth to one side, looking sternly at him. "No kissing in the carriage. And no fighting in the street."

He laughed softly, so she wouldn't notice he hadn't promised. "If you'd feel safer, you can stay here at Greenwood."

"Of course I'm coming with you, and for the same reasons as before as well." She cracked the two pieces of wood together for emphasis and grinned. "You wouldn't dare leave me behind. And if we meet Lord Bolton, we can ask for his opinion on Imperial Crimson versus Peacock Jade."

Chapter Eleven

Cassia leaned back against the seat of the open carriage they had hired for the afternoon in place of the more cumbersome coach, and tried desperately to keep from yawning at the others they were passing as they drove through Hyde Park.

"Haven't we been seen enough, Richard?" she said. "If Lord Bolton were in town, he surely would have heard we're here, too."

Richard lifted the front of his hat and smiled to someone she didn't see. "You've been idle in the country so long that you've forgotten what tedious labor it is to be a lady."

"Tedious boredom is more correct." She twirled the handle on her parasol between her fingertips, hoping the motion would help keep her awake.

When they had left Greenwood, it had seemed so early as to be more last night than this morning, driving along roads thick with farmers bringing their cows and chickens and peaches to the market at Covent Garden. She'd been too excited and on edge to sleep, though Richard had been on his most congenial behavior. At her request, they'd gone straight to the stalls with the used furniture, where she'd had excellent luck with pictures and chairs, and an oversize looking glass.

Then they'd paid a brief visit to her sisters at Penny House, wandered through the shops in St. James Street, viewed the pictures in a gallery, drunk chocolate in one coffee house and dined in another. She and Richard could have pranced across the stage at Vauxhall and not be seen by more of the fashionable world, and if Lord Bolton or his friends had somehow missed them, then it wasn't from lack of trying.

"Wake up," Richard said, prodding her knee with his toe. "I don't want anyone thinking you've tired of me so soon."

She shifted in the seat. "Perhaps I have."

"I don't see how," he answered, and he wasn't entirely teasing now. "You've scarce spent any time in my company these last two weeks."

"Only because I've been toiling on *your* house, trying to meet the ridiculous deadline that *you* have set." She'd also been making sure that the time she spent alone with him was at an absolute minimum to lower the risk of missteps, but she wasn't about to confess that to him. Better to let him think he was utterly resistible.

His smile seemed oddly bittersweet. "I've missed you, you know, even though you've been under my roof…or what's left of it."

She blushed, and wished she hadn't. "Can't we please turn toward home now, Richard?"

"'Home?'" he repeated, unable to resist. "So that's what Greenwood has become to you? Why, I'm touched."

"I'm half-asleep, Richard," she said crossly, sorry she'd made that particular slip. The last thing she wished was to have him making any wrongful assumptions. She'd been working so hard on the house that it almost did seem like hers, if only for this handful of days, but that was as far as it would—or could—go. "I can be forgiven."

"Oh, certainly," he said with a wave of his hand that she didn't believe at all. "But we're not ready to turn back yet. The day is young, especially for London. There's a musicale at Ranleigh tonight. I thought we'd pause to hear a few tunes from the new singers."

Now she did yawn, and didn't care who saw it. "Only if you wish me to snore along in tune with them. Oh, please, Richard, I beg you, can't we—"

"Look at me," he ordered suddenly, his expression perplexed as he leaned close to her. "Rather, let me look at you. My God, Cassia. There are scraps of wood on the brim of your bonnet."

"I know. I put them there." She smiled proudly, touching one of the elaborate curls of mahogany that she'd rescued for a new purpose. "When I saw them on the floor beneath the carpenter's planing bench, they reminded me of spring flowers, almost like rosebuds. So I thought, why not dress my hat with them instead of the tired old silk flowers to be found in every milliner's window?"

"But Cassia," he said, unconvinced and still staring. "That's *wood*. On your *hat*."

"How perceptive of you," she said, smiling as she leaned back. Bonnets were a far safer topic for them than homes and who missed the other more. "And how imaginative of me. Isn't that why you wished me to come to your house? To set the fashion, and not simply to follow it?"

"So help me, Cassia, if you have strewn scraps of that Honduras mahogany across my bed, then I will—"

"Good day, Blackley." The young gentleman on horseback beside them was clearly trying to decide whether or not to lift his hat to Cassia. "I didn't expect to see you here today."

Cassia decided for him.

"My Lord Carew!" she exclaimed, forcing him to acknowledge her. "It's been far, far too long since our paths have crossed! Have you been having a pleasurable summer, my lord?"

"Good day to you, Miss Penny." The hat came off at last, but his smile was perfunctory, almost shamefaced. "My summer has been most pleasant, thank you."

"Are your mother and sister riding with you here in the park, my lord?" Richard was scanning the other carriages around them, but Cassia couldn't tell if he wished to see Lady Anne now or not. "It's such a grand afternoon."

"They're not here, no," Carew said curtly. "Not today. But then they weren't expecting to see you, Blackley, were they? They don't expect to see you anywhere these days."

Cassia listened. So that was how Carew was going to play it, that Richard had been neglecting his sister in favor of her. How vastly inconsiderate and wrongheaded of him!

"I know your mother has shown great interest in Mr. Blackley's new home in Hampshire, my lord." She made sure that she smiled her most winning smile at the young lord. "Mr. Blackley has been making so many improvements in the house that, when Her Ladyship finally visits, she will be amazed by the changes!"

"Has he, Miss Penny?" Carew relaxed enough to return her smile—tight-lipped and reluctant, but still returned. "I'd heard you were the one doing the improving."

She tipped her head and smiled archly. "I suggest," she said, "and Mr. Blackley improves. Isn't that so, Mr. Blackley?"

Richard glanced at her uneasily, as if he feared she was going to make things worse rather than better. She was working day and night to make his house ready for Lady Anne. Did he understand that she wasn't about to let his precious lady-bride escape over a slight as small as this one?

"I'm the one paying for all that improving, if that's what you mean," he said finally. "I tell you, my lord, that there's been more improving going on at Greenwood in these last two weeks than in the last three hundred years. I scarce know what to expect from one day to the next."

"Yet you have given such decisions over to Miss Penny, haven't you?" asked Carew, almost as if Cassia wasn't there in hearing. "That is a deuced great responsibility to grant a, ah, a friend, don't you think?"

"Oh, speak it out, Carew," Richard said with a lazy,

too knowing smile. "The whole town knows it. I won Miss Penny from Ralcyn over the hazard table."

Shocked, Carew glanced at Cassia for her reaction.

"I say, Blackley," he said uneasily. "That's putting it a bit stiff, isn't it?"

"Not at all," Cassia said quickly, not that she was about to show her true feelings here—true feelings that included anger and confusion and plain, ordinary hurt.

She made herself smile again. "Mr. Blackley won my time and services for refurbishing his house," she said with a shaky laugh. "Nothing more, My Lord, and you can tell that to your mother and sister."

"They're above caring about you, sweetheart," Richard said. "They're ladies, you know. Mere mortals like us aren't worth acknowledging."

"You're most welcome to call, Blackley," the young lord said, not following this at all. "My sister would be most pleased to see you—that is, to acknowledge you if you want to be acknowledged."

"She'd have to be damned quick about it," Richard said, "seeing as I'm returning to the country with Miss Penny tonight."

"To continue the renovations," Cassia added hastily. "You see, my lord, Mr. Blackley wants everything done within a month, and considering the great age and disrepair of Greenwood Hall, we cannot squander a minute."

"A month, Blackley!" Carew exclaimed, successfully detoured. "I hadn't heard that you'd set yourself such a task in such a short time!"

"He has his reasons, my lord," Cassia said, determined to salvage the conversation however she could.

She leaned forward, angling her parasol back over her shoulder and inviting the young lord to share her confidence. "I shall tell you, my lord, because Mr. Blackley himself is too modest to reveal it himself."

Richard widened his eyes with mock surprise. "Why, then, tip my hand, Miss Penny, and enlighten us all!"

Cassia glared at him, and smiled at Carew. "It's your sister, my lord. Because of his admiration for Her Ladyship, Mr. Blackley is planning to invite your family down to Sussex as his special guests, and he wants the house to reflect his respect and regard for your noble family."

"I intend to if the lady will acknowledge me," Richard said, watching Cassia with such a curious mixture of amusement and affection that she began to blush all over again. "I can't begin to guess what Lady Anne's wishes are."

What Cassia wished was that Richard would stop looking at her in that strange, inappropriate way, before his lordship noticed. What had possessed Richard, anyway? He should be thinking of Lady Anne, not making idle mooncalf eyes at *her.*

Carew laughed nervously. "I never can tell what Anne wants, either, and I've known my sister all her mortal days. But I shall relay your invitation to her, Blackley, indeed I shall."

Cassia twisted on the seat, focusing more fully on Lord Carew and turning away from Richard. "Once the renovations are done, Greenwood will be a beautiful, beautiful house, my lord, quite the pride of the county. Any lady will be delighted to call it her home."

She'd meant that to reassure Carew, to give him more to tempt his sister, but even she could hear the wistfulness that came out in her words.

"Indeed, Miss Penny." Carew fussed with the reins of his horse to avoid meeting her eyes, for he, too, clearly understood more than she wanted him to. "Will you, ah, will you still be in residence at the end of the thirty days?"

Richard sighed mightily. "Thirty days is all I have her for, my lord. That was the extent of my wager with Ralcyn. Thirty days of hard toil, like a sentence for poaching pheasants out of spite."

"I'll be returning to my sisters at Penny House as soon as the month is done, my lord," Cassia said quickly, understanding what he was really asking. "I can't be excused from my duties there for any longer. And the wager between Lord Ralcyn and Mr. Blackley was most specific in its limits."

"It was, more's the pity," said Richard softly, and Cassia didn't have to look back to know he was still watching her in that inappropriate fashion.

Carew cleared his throat. "I shall be sure to give your regards to my sister and mother, Blackley, especially the part about visiting your house when you're done. I can't imagine anything that Anne would enjoy more. Miss Penny, good day."

She nodded and smiled one final time, the effort making her face hurt. As much as she wanted to, she knew she could not make a scene here in the park, not with so many others around them, and yet she couldn't let this pass without saying something.

But Richard said it first.

"What a sniveling little weasel," he said as Lord Carew rode away from their carriage. "Can you believe he'd dare speak that way to me? Dressing me down as if I were the lowest groom in his stable?"

She turned to face him, stunned. "What I cannot believe, Richard, is what you said to him!"

"What, trying to take the whelp down a peg or two?" His swept his hand through the air with scorn. "Just because his father's a blasted peer of the blasted realm doesn't mean he can treat me like that. I've seen his type all my life, and they don't improve with age."

"Is that all you can think of? How his lordship insulted you?"

He stared at her blankly, his gray eyes wide with astonishment. "What else is there, Cassia?"

"What of this poor girl you claim you wish to wed?"

"Lady Anne?" he asked. "Why, I still have every intention of marrying the little chit, no matter how shamed her family might be of me. Though not of my money. Did you see how Carew's eyes lit when you told him how fine Greenwood was going to be?"

"What I saw was how hard he was trying to defend his sister's honor," Cassia insisted. "Haven't you any regard for her, for what she might be thinking when you haven't called on her for days and days?"

"I've been distracted." He smiled at her. "When I'm with you, sweetheart, I can scarcely recall the girl's face."

"Stop that nonsense, Richard, stop it right *now!*" She slammed her fist against the seat beside her with frustration. "All I've heard from you is how much you want to marry this girl, yet you ignore her completely while you let the world believe I'm your mistress."

"Lower your voice, Cassia," Richard ordered sharply. "People are looking."

"Then let them look, if it makes you see sense," she said. "What must poor Lady Anne think when she reads the scandal sheets? How can she possibly defend her bridegroom to her friends and family when he's seen all over town with the woman he *won* over dice? You must be breaking her heart, and you don't even realize it!"

"Listen to me, Cassia," he said, his voice so tense that she realized he'd finally become as angry as she. "This isn't some cheap tavern ballad. That's not how it's done with the grand folk. They don't marry for love. Neither will I. Lady Anne is as much for sale as that gilt looking glass you bought this morning. She knows how the game is played, and when I make an offer for her, she should be damned grateful to get it, considering how long she's been on the shelf. Love and poetry have nothing to do with this, Cassia, and never have."

"The only thing that matters here is *you*, Richard Blackley." She could feel the tears stinging her eyes, and she gulped them back, determined not to give him the satisfaction of seeing her cry. "You never waste one second on anyone else, do you?"

"How else would I have gotten as far in the world as I have, Cassia?" he demanded. "If I hadn't, I'd still be sitting in that damned collier's boat, with my hands bleeding from the shovel in my hands and my back breaking and not one stinking farthing to my name!"

She stared unseeing down at her lap, struggling to

hide how her own heart was breaking, here, in this carriage in the middle of Hyde Park. He'd never pretended to be anything than what he was. He'd never claimed that he cared for her. All the teasing and jesting and flirting—that meant nothing to him. He didn't realize that by letting Lord Carew believe they were lovers, wanting to thumb his nose at the Stanhopes, he'd cut her to the quick. He didn't see it, and he never would.

"You are the most selfish man I have ever met, Richard," she said finally, still staring down at her lap.

"I'm likely the most successful one, too," he said proudly. "Don't forget that."

"You won't let me," she said. With a great effort, she drew back her shoulders and lifted her head, composing herself. He didn't understand and he never would. "I would like to go back to Greenwood now, Richard. I see no point for us to remain in town and pretend to enjoy one another's company."

She knew he was looking at her again, but she didn't look back.

"For once, Miss Penny," he said at last, "I couldn't agree with you more."

Richard sat on the top of the coach, squinting into the wind alongside the coachman in the dark. He didn't enjoy riding up here, not when he thought of the inside of the coach beneath him, warm and cozy and free of wind, with soft cushions and wine to ease any bumps and the road. But tonight that interior also held a silent, unfriendly Cassia, and given the choice between that and the chilly, rocking perch on top, he'd taken the driver's bench.

He had never considered himself selfish. He'd made his share of contributions to the poor box, and he'd always paid anyone who'd worked for him a fair, honest wage. If working hard to achieve what he'd wanted from life was being selfish, then selfish he was.

But still Cassia's words rankled, nibbling at his conscience. Perhaps he had been less than charitable about Lady Anne and her rabbity little face, but the hard truth was when he looked at her, he thought of her title, not her face or form. He felt absolutely no passion or desire for her, and knew that his wedding night with her would define *uxorial duty.* Yet he'd work hard to be a good husband to her, and he intended to be respectful and kind and generous, so she'd want for nothing in return for bearing his children.

Granted, he felt far differently when he looked at Cassia. Cassia was beautiful and passionate, and she made him laugh and she made him think. She'd even taken Anne Stanhope's side, which made her noble and generous as well. He couldn't remember ever being with a woman who amused him this much, and up until they'd met Carew in the park, this day had been one of the best of his life.

But did that make him selfish? Was enjoying her company for this short time they had together such a mortal sin as she wanted him to think?

"Fine night, guv'nor," the driver said beside him, the first words he'd spoken to Richard since they'd left London. "Fine moon for th' road."

"Yes, it is," Richard agreed, and there the conversation ended.

But it was a fine night, with a nearly full moon and too many stars to count scattered across the night sky. English nights were different from the ones in the Caribbean, and he'd appreciated the difference since he'd returned. He remembered explaining that once to Cassia, how he'd lie in the sweet grass near his run-down house and gaze for hours up at the night sky, listening to the nightingales singing in the orchard. That had been before the wager, and though she'd refused to come with him, he knew she'd been tempted.

Maybe that was what he needed to do now. They only had two more weeks together, and he didn't want to waste them with her being sullen and unhappy with him. Maybe he should try a bit of moonlight and stars to ease her mood. He'd promised not to try to kiss her in the coach, but he'd said nothing about out in the grass. Maybe if he spoke more about her and less about Anne, she'd think he wasn't so selfish.

He wondered what she was thinking, alone in the coach below him. He hoped she was regretting speaking so harshly, and taking Carew's side against him.

He hoped she was thinking of him as much as he was thinking of her.

The coach drew into to the end of the long drive before the house, the weary horses recognizing that they were home. Richard climbed down from the top, his arms and legs stiff and aching from sitting hunched on a hard bench for so long in one position.

But the moon was still there, and the moonlight and stars with it.

"I'll see to Miss Penny," he said to the footman who

had trotted up to open the coach door. "There's one box on the back to be brought in, and then you may go."

Richard waited until the footman had left, then opened the door himself. He could just see her in the darkened coach, sitting in one corner with her arms folded stubbornly over her chest. Her hat with the wood curls lay on the seat beside her, her face masked by the shadows around her.

She did not look like she'd been thinking kind thoughts of him, not at all. Better to stay standing outside here, at least for now.

"Cassia," he began, his voice soft, coaxing. "Cassia, sweetheart, listen to me. Maybe you were right. Maybe I have been selfish. I've had much on my mind lately, and maybe I've put that too much ahead of you."

He paused, hoping she say a word or two of encouragement, or at least give an indication that she was listening. Nothing: only the stoniest of silences, leaving him nothing to do but to plunge on.

"You've been busy, too, I know, toiling away on Greenwood," he continued. "I should have realized that before I dragged you off to London. What you needed was a little peace, not having to watch me square off against Carew that way. I shouldn't have done that to you, and that's a fact. I admit it, Cassia, and I'm sorry as can be."

But still she didn't answer.

He took a deep sigh. He'd come this far. He wasn't about to give up yet. "And maybe I didn't behave as a gentleman should toward Lady Anne. Maybe she does deserve a few roses and poetry from me. I've never courted a lady like that, and I don't know exactly what she's expecting. But for you to come to her defense— that was outright noble of you, Cassia, and I appreciate it. No one would ever come out and call you selfish, not with you behaving like that."

He'd felt sure that would win her over. How could it not?

But still she didn't answer, and at last his patience gave way. He climbed into the coach with her, his weight making it rock slightly on his springs.

"I don't know what else I can say to you, sweet-heart," he began, coming to sit beside her. "Damnation, Cassia, what will it take for you to answer me?"

She shook her head and stretched her arms before her, and yawned.

"You've been asleep," he said, incredulous. "You haven't heard one blasted word I've said."

"Oh, yes, I have," she said, her voice so thick and drowsy with sleep that he was sure she hadn't. "And you're still the most selfish man I've ever known."

Chapter Twelve

"That says more about the men you've known than about me," Richard said with maddening illogic. "If you have been listening, then you'd know that."

"No," Cassia said, refusing to admit she'd been asleep, and she had, too, since before they'd even left London. "No, no, *no*. I don't need to hear any more excuses or explanations from you. I know what I've seen and what I've heard, and that is all the proof I need."

He made a sound that was half derisive snort, half laugh, and complete scorn. "You call *me* selfish, Cassia, and yet you go ahead and pass a ridiculous and unfair judgment on me like that!"

"I'm going inside the house." Now wide awake, Cassia pushed her way past him and hopped from the coach, bunching her skirts to one side to free her legs. "Good night, Richard."

"Not yet, you're not." He caught her by the arm, bringing her to a noisy halt with a little spray of crushed rock from the drive. "It is a good night, sweetheart. Remember when I told you how glorious the nights were at Greenwood? How the moon was bright as silver here, and how there were more stars in the sky than anywhere else?"

They were alone now, the coachman finally able to guide his exhausted team around to the stables. Richard's eyes were the same silver he claimed for the moon, so intense that she could not make herself look away and look up to see if he was telling the truth or not.

"I didn't come here for either your promises or the moon, Richard," she said. He was scarcely holding her now, his fingers only the lightest of touches on her wrist, yet she didn't try to break free. "It was the wager that brought me here, and nothing else."

"No?" He ran his fingertips lightly up the inside of her wrist, tracing little circles over the blue veins that shadowed beneath her skin. "Breathe this air, Cassia, and tell me it's not different from anyplace else."

Without her hat, her hair had come loose, forcing her to shake it away from her face. "You should save your poetry for Lady Anne."

"Ahh, it spills like water from the well when the inspiration's with me." He smiled, his voice dropping lower, as if the words could cast a spell. "Honeysuckle and new-mown grass and the dew that's waiting to fall—it's all there, lass, heady and sweet, all waiting if you'll but breathe deep of it."

She told herself it didn't matter, that country air smelled the same everywhere. Yet she couldn't keep herself from breathing, any more than she could stop the way her heart was racing in her breast because of him.

"There now, Cassia, I told you it was magic, didn't I?" Gently he drew her closer, circling his arm around her waist as if they were beginning a dance. "Breathe and listen, listen close. Some nights I swear I hear King Henry riding by on the hunt, his horses crashing through the brush and the jingle of the little bells on his hawks' hoods. This old house may have mice in the attic and chimneys that smoke, but it's a special place, lass."

His face was near to hers now, so near she knew that she could feel the warmth of his words against her cheek, and so close that in another moment he would kiss her, and she would not stop him.

"You understand the power that Greenwood has, the same as I do," he whispered. "We see such things, you and I. That's why you've put your soul into this, and why your face seemed to glow when you described it to Carew. You called it home, and you meant it."

"I meant nothing," she whispered back. "It was an accident, a slip."

"It wasn't," he said. "It was the truth, lass. You *knew*."

"It was the wager, Richard, I swear to that!" She ducked beneath his arm and spun free of him, her shoes crunching on the crushed stone. Though the servants inside the house had left them alone, the house's tall front door remained ajar, waiting for them to enter, and the candlelight from the lantern that hung in the front hall spilled out down the steps and across the drive, casting crazy shadows where it fell. "Only the wager brought me here, and only the wager makes me stay!"

Richard followed her slowly, matching his steps to hers so she wouldn't escape. "In the beginning, yes, before you'd seen the house, but not now. Now it's more, isn't it?"

"What are you asking, Richard?" she cried, backing

away. "Why do you care what I think about your wretched house? It's yours and your family's, not mine."

He stopped suddenly, and in unthinking response she stopped, too.

"Is that why you speak so much of Anne?" he asked. "Defending her, worrying over her? Because Greenwood will be her home, not yours?"

"What I say about Lady Anne has no bearing on anything," Cassia insisted. "No matter how much time I give to your house, no matter how I feel about this— this *magic* you say is here in the air, it will all belong to Lady Anne or another in her stead. Greenwood Hall is not mine and never will be, and I know that!"

His smile was unexpected, a flash in the moonlight.

"You're jealous," he said softly, his amazement genuine. "My poor little Cassia! Why didn't I see it before? You're jealous of Lady Anne, over me, and over Greenwood."

"Jealous!" The word wrenched out her in a wail of outrage and pain. "How can you ever, ever be so wrong?"

She charged forward and shoved him as hard as she could, both palms flat as they struck his chest. "*Jealous!* Was there ever more proof that you are selfish, that you are alone in the middle of your empty, cursed, hateful heart?"

He grabbed her forearms to stop her, but her anger gave her strength, and her tight fists drummed against his chest.

"No more, Cassia, no more!" he ordered as they struggled. "You'll rouse the servants!"

"And what if I do?" she cried, not caring now that she wept hot, angry tears that stung her cheeks. "Let them come! Let them hear! Why should I care if they do? I've no lasting place here, nor ever will. But you—you believe every woman alive would want to be your wife… or your mistress!"

He jerked her close, holding her so tightly she had no choice but to meet his eye. "I know you cannot lie, Cassia, that it's not in your being. So can you tell me that you haven't imagined yourself here in Anne's place with me? Tell me you never pictured this house as your own?"

She shook her head, her breath coming in furious gulps. "You don't understand, do you, Richard? You want the truth from me, but you are too blind to see for yourself, aren't you?"

"Don't talk in riddles, Cassia," he said. "Damnation, tell me the truth!"

With a sudden effort, she surprised him and pulled free again, darting up the stone stairs ahead of him. "If you want to see the truth, Richard Blackley, then I will show it to you!"

"Damnation, Cassia, come back here!" he shouted, charging up the steps after her. "Come back now!"

But she'd already run ahead, through the hall to the main staircase, her loose hair flopping down her back and skirts flying around her ankles as she ran up the polished steps two at a time. She didn't take the half second to look back to see if he was gaining on her; she didn't doubt at all that he was following her, chasing her hard.

"Cassia!" he roared, his voice echoing against the polished stairs. "Cassia, stop!"

Still she ran, even though she knew where the chase would inevitably lead, and where it must end, past the scaffolding, brushes and buckets of paint. Perhaps the house *had* possessed her, the way Richard had claimed. What other reason could there be for what she was doing now, casting sense and quite likely her honor to the winds to make her point?

She skidded to a halt at the last room of the hall, her fingers trembling as, with both hands, she turned the knob to open the door. She ducked inside, leaving the door open, and swung around to face Richard just as he entered the room after her.

"There!" she cried, throwing her arms out to either side to encompass the entire room. "Here is your answer, Richard, here is your truth!"

He'd stopped, for once struck dumb as he gazed about the room in wonder. "This is my bedchamber? This is mine?"

"The master's," she said, out of breath. She drew her arms in, folding them over her chest. "The first room I began and the first finished, as is proper."

She watched his gaze wander the room, seeing everything that she'd planned and arranged, every last candle chosen with considered care. The old Tudor paneling had been stripped of the peeling whitewash, down to the book-matched black walnut that had been hidden beneath. The diamond panels had been rubbed and polished until the wood seemed to glow, then edged with a brush of gold leaf.

She'd found an enormous bed carved from the same wood, ample enough for King Henry himself, but instead of the heavy velvet hangings such a bed would have had, she'd draped the frame and the windows with a light changeable silk, deepest purple to sapphire shot through with silver threads.

And over the fireplace, of course, hung *The Fortune Teller.*

"The porcelain monkeys along the mantel are to remind you of the Caribbean," she said, unable to keep silent while she waited for his reaction, "and that disc of leaded glass hanging in the window is like the compass, a mariner's rose, meant always to guide you to your home, no matter where you ramble."

He pointed to the fireplace. "And the painting?"

"To make certain you always remember the day you met me." She smiled, challenging, daring him to say or remember otherwise. "And look, here, on the bed."

She ran her finger along the bulbous posts, pointing to the cabochon jewels she'd had backed and set in silver and inlaid into the wood like distant exotic stars.

"You said I could make use of Captain Page's amethysts however I pleased, and here they are." She couldn't keep the pride from her voice as she traced her finger around one of the inset purple stones. "The stone of royalty, on a bed fit for a king."

Slowly Richard crossed the room to the bed, touching his fingers to the same purple stones. "I don't know what to say, Cassia. This is so far beyond what I imagined—beyond what I *could* imagine. I don't know where to begin."

For a fleeting moment, she wondered anxiously if he didn't like it. What if she'd guessed wrong about him, and gone too far? What if she'd let her tastes overwhelm his, and made things too exotic? If she'd failed here, then the rest of the house would be doomed as well.

She shoved her hair back from her face. "You could begin by saying you approve of what I've done, you know."

"I do," he said softly, still seeing more wherever he looked. "And you did this for me."

"Hallelujah," she said. "You finally understand, Richard."

"Understand what?" He turned back toward her, his smile full of wonder.

"Why I did this." She swept her hands around in a circle, feeling like a conjurer who has just stunned his audience. "To be sure, in the beginning, it was the wager that brought me here, but to stay, to work until I could scarce stand, to watch over the painters and plasterers like a hawk, to scour the markets for special pieces, old and new—I did that for you. Not from jealousy or avarice or imagining myself in Lady Anne's place, but for you."

"For me, Cassia?" He moved his hand along the bed-post until their fingers touched, until his hand was covering hers. "You did it for me?"

"Twice you saved my life, Richard." She tried to smile, her mouth suddenly tight, her heart beating as fast and as hard as when she'd run up the stairs. "Even this room could never repay such an obligation. But to please you—that pleases me as well."

"No one has ever given me such a gift," he said, reaching up to tangle his fingers in her hair. "I know I've never deserved it. I'm not sure I do even now."

"Perhaps you're not so very selfish after all," she murmured. "And it should be my decision whether you're deserving or not."

He pulled her face closer to his. "No wonder I can't think of Lady Anne."

"Hush," she whispered, the word husky in her throat. "Then don't, not tonight."

"But you were wrong, Cassia," he said. "I was thinking of you, not myself."

"I told you to hush," she said, arching up against him. "Just…hush."

"At least I've a good notion of what to give you in return," he said, brushing his lips over her brow. "A most excellent notion."

His held her with one arm high around her waist, his other hand lower, fingers splayed over her hip, and as she eagerly turned to meet his kiss, she felt at once the change between them, the shift from simple affection, friendship, to something darker, richer, forbidden and far, far beyond her experience. She'd felt it before when they'd kissed, especially that day in the coach, but even then part of her had held back, more fearful of what she'd learn of herself then of him.

But now, as she felt Richard caress her hip, discovering the curves from her waist to her bottom and back again, she welcomed his touch with her heart racing in invitation.

She murmured with excitement, almost like a kitten purring. "Is your gift worthy of a royal bed?"

"Oh, without doubt," he said, his lips brushing across her face, taking their time before he reached her lips. "Kings and emperors come to me for advice every day. But I suppose you must be the final judge, yes?"

"Yes," she whispered, and smiled wryly, even as he

slanted his mouth over hers. He might not know a single potentate to advise, but she was certain he knew more about kisses than she did.

Infinitely more, she decided as she parted her lips for him to deepen their kiss. She quivered as his tongue found hers and raw, unfamiliar sensations of need flooded through her. She wasn't ignorant of what would happen when she gave in to that need. One of Father's more maternal parishioners had told her and her sisters the basic facts of what happened between husbands and wives; that, followed by the whispered experience of a friend in Woodbury who'd married early and the conversations of Penny House's inebriated patrons had been the last touch on her dubious education.

"My own dear lass," Richard said, his voice rough with longing as he broke away from her lips to kiss her cheek and along her jaw, small, teasing kisses that made her shiver.

She was a dear lass, but not a wife. Was that enough to bring her pleasure?

Boldly, she pressed her lips to the hollow at the base of Richard's throat, silently pledging herself to the heart that beat so strongly there. They'd come this far together, and she wouldn't be the one to halt now.

Together: yes, that was what made it right, wasn't it? What she and Richard had done—what they were doing even now—was done together, two as one. She wasn't "his" whore, any more than he was "her" keeper. For what was left of this month, they could belong to each other, seamlessly, equally. She had trusted Richard with her life, and more of her heart than he'd ever know. All that was left to give him was her body, and with a sweet shudder of resignation she toppled with him to the enormous bed that she'd made his.

He lay half atop her as they kissed, and she sank deep into the downy cloud of the feather bed as the rope springs creaked beneath them, their kisses so heady that she could well have been floating. She slipped her hands inside his coat, restlessly running them along the broad muscles of his back, stretching and wiggling languorously beneath him, her movements an unconscious amplification of his mouth over hers.

"Damnation, Cassia," he groaned, and she froze. Perhaps what she found pleasurable was not to him. Perhaps to be agreeable she shouldn't move, but lie still.

"Forgive me, Richard," she said anxiously. "If I've acted wrongly, or—"

"Not wrong." He brushed his lips across her cheek to reassure her. "Nothing wrong, and everything right."

As if to prove it, he shifted more heavily across her, and she sighed with the rightness of it. He slid his hand over her breast, making short work of unfastening her bodice and easing open her chemise until he reached her skin. Now it was her turn to gasp as his palm teased her nipple into a tight, hot bud of longing. Impatiently she arched against his hand, seeking more, and she felt the deep rumble of his chuckle at her eagerness. As distracted as she was by his caress, chuckling did register as better than a groan.

"My greedy Miss Penny," he murmured, his breath hot on the sensitive place beneath her ear. "That's two of us, eh?"

She wanted to say something clever back to him, but the way he was kissing her throat with his hand moving—*so!*—over her breast made even three coherent words, let alone witty ones, impossible to concoct. Instead she sighed, wordless but blissful, and resolved to be witty later, when her body wasn't so intent on mastering her reason.

She slid her hands down Richard's back, daring to pull his shirt free of his trousers. Her hands dipped lower, beneath the lacing at the back of his breeches to discover the shallow valley of his spine, the twin dimples on either side, and still more taut, unfamiliar muscles for her to explore. His skin was burning as if he'd been too long in the summer sun, her touch enough to make him groan again as he tore away more of his own clothes.

This time she understood. Her heart was racing, her chemise clinging moistly to her body though the hearth was cold and empty. Yet still she wanted more, and more, and *more* of Richard, with a desperation that went beyond desire.

All through her girlhood she'd been admonished to be a proper lady and keep her legs together and her ankles genteelly crossed, but this new urgency was making her forget every ladylike warning she'd ever received.

With another little sigh, she whispered her legs apart and let Richard's body settle there between, and at once that little sigh changed into a startled gasp. Though still protected by layers of petticoats and chemise as well as his trousers, through it all she could feel the rigid heat of that most masculine part of him pressing hard against the place where she was most a woman.

She felt soft and warm and aching, her own heartbeat now concentrated in that same place at the top of her thighs, and instinctively she wrapped her legs high around his hips to draw him toward the aching, heedless of her shoes on the coverlet or how her skirts slid up past her garters and over her knees.

She might not have noticed, but Richard did.

"By the stars, Cassia!" he rasped with a desperation of his own, his breath as labored as if he'd run from town. "You'll unman me if you keep doing that!"

"Then don't wait any longer," she said in a rush, not sure of anything else. "Don't—don't wait."

"I'm not sure I could, sweetheart," Richard said hoarsely, and he kissed her hard to prove it, his lips demanding enough to steal her breath and maybe her soul with it. Certainly enough to make her head swirl, and to make her cling to him as if she were being tossed on a wild, stormy sea. But instead of the ceaseless drone of the waves, the rhythm that drove her was the thumping of her heart and Richard's, mingled with the ragged pace of their breathing.

She felt him shove her skirts higher, into a mass of crushed linen and wool at her waist, and then he was sliding between her legs, touching her, telling her how beautiful she was, how much he wanted her, and stroking that warm, secret place, until she realized that the low, animal sound she'd heard was coming from herself. Her body was tightening, coiling strangely inside, and she shuddered with an odd mixture of relief and disappointment when Richard abruptly sat back on his heels on the bed.

But only for a moment, the single moment that it had taken him to tear off his coat and trousers and return to her. His palms were hot on her thighs, the soft linen of his shirt's tails brushing over her skin like another caress. Then his touch again, the same rising pleasure that made her arch and cry out for joy, and then something blunt, infinitely larger than his fingers, forcing its path into her to stop the pleasure short.

"Richard!" she cried out, panicking, trying to scuttle backward beneath him, away from this sharp pain that pushed into her. "Richard!"

This wasn't anything like what she'd been told. She didn't feel treasured or blissful or transported on the rapturous wings of angels, the way her friend had promised. Instead Cassia felt crushed and stretched and filled in a way that had absolutely nothing to do with angels or rapture.

"Cassia?" whispered Richard hoarsely, propping himself up on his elbows above her. "Cassia, sweetheart, look at me."

She didn't want to cry, not again. Better to concentrate on the one good thing she could find in this entire debacle.

"Richard," she began bravely, "Richard, I—I have never had a—a gift such as this before from anyone."

Gently he smoothed her damp, tangled hair back from her forehead. "I know, sweetheart," he said, "and I'm sorry."

"You're sorry?" That wasn't what she wanted to hear,

not with him buried deep inside her poor, aching body, not with tears fighting a close battle with bravery.

"Not about being the first," he said hastily, "but that I've hurt you."

"No, you haven't," she said with equal haste. "Not much."

"Liar." He kissed her again, more from apology than passion. "But I swear I'll make it better for you now."

She didn't believe that was possible, but because it was Richard making the promise, she would try.

"Rapturous," she said with a sniffle as she reached up to kiss him. "That's how a friend told me this would be. Rapturous, like soaring upon angel's wings."

"Hush," he said. "Enough rubbish about angel's wings."

She stiffened as Richard shifted on his knees to angle himself differently inside her, and she breathed a tiny sigh—not quite of pleasure, perhaps, but no longer out-and-out pain, either. Now that he'd begun moving again, she was surprised at how accommodating her body had become, and as an experiment, she tentatively tried rocking her hips to meet him, the way she had done earlier.

Amazingly accommodating, in fact.

"Little witch," muttered Richard with a groan. "I thought I was the master of this house."

"But not of me," she said, then gasped with startled, breathless delight as he drove more deeply into her. "Not—not here at Greenwood."

"Greenwood, hell," he said, and when he chuckled she could feel the sound vibrate between them. "Give me your hand, sweetheart."

He raised himself a bit away from her, and placed her fingers where their bodies were so intimately joined, her own flesh wet and slick and hot as fire around his.

"There," he said hoarsely as she touched him. "That's us together, Cassia, as close as a man and woman can be, two joined as one."

She looked and touched and felt, ah, such feelings! She wasn't sure that those angels' wings would have much to do with her and Richard right now, tangled together on his bed, with their clothes half off and damp with sweat and desire and her feet in her shoes—in her red-heeled, still-buckled shoes—hooked high around his waist, and both of them half laughing and half weeping as they moved together, together, yes, until they'd both found the joy that would bind them together.

And when they lay together afterward—a long time afterward, after they'd managed finally to shed their shoes and the rest of their clothes, after they'd wiggled down beneath the coverlet and into the new bed linens, after they'd laughed again about advising royalty and *The Fortune Teller* watching them and gifts given and taken—content and exhausted, Cassia drowsily decided there was nothing better in life than to be here, now, with Richard Blackley's chest against her back and his arm around her waist and his heart beating in time with hers.

"You kept your promise, Richard," she whispered sleepily, not even sure if he was still awake, either.

"Umm," he grunted, barely proving that he was. "What promise?"

"You said it would be better, and it was. Much better."

"Oh, yes," he said, and kissed the nape of her neck. "I told you I knew what to give you, didn't I?"

She laughed softly and snuggled closer to him, and her last thought before she fell asleep was of the other rare, unselfish gift he'd promised for the morning.

And not a minute beyond.

Luke shuffled along with the others in line, willing to wait as long as he had to.

"So why would a great lady living in a house like this give away her food to poor folk?" he asked his new friend Matt, met that morning when they'd both been chased from Covent Garden for trying to filch apples. "Why wouldn't she keep it for her own people?"

"Because she's a bloody saint." Matt rolled his eyes to the heaven and sighed with exasperation. "She does it 'cause she wants to, Luke. I'm not askin' why 'cause I don't care, as long as I get my share."

Luke looked up at the enormous house before them, the pale stone gleaming in the morning fog above the shuffling queue of poor folk snaking to the kitchen door. He couldn't begin to imagine what life must be like inside a house like that; not even the governor of Martinique had lived on such a scale.

"But doesn't her husband—"

"I told you, Luke, this isn't a reg'lar house, with a reg'lar wife an' husband an' tiny little babies in their beds." Matt leaned closer, confidential. "It's a private club for the swells, with no ladies admitted, if you catch my meaning."

"You mean it's for—for whores?" Luke hated that

word, knowing what it meant and having heard it too often. "This house? This lady?"

"Nay, don't be daft!" Matt poked him in the arm to shake some of the stupidity loose. "It's a gaming house, for playing cards and tossing dice and such all the night long. They say some nights a lord will lose a thousand gold guineas, and not even flinch, he don't miss it that much."

Luke whistled with appreciation.

"The food Miss Penny gives out's what the gentlemen don't eat," Matt continued. "Her kitchen sends up food fit for His Majesty himself, but the lords are worrying so much about their cards that they don't eat it, and she saves it all for us. Dining like a king, that's what you'll be, Luke."

Luke nodded again. Hearing about so much food was enough to make him drool like a mongrel dog. He hadn't had a full meal since he abandoned the security of the *Three Sisters* and jumped into the Thames, and his hollow stomach growled in anticipation.

But once he found his father, everything would change. His father would see to it he'd never be hungry again, or sleep in a doorway, or hide shivering in the river's shallows to dodge the men who gathered up unwanted boys and sold them for bones and gristle.

Once he found his father...

"Step up, Luke!" Matt ordered, giving him an extra shove for good measure. "Don't keep the lady waiting!"

The lady was as beautiful as an angel, with pale skin and red-gold hair that curled beneath her ruffled cap and around her full cheeks. Her apron was as white as a gull's wing, and she was so tidy and clean that Luke hung back, ashamed of his own grimy hands and clothes.

"You're new, aren't you?" she said, bending over. "I'm glad you've come. I like to see hungry boys eat."

She smiled again, and handed Luke a makeshift bowl fastened from a folded newspaper. The newspaper was warm in his hands, steaming and full of so many delicious things that Luke was overwhelmed, unable to remember to say thank you, the way Mama would have wanted.

But the lady wasn't angry, and she even reached to ruffle his hair, not caring that it was filthy and full of crawly things. Matt jabbed him again and Luke moved on, cradling his newspaper bowl in his arms.

"I told you it's a miracle," Matt said, sitting beside him on the step. Luke was already wolfing his food, eating so fast that to his sorrow it vanished before he'd had time to taste it, the way the lady would have wanted. He licked the paper clean, same as Matt did, then turned it over, looking for anything he might have missed.

And then he saw the name: Richard Blackley. His father, here on this newspaper like the great gentleman Luke had always known him to be. His father, and his grand country house in Hampshire. His father, keeping company with some beautiful lady whose true name was hidden behind a row of printed stars.

His father, alive and waiting for him, Luke, his son, to find him and come up and say good day.

"Miracles, that's what the lady gives out at Penny House," Matt said, licking his fingers. "Didn't I tell you right? A bloody, righteous miracle, and it's not even noon."

Chapter Thirteen

Richard stood at the window, watching four men wrestle a grimy, life-size marble statue of Hercules from the back of a cart while Cassia hovered around them, offering advice and suggestions that Richard suspected they didn't need to hear. She'd told him the story of the statue that morning over breakfast—how she'd rescued poor Hercules from a local barn where he'd been hidden since Cromwell's day as a banished heathen, how he'd been so covered with filth and pigeon leavings that she'd gotten him for next to nothing, how she meant to restore him and place him with honor in the front hall as a symbol of Richard's own strength and omnipotence—oh, yes Richard had heard so much of this Hercules that he felt as if they were already the best of friends.

The men staggered beneath the statue's weight, while Cassia hovered beside them, ready with the scrub brush to begin Hercules's cleaning the moment he touched the ground. Richard smiled. A week ago, he would have begrudged her the time spent with Hercules and not with him. But now, with the house nearly done, he could let Greenwood have her by day, because by night she'd belong to him, in the great king's bed upstairs.

He still marveled at all she'd done for him, not for money, but because she cared for him. For *him.* When he'd thought about it, she was right: he had been selfish. He had made his own way, and in the process he'd taken what he'd needed or wanted. It might not have been pretty or genteel or even moral, in some instances. But how could he have been otherwise, when no one else in the world cared whether he'd lived another day or not?

But with Cassia, everything was different. Oh, he still was selfish, at least by her definition. He would still do the things that benefited himself and his trade, for he'd no intention of becoming a happy-go-lucky pauper. But because she was thinking of him, he'd found it was easier and easier to think of her in turn. Not just the grand gesture of saving her life, but smaller ones as well, bringing her tea himself instead of a servant, or leaving a bunch of wildflowers he'd picked beside her comb and brush, where she'd be sure to find them, and think of him.

And when she came to him each night—ah, that was the best give-and-take of all.

He was smiling still as he turned back to the packet that had come for him from London. Most of it was the usual letters and reports from the countinghouse and from his captains, but there were three things this time that were far from usual.

The first was another unsigned threat from Lord Bolton, or his friend, or whoever it was that was sending them. This one was even more vile than the last two, full of obscenities in addition to the threats to both Richard and to Cassia. While Richard's first inclination was to toss it straight into the fire where it belonged, instead he carefully refolded it and set it aside. One never knew when such proof might unfortunately be necessary, if the writer ever decided to match his words with action.

Richard glanced out the window again, this time past Hercules to the distant stand of woods that marked one border of his estate. He'd hired a small group of local men to patrol those borders, men who knew the land and which outsiders should and should not be on it, men who weren't afraid to use their rifles to enforce the difference. Richard regretted having to take that step in the place he regarded as his country retreat, but the threats gave him no choice.

And though he'd never tell her, the guards were one more thing he'd done for Cassia, to be sure she was safe.

The next letter was perplexing in its own way, though without even a breath of menace. This one, written in a flawlessly elegant hand on creamy paper so heavy its folds were stiff and thick, was from Her Ladyship the Marchioness of Denby. Clearly Carew had relayed every word of their last meeting in the park to his mother and sister, and the marchioness had waited a respectable week before she'd written, not wanting to seem overeager.

Which was, of course, exactly how she seemed to Richard.

Her Ladyship was delighted to hear he was well, delighted that his renovations of Greenwood Hall were moving along so swiftly, delighted, really, by everything to do with him. Lady Anne was apparently delighted, too, though far too demure to add a bold word of her own. She hoped they'd see him again soon, the sooner the better. She couldn't wait for their sure-to-be delightful visit to Greenwood. She was as good as offering Anne to be offered for, if only he'd come ask.

And there wasn't a single word in all that delight that related to Cassia Penny. Gentlemen were allowed certain peccadilloes, so long as they were discreet, and obviously Lady Stanhope had decided that Richard's fortune entitled him to that sort of lenience. Not only was Cassia not mentioned in her letter; her name would never be spoken aloud.

Richard sighed and tossed the letter back onto the table. The way matters stood now, Cassia would leave Greenwood in a week, never to return. Then the Stanhopes would descend, as determined—and as welcome—as a plague of locusts, and he was quite sure they wouldn't leave again until an engagement between him and Lady Anne had been arranged and announced.

Exactly as he'd always wanted. The country house and estate, the titled family, the lady-bride, everything as he'd planned. How many other men could make such a claim about their lives?

He grumbled to himself, a wordless mutter, and turned to the last thing to come in the packet. This wasn't another letter or a draft or a bill, but a flat, plush-covered box. He clicked open the tiny brass hook that held it shut, and lifted the lid with his thumb, and smiled with satisfaction.

The jeweler had done precisely what he'd asked. The five large oval amethysts had been ringed with gold, then surrounded by brilliant-cut diamonds, and finally linked together into a necklace. The purple stones were far better than the ones Captain Page collected—clear and rich in their color—but Richard hoped Cassia would still make the association with their royal bed, just as the diamonds were supposed to represent all the stars that they'd seen together.

At least he hoped she would, anyway. He couldn't be sure with Cassia. This was a woman so unconcerned with the usual expensive feminine fripperies that she put wood shavings on her bonnet. But if *The Fortune Teller* was supposed to remind him always of meeting her, he'd wanted to give her something in return that would remind her of him.

And perhaps, if he was truly lucky, the necklace might help convince her to stay in his life after next week.

"I know it's not a good and humble thing for you to believe that you're right, Richard, but about this you are." Cassia held her glass up to the night sky overhead. "The heavens are more glorious here at Greenwood than any other place on earth."

"I told you so," Richard said, leaning back on the coverlet with his head resting comfortably on his bent arms. "Even if you hadn't been drinking that wine, you'd agree with me."

"Once in a great while, it's bound to happen." Shoving back her hair, Cassia set the wineglass in the tall grass and twisted it gently into the soil so it wouldn't spill. "Even two such strong-willed persons as ourselves will, in time, agree."

"Strong-willed, indeed," Richard muttered. He circled his arm around her waist and pulled her back down onto the coverlet next to him. "Speak for yourself, Miss Penny."

"Oh, you know I will," she answered. She leaned over to kiss him, giggling as her hair fell around them like a copper curtain. "When have I not?"

"Not in my memory, anyway." He threaded his fingers into her hair and kissed her back, her sigh of happiness reverberating between them.

She rested her hand on his chest, feeling his heart beat beneath her palm. They had already made love once here on the coverlet, and she was sure they would again at least once more before they returned to the house, but now they were lazy and warm and sated with wine and contentment. Without stockings or shoes, their clothes still unbuttoned and unlaced and half off, they looked like any other summer lovers, high-bred or low. The quarter moon and the stars smiled down on them, and the nightingales sang exactly as Richard had described.

She chuckled softly, and flopped over, resting her head on his chest while he curled his arm protectively around her, his hand over her breast. They'd spread the coverlet on a hillside, shielded by the tall meadow grass and nodding white wildflowers, their fragrance sweet and mingling with the musky scent of their lovemaking.

"I can see the house from here," she said, then giggled at having made such an idle, empty observation. "Can you?"

"Only the roof and the chimneys," he said. "I'd rather look at you, anyway."

She sighed happily. "The chimneys are much improved, and so is the roof. Seeing them should please you."

"Not now," he said. "Only you do that."

She linked her hand into his, bringing it up to her lips. "You should have a great ball. You should invite everyone in the county, and your closest friends down from London."

He yawned. "I don't have any friends in London. None that I'd like to have invade my house, anyway."

"You know the Stanhopes." There, she'd said it, and as soon as she had she felt her joy begin to deflate. Maybe he could go on pretending that this month would never end, but she couldn't. "You've already invited them to come."

"You invited them, if you recall," he said, and closed his eyes. "Through Carew. I didn't."

"Because that was what you'd told me you wanted!" She sat up, away from him, linking her arms around her bent knees. "If you don't want to marry Lady Anne, then don't. The world will go on either way. But you can't keep saying you want to, and then acting as if you don't. It's not fair to her."

Or to me...

"You're taking her side again, sweetheart," he said without opening his eyes.

She pressed her cheek against her arms. "I'm not taking anyone's side."

"No?" He sighed. "Maybe it's just that I don't want

to marry her now. Maybe I need more time to consider, to be sure."

She didn't answer. How could she, without saying things she knew she'd regret?

He reached across the coverlet to caress her hip, running his hand up and down the full curve to the top of her thigh. "Come back, sweetheart. Please."

She sighed, and turned her face toward him.

"Didn't it occur to you that I don't want Lady Anne to come here because it would mean that you had left?" he asked softly. "I want you to stay, sweetheart. Stay here with me."

"You know I can't, Richard," she said, trying to be firm. "I belong back with my sisters. When the wager's done and the house is finished, I'll have no excuse for keeping away."

"The house will never be done," he said, his smile wry. "There will always be something more here that needs improving. Me, for example."

"Don't, Richard," she said softly. "Please."

But he'd sat up, too, and was now rummaging through the willow basket that they'd brought to carry the wine. He turned and pressed a flat, square box into her hands.

"What is this?" she asked, though she could already guess. Even in a country rectory, girls knew what came in shaped, hinged boxes covered in leather or velvet.

"Open it, and see for yourself." He sat back on his heels, eager for the reaction. "Go on. Nothing's going to jump out and bite you."

"How reassuring." But she still didn't open it, knowing that as soon as she did, everything would change between them.

"Then open it, lass," he said, clearly wondering why she hadn't. "The little hook's there in the front."

"So it is." She laughed nervously, knowing she couldn't put it off any longer. She flipped the hook, opened the top, and gasped.

The necklace was beautiful, unlike any she'd ever seen. Amethysts and diamonds and gold, glittering to rival the moonlight above.

"I had it made for you," he said proudly. "Amethysts so you'd always recall the bed you'd made for me, diamonds like the stars over us, and gold because—well, I suppose because it's gold, and precious, like you. Here, let me fasten it for you."

Before she could stop him, he'd settled the necklace around her throat and fastened it, centering the largest stone before he sat back to admire the affect.

"There," he said, his smile wide and pleased. "A most beautiful necklace for a most beautiful woman. You do like it, don't you?"

She tried to smile; she really did. She'd never worn anything as rare, as costly as this necklace must be, and the stones sat cold and heavy on her skin, almost as heavy as the guilt that came with them.

"You've given me so much, Cassia, that I wanted to give you something in return that was special, too," he said. "Something that would show you how much I've come to care for you, something that—"

"I can't accept it, Richard," she said hurriedly, her head bowed as she fumbled with the clasp to take it from her throat. "It is very beautiful, as you say, but I—I can't accept such a gift from you."

"Why the devil not?" he demanded, stunned by her response. "Why can't I give you something I know you will like?"

"Because of what it is," she said, tumbling the necklace back into the box. "Because it is one thing for me to be here, working for you, but quite another to—to accept a necklace like this."

"I still don't see why!"

"Because this is a gift a gentleman gives his mistress," she said. "And if I took it from you, that is what I would be."

She snapped the box shut and set it on the coverlet before him. "I can't, Richard. I can't."

"Damnation, it's not like that between us, Cassia!" he said, rising to his feet. "We're more equal than that. You said yourself that I'm not your master. If anything happens to you, then I'll take care of you, as a friend would any friend."

"If those friends lie together?" she asked, the bitterness of her situation welling up within her. He'd never said he'd loved her, or given her any genuine reason to trust him. He'd never said he'd marry her instead of Lady Anne. She'd been the one who'd been the fool for love, the fool of a woman who'd let herself be ruined for hope and a future that never would come. "If together they conceive a child, a most inconvenient child if you were to marry Lady Anne? How can I trust you, knowing what I know?"

"You know I would look after you, Cassia," he said,

holding his hand out to raise her up. "The child would be as much my responsibility as—"

But the gunshot ended whatever he'd say next, echoing close to them. Cassia gasped, not sure what was happening, and then Richard dropped face first to the grass beside her.

"Richard!" she cried frantically, pulling at him, clinging to him, grabbing at his arm to turn him over. He must have been hit, shot to fall so hard, but oh, please God, please God, he wasn't dead, please God that her last words to him would be something better, something finer! "Oh, Richard, please, please, live for me, live for—"

"Get *down,* Cassia!" Richard ordered, his arm reaching out to jerk her down beside him. "For God's sake, keep low, below the grass! You don't know who or where they are!"

The gun cracked again, the acrid smoke from burning powder drifting toward them.

"Oh, Richard," she whispered, pressing close beside him. "I thought you'd been shot, I thought you were—"

"Well, I'm not, am I?" He inched his head up a fraction, trying to peer through the grass and weeds. "What I want to know is what bastard has decided to open fire at me on my own land?"

"Don't you think it's Bolton?" After fearing she'd lost Richard forever, she now couldn't get close enough to him to reassure herself, her body touching his every place she could. "Who else could it be?"

"I don't know," he said furiously, "but I'm sure as hell going to find out."

Another gunshot, closer this time. She heard the footsteps running through the rustling grass toward them at the same time he did, and with a desperate little cry she closed her eyes and buried her face against his shoulder as he held her tight.

"Down," he said in a hoarse whisper. "Stay down, sweetheart, and everything will be all right."

"I love you," she breathed, the tiniest of whispers that she doubted he'd even heard. But she'd wanted to say it to him, whatever happened. She'd needed to say it, if she never said anything else in this life. "I love you, Richard."

"Master Blackley!" the man called. "Master Blackley, sir, it be Hudson! Shout an' let us know where you be, sir!"

"Hudson, here!" Richard pushed himself up and waved. "We're here!"

"Who is it, Richard?" As quickly as she could Cassia worked to button her bodice and pull her skirts down over her knees. "Do you know him?"

"He's one of the men I hired to walk the borders," he said, reaching down to scoop the amethyst necklace, spilled from its box, into his pocket. "Hudson! You're a welcome sight, I can tell you! Did you see who fired on us? Did you get the bastard?"

"No, sir." The man loped toward them with his rifle still ready, his leather weskit and brown homespun shirt making him blend into the night's twilight. All the time he spoke to Richard, his eyes kept moving, scanning the fields and trees for their phantom attacker. "Sorry, sir."

Belatedly the man acknowledged Cassia at Richard's

side, touching the front of his cap to her. Not that Cassia felt slighted. She was still too frightened to care, willing to give anything to be far, far away from here with Richard beside her.

"A shadow's all I saw, sir," Hudson continued, "rushing through the alder trees, though I heard the gunshot clear as can be."

"Then find him, Hudson," Richard said, his words clipped with anger. "I don't care who it is, or what his rank may be. I want him taken, and brought before the courts so they can send him to the gallows."

Another man came running, too, with a third close behind him with a pair of panting dogs on a lead. Hudson whistled low, and they froze, and nodded, their guns at the shoulders. Cassia shivered, her arm tightening around Richard, and wondered what had become of the happy Greenwood where she'd felt so safe.

"We'll find the rascal, sir," Hudson said. "He won't get far before we take him, one way or another.

Luke sat high as a squirrel in the ancient oak tree, pressed against the trunk and surrounded by leaves where he prayed the men wouldn't look up and spy him. When Luke had seen the dogs below, he felt sure he'd be taken, but though one dog had nosed and snuffled around the fallen leaves and roots of the tree, he hadn't barked, and moved along with the man, leaving Luke safely behind.

He didn't dare come down, not yet, no matter how stiff his arms and legs were nor how hungry and thirsty he might be. He must have been in the tree for at least an hour by now, but he could still hear the men's voices in the distance, and the swinging lights of their lanterns as they searched the surrounding fields and meadows.

He sighed, turning up the tattered collar of his coat. He'd been chased away before, sure, but he'd never had anyone shoot at him before, and couldn't say he'd enjoyed it. The ball had come so close he swore he'd heard it whistle past his right ear. He'd have a story to tell his father, true enough.

He leaned back and braced himself in a crook of the tree, the bark rough against his spine. But from here he could just make out the four tall chimneys and the roof of his father's house. The old tinker who'd given Luke a ride in his wagon had pointed it out to him. Greenwood Hall was the house's name, the tinker had said, as if every house had a name of its own. The tinker had also told him how Blackley had won the house on a hand of cards, won all the land with it, too, and if that wasn't a lesson to be learned against gaming, then nothing was, and make no mistake, wasn't that Blackley a clever character, too? The tinker had sipped freely from a bottle of gin, letting his horse decide the pace, but Luke had been so grateful for the ride—and the information about his father—that he hadn't minded at all.

Luke still wasn't sure exactly what he'd say to his father, or how he'd introduce himself. He never did know what older people were going to say, and this was going to be a righteous surprise for his father, any way Luke looked at it. After all, his father never even knew he'd been born.

But Father would know soon enough. He'd know tomorrow. With a sleepy yawn, Luke settled back into the tree, and drifted off to sleep staring at the tall chimneys of his father's house.

The next morning, Cassia stood before the mantel in the front drawing room, a tall silver candlestick in each hand. She was determined to continue this day as if nothing had happened, as if nothing had changed, as if making the final decisions for the drawing room were all she had to consider.

She'd made this room all pale washes of color, pastel blues and greens and pinks, sparked with silver. The frames on the looking glasses were Venetian silver, and the curtains were tied back with silver rosettes. Even the hardware on the doors had been switched from brass to silver. Instead of using matched candlesticks, Cassia had collected an assortment of differing styles and heights, and now she was working on how to arrange them to be displayed to their best advantage.

She frowned, switching them around yet one more time. As tasks went, this wasn't taxing, but then after all that had happened the night before, arranging candlesticks seemed more than enough of a challenge.

"What would you say, Bess?" she asked the maidservant, standing dutifully by with her arms full of more candlesticks. "Short ones at the end, or tall? What does your eye say?"

"My eyes don't talk, miss," Bess said. "But if they did, I vow they'd like the tall ones fine, same as you had it first."

Cassia nodded, satisfied. "Tall on the outside, moving in to the short. So it shall be, Bess."

She turned to take another tall candlestick from Bess's arms, and stopped. A small bedraggled boy was trudging up the drive alone, his head down and his steps weary but determined.

"Who is that boy, Bess?" she asked. "He's not from the house, is he?"

"No, miss," Bess said, skeptical. "He has the look of a gypsy brat, miss, all greasy and dark, and not the sort we welcome here. I'll go turn him off before he causes any mischief."

"No, wait, don't." There was something oddly familiar about the boy, though his face was still downturned beneath a filthy knitted cap, and the way he was climbing up the center of Greenwood's front steps as if he'd as much a right to do so as any county squire, struck her as both brave and ridiculously bold. "I'll go speak to him myself."

"Wait, miss!" Bess hurried to follow. "You know what Mr. Blackley said about you taking double care today, and not looking for dangerous risks."

"I hardly think a small, presumptive beggar boy qualifies as a dangerous risk, Bess," she said. "I'll speak to Mr. Blackley myself if he objects."

She opened the door just as the boy was reaching for the knocker, catching him on his toes with his hand raised. Quickly he lowered his arm, hiding the gaping hole in his coat, and pulled off his cap. Surprise and hunger made his gray eyes seem huge in his gaunt little face, but he recovered fast, bowing low from the waist the way that someone had taught him to do, his lank black hair flopping forward over his face.

"Good day to you, mistress," he said gallantly. "I hope you are well."

"Well enough," Cassia said, ignoring how Bess was clucking her tongue with outrage at the boy's impudence. "Might I ask your business with this house, lad?"

"You might indeed," he said solemnly. "Please pass word to Mr. Richard Blackley that I am here."

Cassia raised her brows. "Is Mr. Blackley expecting you?"

"Not at all." The boy raised his chin and squared his narrow shoulders, and even before he spoke, Cassia realized the truth. "Please tell Mr. Blackley that his son Luke is here, and ready to make his acquaintance."

Chapter Fourteen

"To have you two gentlemen from the county offer me your assistance means a great deal to me," Richard said, hands clasped behind his back. He was surprised by how quickly the word of last night's shooting had spread among his neighbors, and gratified by their response. Perhaps he'd friends to invite to a ball after all. "A great deal."

"It's the least we can do, Blackley." Mr. Peterson, the squire from the estate north of Greenwood, shook his head. "We cannot have these blackguards running about the county, shooting at whomever they please. We'll have outright murder next if we don't take care."

The second gentleman, Mr. Garth, struck his fist on the arm of his chair. "It's simply not to be borne, Blackley, not to be borne! We must arrange patrols, a watch, a schedule of— Eh, who could that be?"

"Only a brief interruption, I'm sure," Richard said, scowling at the door where the knock had come. He'd left strict word among the servants not to be interrupted,

and here he'd not been ten minutes with these gentlemen before someone came thumping on the door.
"Enter!"

Cassia's face was so pale and upset that at once Richard rose, fearing the worst. "What is it, Cassia? What
has happened? The gunman—"

"This is another matter altogether," she said, her
voice strained. "Forgive me, gentlemen, but I must take
Mr. Blackley from your company for a moment."

The gentlemen rose and bowed and murmured,
watching Cassia with obvious interest as Richard hurried her from the room.

"What is it, Cassia?" he asked, taking her by the arm
to steady her. "Is it Bolton?"

Distraught, she shook her head. "It's something different, Richard." She clasped her hands before her, then
took a deep breath. "Do you recall a woman named
Marie-Claire? Long ago when you both were young, on
Barbados?"

"Marie-Claire?" The name called up nothing in his
memory. "There were many girls on Barbados, Cassia, and
many with French names, and if it was so long ago—"

"Ten years," she said, her face somehow growing
paler still. "Not so long, considering."

He guided her to a chair in the hall, afraid she was
going to faint. "What is this mystery, sweetheart? Why
ask me of things that happened so long ago?"

"Think harder, Richard," she insisted. "Marie-Claire.
She must have been scarcely more than a child herself,
but beautiful, and—"

"Marie-Claire Lenotre!" Richard smiled, please that

he'd recalled her after all, though he'd no intention of telling Cassia all of what he was now remembering. "She was a pretty little thing, a Creole from Martinique with hoops as big as saucers in her ears. She worked in the kitchen where I was one of the overseers."

"Did you oversee her, too?"

"Not directly, no," he said slowly, wondering where all this ancient history was leading. Cassia was too practical to ask questions like these if she hadn't a reason. "But because she'd slavery somewhere among her blood family, she would by island law have to obey me."

"Obey you by *law?*" She pressed her hands to her cheeks. "Oh, Richard, how little I know of you!"

"Cassia, please, tell me what—"

"I won't tell you, because I do not know, not for certain," she said, rising to her feet and taking his hand. "But if you come with me to the kitchen, I will show you."

He glanced uneasily back at the room he'd just left, thinking of the two men he'd left there. "Can't this wait, sweetheart? I'm in the middle of—"

"This has waited ten years, Richard," she said, pulling him with her toward the back stairs to the kitchen. "It shouldn't have to wait any longer."

He followed her, his mind racing through a sea of disastrous possibilities. "She's not here, is she? Marie-Claire Lenotre? She hasn't found her way to—"

"Marie-Claire is dead," she said, making the last turn in the stairs before they reached the kitchen itself. "She's past troubling you now."

"Then what in blazes is this about, Cassia?" The kitchen staff had expanded dramatically these last weeks, with dozens of extra hands helping prepare the meals for the workers in the house. Usually at midday like this, the kitchen was teeming with activity and noise, but as soon as he'd entered, everything stopped— the clatter of the pans, the shouted orders and the running footmen—and everyone turned to stare at him. Then one by one, they all stepped aside, making a passage for him, until he reached the farthest table.

"Marie-Claire couldn't come to you," Cassia said, "but her son is here."

"Her son?" Richard smiled, imagining a child in the likeness of his sunny mother. "Here?"

"Here, sir." The small boy slipped from the tall chair and stood at attention, his arms flat to his sides. His clothes were little more than dirty rags, with no socks and shoes held together with snippets of rope, but he knew how to bow. "My name is Luke Lenotre, sir, and I am most honored to meet you, above all things."

"Marie-Claire Lenotre was your mother?" Richard asked, though the truth already had him by the throat.

"Aye-aye." The boy's silver-gray eyes were so bright that Richard knew he was about to shame himself and cry, and for that matter, Richard might well cry, too. "She was my mother, and you—you, sir, are my father."

"So I am, Luke." There was no point denying it. The more he looked at the boy's face, the more he saw of his own. "So I am."

"Yes, sir." The boy swiped his sleeve beneath his nose, waiting for—for what?

In desperation Richard looked around for Cassia, who'd vanished most inconveniently from his side. She was the one who'd orchestrated this reunion, and she was also the only one who'd know the proper thing to say and do. How in blazes did one deal with a newly discovered bastard son, anyway?

He cleared his throat, especially all those emotional cobwebs. "Your name is Luke?"

The boy nodded, clearly still uncertain of his welcome.

"And you're ten?"

"Eleven in August, sir."

"Yes, of course." That would be right for when he'd known Marie-Claire. It hadn't lasted long between them, only a month or so during the season for hurricanes, when it had seemed to blow and rain day and night and they'd been cooped up together in the big house. She'd disappeared from the plantation soon after the storms stopped, the way so many of her kind did, and she'd slipped from his mind, too.

"So did Cook make you something tasty?" he asked. "You look like you could use a bit more on your bones."

"Aye-aye, sir." The boy glanced back longingly to the bowl of mutton stew he'd left on the table. "Might I finish it, sir?"

"Of course you can," Richard said with overblown heartiness. He glared around at the others who were so shamelessly watching and eavesdropping. "On with you now, the whole idle lot of you! Go about your work!"

He watched the boy devour his food, his face so close to the bowl that he scarcely needed the spoon. "Bring me a bowl of whatever Luke here is having."

"But that's mutton stew and onions for the laborers,

Mr. Blackley!" Cook said, scandalized. "'Tis not fit for the table upstairs!"

"If it's fit for the boy, it's fit for me." Richard sat on a stool beside him, waiting for his stew. He hated to keep the child from eating, but he'd so many questions that he couldn't help it. "So how did you learn to *aye-aye* like a sailor-man?"

The boy looked up and grinned. "I was cabin boy on board the *Three Sisters*, for Captain Rogers. That's how I came here from Martinique, looking for you. I told them I was older than I looked, and I told them I was English."

"You must be my boy, with a tale like that," Richard declared proudly. "How long ago did your mother pass along?"

His face fell. "Last summer, from the fever."

"I'm sorry," Richard said softly, and he realized that he meant it. "I liked your mother."

"I know you did, sir," he said, looking back down at the stew. "But she loved you."

Now it was Richard's turn not to answer. He had needed ten minutes to recall Marie-Claire's face, and yet she'd borne his son and spent the rest of her life loving him and his memory.

You are the most selfish man I have ever known....

"Your mama never told me about you, you know," he said defensively. "It's not something I would have guessed on my own, not after she left the plantation and went back to Martinique. But I would have helped any way I could, if I'd known."

"Aye-aye, sir." The boy's face went scrupulously

blank. "She always let me think you were dead, sir, on account of you not looking after us, but I knew you weren't. That's why I came to find you."

How can I trust you, knowing what I know of you?

She let me think you were dead, on account of you not looking after us....

"Is that red-haired lady your wife, sir?" Luke asked. "She opened the front door for me, and let me in."

"She's not my wife, no," Richard said, wishing the boy hadn't asked that particular question. "She's a friend who's been, ah, staying here a bit to help me refurbish this house."

Luke nodded, his face turning blank again. The boy knew too much for his age; clearly he already understood the difference between a woman who was a wife, and one who was merely a gentleman's friend.

"She was kind to me, sir," he said, swinging his legs in the tall stool. "She brought me here to the kitchen."

"She's kind to everyone that way." Richard glanced around the kitchen for Cassia, wondering why she hadn't returned. He couldn't blame her for being surprised by Luke's arrival—God knows he was—but this had nothing to do with her.

Did it?

"Beggin' pardon, Mr. Blackley," Bess said as she bobbed her curtsey beside his chair. "But Mr. Peterson and Mr. Garth are asking whether you're returning to talk more about the shots this morning, or whether they should leave?"

Oh, hell, he'd forgotten clean about them. "Tell them

I'll be there directly, and give them my apologies for making them wait."

"Someone shot at *me* this morning, too, sir," Luke said, his mouth full of stew. "Near the tall trees, not far from the road."

"They did?" At once Richard's attention swung back to the boy. "Did you get a good look at the rascal that did it, Luke?"

"Aye-aye, sir, I did," he declared. "He was stout, and—"

"Hold now, and save it for another minute or two," Richard said, grabbing the boy by the shoulders to lift him down from the stool. "Bring your bowl if you want, but you're coming upstairs with me to tell the other gentlemen exactly what happened."

With few belongings, Cassia packed quickly, the trunks ready before the footman came to take them downstairs to the chaise. She walked briskly down the stairs, wasting no time taking her leave of the house. She was sorry not to see everything she'd planned finished and done, but it was far more important now that she leave at once, without meeting Richard again, than that she see the molding tacked in place around the wallpaper in the dining room.

She'd left the note where she knew he'd find it, tucked into one corner of *The Fortune Teller's* heavy gold frame. She hadn't written much. There hadn't been much to say. She'd thanked him for this last month, and though she regretted leaving a few days shy of the arranged month, certain things had occurred that made it impossible for her to remain. She was confident that time would prove this separation would be best for them both. Then she'd wished him much joy in his upcoming marriage, and she'd signed her name.

Simple, direct, polite, a farewell letter with no anger or recriminations. Even Father would have been proud.

And not one word to betray how her heart was breaking with every step she took, down the stairs, to the chaise, and away from Richard Blackley and Greenwood, never to return to either.

"Neuf!" Richard shouted, pulling off his shoes without unbuckling them. "Neuf, where in blazes are my riding boots?"

Garth and Peterson were already waiting for him downstairs in the drive, his one horse called from the stables. Together the three of them would ride out to where the shots had come, and inspect the area again in daylight in light of what Luke had told him. Though Hudson and the others had been thorough, it wouldn't hurt to have another look.

"Here they are, sir." Neuf appeared, the boots in his hands, not hurrying one whit more than was necessary. "As you wished, sir."

"More as you wished, Neuf," he said as he dropped into the nearest chair, thrusting out his stockinged foot for the first boot. "I won't be gone long, an hour or two, but I want you to check in on the boy, Neuf. He's from Martinique, so you'll speak his lingo."

"Yes, sir," Neuf said. "He looks to be a good boy, sir."

"He is," Richard agreed, thinking how well Luke had

just done telling them about the shooting. "Carroll is supposed to be seeing to his washing and rigging him out in something more decent, but I'd like you to take a look in on him as well, to see if there's anything more that can— What's that?"

"What is what, sir?" asked Neuf, presenting the second boot.

"There in the painting." He pushed himself out of the chair, hobbling across the room with one foot in a boot and one without, and snatched the folded white paper from the corner of the picture's frame. He didn't even need to see Cassia's neat, rounded penmanship on the front to know that however bad this day already seemed to be, it was going to become considerably worse. The old bawd in the painting smirked down at him.

It didn't take long to read her note, and so he read it again to make sure he hadn't missed anything. How could she leave with only this as a goodbye? Where was her passion, her spirit? Where was Cassia herself in this handful of words that were icy-cold and without feeling, as formal as a solicitor's brief? No reasons, no explanation, no endearments to soften the blow: that couldn't be the Cassia he'd come to care for so much, the Cassia he needed in his life!

With the letter still in his hands, he looked up for Neuf. "How long ago did Miss Penny leave?"

Neuf shrugged, the second boot still waiting in his hands. "An hour, sir, perhaps more. You were with the other gentlemen."

"Hang the other gentlemen!" he cried. "Why wasn't I informed she was leaving?"

"Miss Penny asked specifically that you not be told, sir," Neuf answered, unperturbed. "She said she'd explained everything in a letter to you—that letter, sir—and that you would do better going about your life without being interrupted."

"The hell with her interruptions!" He thumped back to the chair. "The other boot, Neuf, the other boot! I can't ride a horse like a one-legged jackanapes, can I?"

"Forgive me for speaking, sir, but is that the best course?" Neuf asked as he braced the boot against his shoulder for Richard to push against. "After the lady has asked you to forget her?"

"The lady asking doesn't mean I'll obey." She couldn't leave him like this, slipping away from his life with as little trace as a wave from the shore. She *couldn't*. Damnation, he wouldn't allow it. "I'm going after her to try to change her mind."

Neuf bowed. "Then good luck to you, sir. And good luck to Miss Penny as well."

The driver of the chaise stopped at the same inn where Cassia and Richard had stopped before. This shouldn't have surprised her; it was a good distance from Greenwood to pause for the horses' sake, and if a change was needed, Richard had a standing arrangement with the stablemen. But to Cassia the place held too many memories for her comfort, and while the horse was watered she chose to walk outside the inn, pacing back and forth with a cup of tea in her hand, and trying not to think of all she'd left behind at Greenwood Hall. With her free hand, she plucked a piece of tall grass from the bushes, absently whipping it back and forth as she walked.

She knew she'd made the right decision. She knew that, deep down, she'd made it long before Richard's son had appeared on his doorstep. The guilelessness of the boy's story—of how Richard had dawdled with his mother, then cast her off without another thought for her or their unborn child—had chilled her to the quick, and had served as a spur to her conscience. She loved Richard, but she'd never find lasting happiness with a man who could be so callous, so thoughtless of the needs of everyone else.

One of the inn's boys trotted up to her. "Miss Penny, if you please, the driver says he's ready to leave whenever you are."

"Thank you," she said. She tossed the blade of grass aside, and reached into her pocket for a coin for the boy. "Tell the driver I'll be there directly."

She finished her tea, and stepped inside the inn to return the cup. In the road outside, a single horseman came to a racing stop in the stable yard, scattering shrieking passengers and squawking chickens in his path, while everyone inside the tavern rose from their tables to try to catch a glimpse of the rider.

"Reckless idiot," muttered the man who took Cassia's cup. "The yard's no racecourse, no matter what fools like that think. It's a wonder he doesn't trample someone outright."

"Let's hope he doesn't," Cassia agreed. "Impatience like that never will—"

"Cassia!" Richard's voice thundered through the

inn, silencing every one of the noisy diners. "Why did you run away from me?"

She turned quickly to face him, indignation making her own voice ring through the crowded room. "And why have you come chasing after me, Richard Blackley? I told you why I was leaving, why I—"

"The hell you did!" he shouted back across the room at her. "You left me a coward's letter, Cassia, a letter than said nothing and explained less."

The innkeeper came rushing between them, his hands outstretched as he begged for peace. "Miss, sir, I beg you, might I suggest that you move your, ah, your discussion outside to the yard for the sake of the other guests?"

Several of the guests hissed at this suggestion to spoil the entertainment, but Cassia scarcely heard it.

"I'm not going back with you, Richard, no matter how loudly you shout and bluster," she said. "You can't make me do it against my will, and my will is against you!"

A small round of applause followed, drowned out by Richard. "You're riding in my chaise. I've every right to take it back with me."

She tossed her head with defiance, the wood curls on her hat rustling together. "Then I shall hire another chaise here."

"No, you won't," he countered. "Not if I tell the stablemen not to."

"Then I shall walk. Or have you ordered my legs to do your bidding, too?"

"It's your head that I want to make listen to me!"

"Then you must resolve yourself to be disappointed,

sir," she declared furiously, every bit as angry as he was. "You will not humiliate me like this any longer. I am not your wife, nor your mistress, nor your daughter, nor your housemaid, meaning that no part of me is required to obey you in any way."

She turned her back and marched from the side door, away from him and the cheers of the other diners. It wasn't until she was outside that she realized she was shaking, her heart pounding, and her hands damp inside her gloves. The chaise was still waiting for her. If she hurried, she could be inside it before—

"Talk to me, Cassia," Richard said hoarsely, blocking her way, his hat in his hands. "I'm begging you, lass. Just—just talk to me."

She'd never seen this look in his face before, despair and desperation and loneliness all tumbled together.

"There's nothing left to say, Richard," she said, trying to step around him.

He blocked her again, his feet spread wide. "That's not true, lass, and you know it. Tell me why you left."

"Because in the end, Richard," she said, stepping around him again, "you still put yourself first, and always will."

How could she ever explain it more clearly than that?

"Tell me what will make you stay," he said urgently, still not understanding as he took her by the arm, his touch as gentle as if he feared she might shatter. "Anything you want that will make you happy, and make you stay. Tell me, name it, and it's yours."

She looked down at his hand on her arm, and smiled sadly, the heat of her anger fading. If only he'd tell her he loved her, and meant it! If only he'd offer her that, then she'd stay.

"What I want—what I need—I can't ask for it, Richard," she said. "You'd have to give it freely, without prompting from me."

She slipped free of him, and began walking toward the chaise, trying to keep her eyes straight ahead.

He fell into step with her, still refusing to let her go. "If you didn't like the necklace with the amethysts, Cassia, then tell me what would please you instead. Diamonds, or pearls, or—"

"I pray you'll be kind to that lost little boy, Richard," she said, "He's come so far to find you. Don't disappoint him."

He stopped short. "Of course I won't. There's no doubt the boy's mine, and therefore my responsibility."

"You didn't feel that way for his mother," she said softly, imagining the suffering and misery he'd so carelessly caused. "You used her for your—your pleasure, a poor young woman who could not refuse you, and then you forgot her."

"Cassia, that was more than ten years ago!"

"Yes, and in all that time, you never once considered that you'd fathered a child with her," she said. "How many others are there like her, Richard? Would I be just one more?"

"But you're not Marie-Claire, Cassia," he exclaimed. "You're different, far different, different from any other woman I've ever known!"

"I know," she said, climbing into the chaise. "Which

is why I'm leaving now. I must, to save myself, and my heart. Goodbye, Richard. Goodbye."

And before she could change her mind, the chaise drove away, and left him behind.

It was late, very late, the big house quiet except for the ticking of the tall case clock in the stairwell, yet Luke couldn't sleep.

He should be. He knew that. He had no excuse to be awake. He hadn't slept much the night before, wedged up in that old tree. But now he was cleaner than he'd been in months—maybe even in his whole life, after Mr. Carroll had gone after him with the washrag himself—and his belly was full and content.

He was wearing a clean nightshirt, lying in a feather bed so soft it might as well have been a cloud, and the room he'd been given all to himself was larger than the entire little house he'd shared with poor Mama. He was safe from all the ills and misfortunes and villains that could claim a boy with no money and no friends in a city like London.

And best of all, he'd found Father.

But as happy as that had made him—along with making him clean and well-fed and safe and snug in this bed—he in turn had made trouble. He'd seen that for himself, even when everyone else had been fussing over him.

Because of him, the beautiful woman with the coppery hair had left Greenwood. That had made Father furious and hurt, and sent him racing off after the woman. The rest of the staff left here had been upset, too, wondering and worrying about whether the woman would come back or not, and what would become of them if she didn't, and what the master would do next if she did.

All he'd wanted to do was find his father, but all he'd done was ruin everything for everyone else.

He slipped from the soft bed and padded barefoot to the window. It took him only a moment to open the shutters and find the North Star, ready to guide him wherever he chose to go.

He sighed, resting his chin on his arms as he gazed up at the stars. Maybe he'd been figuring all this wrong. Maybe finding Father was only one part of his journey, not his final destination. Since he'd caused so much sorrow by coming here, maybe he was meant to keep wandering, at least for a bit. Maybe he'd even find another ship like the *Three Sisters,* and sail around the world.

Still the star smiled down at him, the way it always did. Luke closed the window, gently, so he wouldn't wake anyone else, and began to dress.

Chapter Fifteen

It took the chaise's driver a quarter of an hour to maneuver through the crowds of carriages and hackneys on St. James Street to reach the door of Penny House, lit up as brilliantly as a giant lantern in the London night. The club must be thriving, Cassia thought as she gazed from the window, though exhausted and upset as she was tonight, she wished could make a less public return home.

"Miss Cassia!" Pratt exclaimed as she came through the door behind a boisterous trio of young lords. "Good evening to you, miss! I wasn't told to expect you back among us tonight."

"Good evening, Pratt," she said, nearly in tears at the sight of his familiar face. Oh, this was not going to be an easy evening for her, if her emotions were that close to the surface! "You weren't told I was coming because no one knew. Will you have someone help this man with my things?"

"Cassia!" Amariah rushed toward her through the sea of gentlemen, throwing her arms around Cassia. "Oh, how vastly good it is to see you! Did you finish your work early? We didn't think you'd be back until next week."

"Greenwood is done for me," she said. "I—I had to leave early."

"Early?" Amariah stepped back, her hands on Cassia's shoulders and her face wreathed in worry as she studied Cassia's face. "What has happened to you, lamb? What's wrong?"

"Nothing," Cassia said, her voice quavering. "Nothing at all."

"Nothing, my foot," Amariah said, taking Cassia by the hand the way they had when they'd been girls. "Pratt, watch the floor for me. We'll be down in the kitchen with our sister."

"I can't take you away now," Cassia protested as Amariah led her down the back stairs. "This is the busiest part of the evening. I can talk to you later."

"We're going to talk now," Amariah said, quickly finding their sister in the middle of the kitchen. "Bethany, Cassia's back, and we all must talk now."

"Please, Amariah, I can wait," Cassia said, but Bethany was already taking them into her tiny room off the kitchen. They'd have to stand—there wasn't room for three chairs—but once Bethany closed the door, no one would disturb them.

"It's Mr. Blackley, isn't it?" Bethany said. "Oh, we should never have let you go because of that ridiculous wager!"

"I had to go," Cassia said. "And none of it is Richard's fault."

"But you fell in love with him," Amariah said softly. "Don't say otherwise, because I can see it all over your face. Oh, Cassia."

Bethany gasped with indignation. "Has he taken advantage of you, Cassia? Has he—has he used you while you were in his home? Because if he has, then he'll—"

"He did nothing wrong," Cassia said, her voice no more than a miserable whisper. "He thinks only of himself, to be sure, but he's hardly to blame if I fell in love with him, but not him with me."

"Oh, the scoundrel, to do that to you!" began Bethany, but Amariah held her hand up for silence.

"Was he cruel to you, then?" she asked. "Did he send you away when he realized you felt affection for him?"

Cassia shook her head, pressing her well-used handkerchief to her eyes. "He begged me to stay, but I was the one who insisted on leaving. I've never been so happy, and he said he was, too, and I'll never love any other man as much as I love him, but he—he never will love me back."

Amariah frowned. "I'm sorry to be thick-witted, lamb, but I'm not following your tale. You were happy with him, and he begged you to stay, but you left? What did he say when you told him you loved him?"

"I never did," Cassia said with a little sob. "He never said it to me, and so I—I didn't, either."

Bethany handed her her own dry handkerchief. "I have heard that those words can be most difficult for gentlemen to say."

"That is true, Cassia," Amariah said. "Sometimes gentlemen can be very thick that way. Did he show you in other ways, by his actions, that he cared for you?"

"Oh, in a thousand ways!" Fresh tears welled up as Cassia remembered how Richard would smile when he looked at her, his eyes full of desire and a kind of wonder that she was with him. "He would bring me my tea himself when I was with the workmen, and he'd agree to anything I proposed with the house, and he made me feel safe and cherished and he made me laugh, and—"

"You've shared his bed, haven't you?" Amariah asked.

Cassia bowed her head, unable to meet her sisters' eyes. "He didn't—didn't force me, or seduce me. I went to him myself, because I wanted to. We were friends, equals, and it was—*glorious*. But then he tried to give me a gold necklace set with amethysts and diamonds, the kind of gift that men give to their mistresses, and spoiled everything."

Neither Amariah nor Bethany spoke, leaving a silence that yawned like a canyon of experience between them and Cassia.

At last Bethany cleared her throat. "Gentlemen also give that kind of gift to ladies they love and respect and plan to marry. Mr. Blackley may not have meant the necklace the way you feared. But wasn't he going to marry some other lady, a peer's daughter? Isn't that why he wanted you to refurbish Greenwood in the first place, so he could bring her there?"

"Lady Anne Stanhope," Cassia said. "She's the daughter of the Earl of Stanhope. At first Richard claimed she was the one woman he wished to marry, and her family seemed agreeable to the match. But lately he seemed to be disenchanted with the lady, and wished to put off seeing her and her family, let alone marrying."

"That's because he met you, Cassia. Even the daughter of a peer would lose her luster beside you." Amariah sighed. "Is it possible that you are already carrying his child?"

"I don't know, not yet," Cassia confessed. She took a deep breath, steeling herself for the rest of the story. "But this morning, a poor, bedraggled boy appeared at the door, and as soon as I saw his face, I knew he was Richard's son. Richard didn't even know the child existed, or that the mother had died."

"Oh, the poor boy!" Bethany shook her head. "I see so many orphaned children without homes each day in our alley at the kitchen door, yet each one still breaks my heart. How fortunate he was to have finally found his way to Mr. Blackley!"

"And Mr. Blackley did take him in, didn't he?" asked Amariah with concern. "I know you said he was a self-centered gentleman, but he certainly seems to have been generous and kind to you. I cannot imagine he'd be otherwise with his son, legitimate or not. The sins of the parents can hardly be visited upon the innocent child."

Cassia didn't answer. She'd always considered Richard to be exceptionally selfish, but suddenly he didn't sound like that as she described him to her sisters. In fact, the more she thought of what she'd said, free of the anger that had added heat to her arguments, the more she realized she was the one who'd sounded more to blame, not Richard.

What if she'd let herself be led by her temper and her pride, and had made a conclusion that was wrongfully disastrous? What if she'd ruined not only her future, but Richard's, too?

"But Richard never supported the boy, or his mother," she said. "He had an—an intrigue with the woman, then never bothered to find her, or learn if a child had resulted."

"That is *not* admirable behavior," Amariah agreed, "and Mr. Blackley should be shamed by it, no matter what the circumstances."

Cassia nodded, gratified that she'd gotten at least that much right. "I believe he does repent, yes."

"A good thing he does, too," Bethany agreed. "But he is hardly the first man with such a sordid secret in his past. Gentlemen are…well, they are different, even if the poorhouses and orphanages are full of the results of their secrets."

"And he did say the girl disappeared without telling him of her plight," Cassia admitted, fairness making her tell the whole story. "He swears he would have behaved with more honor if he'd known."

"That is good, considering your own situation." Amariah glanced pointedly at Cassia's belly, as if she could already see an unborn child, then reached out and hugged her again, patting her on the back. "I must go back upstairs now, Cassia, before Pratt has an apoplexy, and I'm sure Bethany must return to her tasks as well. Take yourself up to our quarters and go to bed, and we'll talk more tomorrow."

"You rest," Bethany said, giving her own hug. "Everything always seems better in the morning, you know."

But as Cassia climbed the long stairs to her room, all she could think of was how she had made the worst decision of her life.

Richard lay in the middle of his bed, trying very hard not to move so much as an eyelash. Though his eyes were closed as tightly as he could close them, he knew to his sorrow that he was not asleep. If he were asleep, then he would not be feeling this ungodly pounding in his head, or the restless churning in his stomach, or the room spinning around him like a pinwheel, even though his fists held tightly to the coverlet. Were he asleep—a place he desperately wished to be—then he would be far removed from the torments that plagued him, and far, far from all his resolutions to never, ever touch a drop of cheap tavern rum again.

His downfall had begun innocently enough, or at least with a good reason behind it. Cassia Penny had scorned him, and cast him aside in the most public way imaginable, with an entire audience cheering her every speech. She had called him a selfish brute, a cad, and sworn never to see him again. As her chaise—his chaise, in fact—had clattered off down the road, her ridiculous hat with the wood chips only a silhouette through the back glass, the innkeeper himself had come to stand beside him and clap a commiseratory hand on his shoulder. A drink, he suggested, to soothe and comfort, for forgiving, and, most importantly, forgetting.

Richard had agreed on the prescription, taking a dose of lime and orange juice, and a healthy dose of island rum. Another soon followed, and another after that, until his forgetting was so complete that he'd needed two helpful grooms from the inn's stable to pour him home to Greenwood. He supposed Neuf had taken over from there. Thanks to the forgetting, he wasn't sure of that, either.

But no matter how much he felt like the lowest, most miserable inside portion of a dead goat's stomach, he still hadn't forgotten Cassia, or what she'd said to him. She'd only been with him for a month—one month out of his entire *life*—yet now he could not conceive of the rest of his life that would follow without her.

Not the high-born lady of his dreams, but Cassia, the flesh-and-blood reality who belonged in his bed—their bed, now—studded with amethysts and marked forever by their lovemaking. He'd never bring another woman to this bed. After her, how could he? And why didn't she understand that? He with her, and now Luke there, too, together at Greenwood for the rest of time. Why was that so blasted hard to comprehend?

Cassia: he had offered her everything he had to make her stay, and still she'd left. It wasn't enough. *He* wasn't enough, and now she'd never come back.

If it wouldn't take such an infernal effort, he'd go stand in the middle of the north field with his arms out and his hat off and beg Bolton to finish him off, now, and be done with it.

"Sir?" Neuf's voice pierced through his ears loud as a steam engine's squeal. "Sir?"

"Damnation, Neuf," he croaked, wincing at the effort even that much took. "I told you not to disturb me."

"Forgive me, sir," Neuf said, refusing to go away. "But there is something—"

"Neuf, I do not care if General Napoleon and all his armies are on the beach at Dover!"

"Yes, sir," Neuf took a deep breath. "But I thought you would like to be informed that the boy Luke has disappeared."

The sun was high in the sky when Luke left the road, cutting through the reeds to the stream that ran beneath the bridge. He set the small bundle of his belongings on the bank before he bent and drank, then dunked his head into the cool water. The day was warm, the sun hot on his back when he'd been walking, and he pulled off his new shoes and stockings to dip them in the water, too. Gingerly he poked his thumb at the pink, puffy blisters on the backs of his heels. That was what came from wearing shoes, and after lunch he decided to go back to walking barefoot, the way he had before.

He moved beneath the arch of the stone bridge, hidden from the road and any travelers, and ate the cheese, bread and plums he'd taken from the kitchen at Greenwood. He forced himself to eat as slowly as he could with tiny nibbling bites, wanting to make the food last, for he'd no idea when he'd have anything so good again.

He wouldn't let himself think of how kind Cook and the others had been to him, and especially wouldn't think of the red-haired lady or Father. Captain Rogers had always said that there was never any use in looking back to where you'd been, only in looking ahead to where you were bound, and right now that seemed like the best advice in the world.

It was cool beneath the bridge, and the stream rushing over the stones and around the rushes made a peaceful, soothing sound. He felt his eyes growing heavy, and tucking the rucksack with his few belongings beneath his head for a pillow, he let himself drift off to sleep.

"What have we here, now?" The man's voice echoed under the bridge, waking Luke with a start. "Some dirty little monkey, spying on his betters?"

The man dumped a mug of water over Luke's head, soaking him, and then roared with laughter.

"Oh, leave him alone, Bolton," the other man said. "That sprat's not worth your trouble."

But Luke had already grabbed his shoes and his rucksack and was scrambling up the bank, away from the two men. When he'd seen them before, he'd been hiding in the tree and they'd been below him, in the dark. Most likely they wouldn't recognize him, but he'd known at once who they were, and he wasn't going to take any chances. They were gentlemen, and they had horses and they had guns on their saddles, and he wanted nothing to do with them at all.

He was nearly to the top of the bank with the road in reach when his foot tangled in a vine and he tripped backward, rolling and sliding over the grasses until he stopped near the feet of the heavyset man, who once again began to roar with laughter.

"Clumsy little oaf, aren't you?" he said, prodding Luke with the toe of his well-polished riding boot. "Hah, maybe it's a maid in rags, not a boy at all, to be such a puling little weakling."

That made Luke mad, madder than he should have been. "Better that than a stinking fat toad like you!" he shouted back at the man. He turned and scurried up the bank, this time taking the bare side without the grass. "Better than being you!"

"Come back here, boy!" the man roared, the tone of his voice abruptly changed. "Turner, stop him! It's Blackley's little bastard, the one they were hunting for at the last inn! Catch him! Catch him now!"

Too late Luke knew he shouldn't have taunted the man, shouldn't have looked up so Bolton could see his face. He ran as fast and as hard as he could. His bare feet thudded on the dirt road, and startled birds chattered and flew from the trees overhead. He didn't stop and he didn't look back, counting on his speed, the way he always had before to outrun the older, heavier—

"Got you now!" The man threw his weight on top of Luke, tackling him into the dirt and knocking all the wind from his chest. Thrashing weakly as he gasped for air, Luke couldn't fight back as the man twisted his wrists behind his back.

"You're mine now, you little black bastard," the man said, leaning his face so close that Luke could smell the stench of old drink on his breath. "Now we'll see what price your father will be willing to pay to get you back, eh?"

It was as if Cassia had never left Penny House, as if the time she'd spent at Greenwood had been nothing but an agreeable dream. She threw herself back into the rhythm of the house's operation, joining the daily meeting to review the highlights of the night before, helping count out the markers to make sure none had vanished, arranging fresh flowers for the mantels in the downstairs rooms. She'd have to plan a trip soon to the used furniture markets: while she'd been gone, two porcelain vases had been broken in some scuffle, and several smaller decorative figures had simply disappeared.

But not once during the day did either Amariah or Bethany say anything to her about her sudden return, or her parting with Richard, or anything at all out of the ordinary. Twice Cassia had tried to raise the subject of her visit to Greenwood with her eldest sister, and both times she had looked away and begun another conversation, as if Cassia hadn't spoken in the first place.

But finally, after supper, Amariah came to her bedchamber. Cassia was dressing in the familiar dark-blue gown for the first time in nearly a month, arranging her hair before the looking glass.

"Come sit with me, Cassia, for a moment or two," Amariah said, patting the edge of the bed beside her. "I know you're dressing, but I have some things that must be said, and I promise I won't ramble on too long."

Cassia thrust the last pin into her hair and sat on the very edge of the bed, striving to look contrite, yet still confident that she'd made the right choice.

Which, by now, she wasn't sure at all that she had.

"My first thought, Cassia," Amariah began, "was that you had behaved shamelessly and irresponsibly with Mr. Blackley, bringing dishonor both to yourself and to

Penny House, especially if you did conceive a child out of your—your frolic in the country."

Cassia didn't answer. What defense could she possibly offer, considering how every glorious misstep she'd taken with Richard had gone against her upbringing?

Amariah sighed, frowning down at her clasped hands—a sure sign that this conversation was no more easier for her than for Cassia.

"But then I began to see deeper," she continued, "the way that Father would have. It appears that while Mr. Blackley has done his best to please you, you have found him lacking for not guessing what you wanted. He has tried to win you fairly, but you have turned his appeals into a game. What man wants a riddle like that?"

"But Amariah—"

"Hush, and hear me first. You say you love him, and that he makes you happier than any other, and yet because you wish to protect yourself from being hurt, you won't tell him so, but insist on waiting for him to tell you first. You say he is stubborn and selfish, but isn't that exactly how you are behaving toward him?"

"But it's not like that, Amariah," she protested weakly. "I'm not like that."

"And I say you are, lamb." Amariah smiled wryly. "I've known you as long as anyone, Cassia, and you've always wanted everyone and everything to march exactly to your tune. Perhaps in Richard Blackley, you've finally met your match, and your fate."

Cassia rose from the bed, pacing across the room to the fireplace. "Is that what you believe Father would have said?" she said with undisguised bitterness. "That

I should not have left Richard, because I *deserve* whatever unhappiness and misery he might inflict upon me?"

"I'm saying you deserve the happiness as well as the sorrow, because in truth you and Mr. Blackley deserve one other. Your stubborn pride masks warm and giving hearts, sometimes even from yourselves."

"But *I* don't know that!" Cassia cried, striking her palms with frustration on the edge of the mantelpiece. "You're telling me to cast my life with Richard's, even if I don't know anything for certain!"

"What you do know is in your heart already, isn't it?"

Cassia turned, looking over her shoulder. "But what of my head, my life, my future?"

Amariah smiled, and shrugged with her hands spread.

"Haven't you learned anything from the gaming at Penny House, Cassia?" she asked wryly. "Take no risks, and you'll never win. To be sure, you'll never lose, either, and what you already have will remain safe, but you'll never gain more unless you're willing to seize the chances that luck will offer."

"So Richard is my chance?" asked Cassia softly, already sure of the answer.

Amariah's shrug widened. "Luck cannot be explained or reasoned, not if— What is that racket?"

Cassia could hear it now, too, someone running up the stairs and arguing with Pratt with every step.

"I must insist, sir," Pratt was calling after the intruder, huffing and puffing. "No gentlemen are admitted to the ladies' quarters!"

"Damnation, Pratt, she'll see me!"

Cassia's face lit at the sound of his voice, and Amariah smiled.

"It's luck, Cassia," she said. "Pure and simple."

But Cassia was already at the door that separated their private rooms from the stairway, throwing it open to greet him.

"Richard!" she exclaimed, ready to throw her arms around him and beg his forgiveness for however he desired.

But then she saw the expression on his face.

"Cassia," he said hoarsely. "Bolton has Luke."

Richard stood close to Cassia, not letting her stray far from his reach. He'd already lost Luke; he'd no intention of losing her, too, even for a moment.

And Penny House was crowded tonight. In the three weeks since they'd been away, the membership had grown and become more fashionable still. But there were more than the usual gentlemen and nobles in the crowd tonight, too. The club's customary guards had been doubled, and there were others masquerading as guests in evening clothes. Richard was leaving nothing to chance, nor risking Luke's life at the hands of some bumbling magistrate. He'd handle this himself. The law would come later, after the boy was back safe with him.

Delivered to Greenwood, Bolton's scrawled note had been clear: he had Luke in his possession and would bring him—and his demands—to Penny House tonight. Though banned from the club for life, Bolton was shrewd enough to realize that such a letter would get him admitted this once, and he was right. What happened after that, though, was anyone's guess, and Richard struggled to control his fury as he thought of his son in the hands of a bully like Bolton.

Restlessly he scanned the crowded front room again, looking for anything that wasn't as it should be as he waited for Bolton to appear. Word had miraculously spread through town that Cassia was back at Penny House, and well-wishers swarmed around her, many begging for her to recite one of her "pieces," others just wanting her to remember their names and smile their way. Richard stood to one side, hating the attention she was receiving, but knowing he'd no right to stop it.

He looked at her now, her fan fluttering in one graceful hand and her head tipped to one side, and his heart tightened at how beautiful she was with the candlelight washing over her luminous face. When he'd come here to her today, turning to her before anyone else, she hadn't sent him away. She'd shared his shock and his outrage over Luke's kidnapping, comforting him, planning with him. That was a start, wasn't it? Perhaps there was still hope for them.

As if she sensed his thoughts, she excused herself from the ring of admirers around her and came to Richard, taking his hand and shutting out all the others.

"I hate this waiting," she whispered for his ears only. "Why hasn't he come with Luke? What if he doesn't come?"

"Don't worry, sweetheart, he will," Richard said firmly, squeezing her fingers fondly in his own. "It's exactly the sort of grand gesture he relishes. He'll be here."

She tried to smile. "I'm scared, Richard. Luke's just

a child, and he's done nothing to that man. He's already suffered so much. What if Bolton hurts him, from spite or meanness? Oh, if only I'd stayed at Greenwood, if I'd made Luke feel more at ease, then—"

"Then it likely would have happened some other way," Richard said, reaching out to stroke her cheek. "There's nothing to be gained by raking over the past, Cassia. We can only do our best with what's before us."

She flushed. "I know that now, Richard. It's only that—"

"Marry me, Cassia," he said, forgetting everyone else in the crowded room around them as he drew her closer. "I love you, and—"

"You *love* me?" she asked, incredulous, her eyes wide as she searched his face. "You love *me,* Richard?"

"Of course I do," he said. "Surely you must have realized that by now. Why else would I be asking you to marry me?"

"To marry you?" she whispered. "Oh, Richard, I—"

"So where the devil's Blackley?" Ripe with liquor and bravado, Bolton's voice boomed from the front hall. "Or has the bastard turned coward on me and run?"

At once conversation stopped, and a murmur of surprise and indignation ruffled through the room. For all that Penny House was a respite for gentlemen away from the restraints of their homes, it was also a civilized place, where Bolton's behavior was unwelcome.

"In here, my lord," Richard answered, his voice loud and clear with confidence. Gently he pushed Cassia behind him, shielding her from whatever might happen. "In here."

"Oh, Richard, please don't be foolish and manly!" she cried, holding on to his arm. "Love, love, don't do anything dangerous!"

He smiled without turning, his gaze focused on the doorway, but that *love* soared in his ears. "I'll be fine, sweetheart. And I promise I'll do only what I must."

"I should have known you'd be hiding behind your whore's petticoat's," said Bolton as he swaggered into the room in a long, dark cloak. His face was florid, his movements exaggerated, and other men melted to each side to clear his view of Richard. "Though I'm surprised you'd dare show your face at all."

"Where's the boy?" Richard demanded sharply. "That's the only reason you were given permission to enter. Where is he?"

"Here." Bolton swung around long enough to grab the boy from behind him, shoving him forward while he jerked him by the arm, the rest of the room crackling with excitement. "I wouldn't forget to bring your bastard, Blackley."

Luke's expression was blank, his suffering silent, that careful blankness he used to shut out a world that was seldom kind. His new clothes were torn and dirty, and there was a bruise as hard and purple as a plum above one eye that made Richard's anger blaze hotter.

"Let the boy go," he said curtly. "You've no quarrel with him."

"But he's yours, Blackley." Bolton's smile was a lopsided smirk of triumph as he twisted Luke's arm behind his back. "Why should I give him up before you agree to do what I want?"

"Because you've no right to injure an innocent child for sport!" cried Cassia behind him.

"The lady's right, my lord," Richard said slowly, unable to look away from Luke, his breathing ragged as he struggled not to whimper or cry out. "You've hurt the boy. By God, you've hurt my *son*."

Unable to keep still any longer, Richard took a step toward Bolton and Luke, and the guards on either side began to close in as well.

But as soon as Richard moved, Bolton flicked back his cape and swept a long-barreled dueling pistol from his belt. He jerked Luke back against his chest and pressed the barrel against the boy's temple. This time the boy gasped, his narrow shoulders shaking with a quick shudder of terror beneath his torn shirt. Now his wide gray eyes gave Richard only one silent message: *Save me, Father. Save me!*

"There now," Bolton said as everyone in the room froze. "That makes it more interesting, doesn't it?"

"You can't do this!" Cassia cried furiously. "This room is full of witnesses who will swear to what you're doing, that you're willfully risking the life of a boy!"

"What, they'll swear against me in court?" Defiantly Bolton glanced around the room, making eye contact with anyone who'd dare. "They'd do that over the worthless life of a gutter-born wretch, a half-blood bastard?"

"Damnation, Bolton!" demanded Richard. "Why are you doing this? What do you want from me?"

"The one thing you stole from me, Blackley," he answered. "My honor."

Bolton gave a quick jerk of his head, and the man behind him who'd been holding Luke now stepped forward with the other pistol. With a bow, he held the polished butt out for Richard to take, and it felt as if the entire room was holding its breath as one.

"In the park, sir, if you please," the man said as pleasantly as if he were offering tea. "The distance is short, but in the dark that is a wise thing."

"It's against the law, you fools," someone said, and was immediately hushed into silence.

But still Richard shook his head. "I'll not do it. I've never fought a duel, and I won't begin now, even though killing you would benefit the entire world."

"You could try." Bolton laughed softly, not taking Richard's refusal seriously. "More likely I'd kill you first. Or I'll kill your son if you don't. Your choice, Blackley."

Richard looked at the offered pistol, then Luke's pleading face, and back to the gun. He was as sure as he could be that he would aim accurately, pull the trigger first, and win. He was sober, and his arm had always been steady with a pistol, while Bolton was drunk, and at least half mad. He'd win, and save Luke.

But then he thought of how he'd just told Cassia he loved her, and she him, and he thought of the long future they wanted to share together. Winning such a duel against a lord would answer nothing; he'd become a fugitive, forced to flee to Calais to hide for the rest of his life. He'd never see Greenwood again, and the promise of his life with Cassia would crumble like ashes.

"Come along, you bloody coward," Bolton taunted. "Take the gun. Test your courage, if you have any. See how a real *gentleman* satisfies a debt of honor."

A gentleman. That was what he'd always wanted to be, what he thought he'd become by now. Richard had never doubted his courage or his skill, but as for being a gentleman...

He caught the flurried motion from the corner of his eye, from behind him, and then the pair of dice were dancing and clattering across the bare floor between him and Bolton. Startled, Bolton swung the pistol away from Luke toward the dice.

That was all that Richard needed. He lunged forward and struck Bolton's wrist, knocking the gun from his hand and sending it sliding harmlessly across the floor after the dice. Bolton swore, letting Luke go as he turned on Richard, driving his fist hard into Richard's jaw. Richard staggered backward from the impact, but as Bolton came toward him again, Richard caught him under the chin once, then twice. Bolton's head jerked back and his arms flung upward like a broken puppet's before he crashed backward to the floor and lay still.

At once everything seemed to spin into motion, with one guard seizing the other pistol from Bolton's second, while two more were crouched down beside the lord, making sure he didn't rise again. Luke was hanging on to him as if he never wanted to let go, and fiercely Richard hugged him back.

"No more running away, lad, mind?" he said into the boy's hair as he held him. "You stay home with me, where you belong."

And then there was Cassia, hugging him, too, and kissing him and laughing and crying at the same time, which seemed like something only Cassia could or would do.

"Oh, yes, I will," she said between the kisses. "I will!"

"Will what?" he asked back, not wanting to be distracted from kissing her.

"Will marry you," she said, and laughed again at having confused him. "I *will* marry you, and I *do* love you!"

"Well, good," he said, and smiled, knowing that everything now *would* be good. "Those dice—"

"Were in my pocket," she said. "Oh, Richard, you were being so brave and strong that I knew I had to do something to help."

His smile wobbled, though he wasn't sure if it was from being punched, or from realizing Cassia, his Cassia, had most likely saved his life. "I'm glad you did, sweetheart."

"Well, yes," she said, and managed to smile back through her tears. "Sometimes, even at Penny House, it's best to leave nothing to chance."

Epilogue

❦

Later that same summer…

No one in St. James Street could recall a wedding quite like it.

For three nights, Penny House was closed to its members, the lights over the hazard table unlit and the card tables quiet as the Penny sisters and their staff devoted all their energies toward the wedding preparations. Even though the Season was nearly done, the writers for the scandal sheets published endless speculation about who was invited and who wasn't, the lace on the bride's gown and the groom's gift to her, and the scandalous notion of the groom's recently discovered illegitimate son acting as his best man. There was even a fantastic rumor, stubborn but unsubstantiated, that the bride's headdress included curls of wood from a carpenter's lathe, dipped in silver and gold. But only those inside the house knew for sure, and they weren't telling.

There were, of course, those spoilsports who said the wedding should not matter, that neither Miss Penny nor Mr. Blackley were people of consequence or breeding. But they were undoubtedly People of Fashion, the people who set the styles instead of following them, and London couldn't get enough of the tales of how they met and how they very nearly didn't have the chance to marry at all.

But for the fortunate guests who crowded into Penny House's front parlor for the wedding, it wasn't the gown, the flowers, the jewels, or the bride's two beautiful sisters beside her, that they remembered first. It was instead the rare love that the bride and bridegroom displayed for each other, the devotion that seemed to glow as bright as any flame from them as they said their vows.

And when at last the minister, an old friend of the bride's late father, had declared them inseparably bound, the kiss they exchanged was hot enough, wanton enough, to make the lady guests sigh and the men groan, and all wish they'd a share of such passion in their own lives.

But though the celebration that followed lasted far into the night, the newlywed couple escaped early in a carriage festooned with garlands of summer flowers, eager to be on their way back to Greenwood Hall.

"I'm not sure how wise it was to marry in a gaming club, Richard," Cassia Penny Blackley said as she lolled across her new husband's lap, then paused to kiss him again with languid, leisurely wantonness. "What are the odds of us having a happy marriage, I wonder?"

"Oh, so much in our favor that I cannot even calculate it, love," he said, idly pulling the pins from her hair so the copper curls spilled freely over her shoulders. "So great that not even the most foolish gamester would dare wager against us."

"Oh, I like the odds just fine." She grinned up at him, beginning to unbutton his waistcoat. "And I should venture that the odds of us not waiting until we reached Greenwood before we, ah, consummate this union are much to our advantage, too?"

"As a wild guess," he said, slipping his hand inside her bodice, "I should have to agree."

She laughed as they kissed, their joy and love vibrating between them. "Oh, Richard, what splendid good luck it was that brought you into my life!"

"The very best luck in the world," he agreed as he pulled down the curtain in the carriage window. "And that is why, sometimes, it's best to leave everything to chance."

* * * * *

THE STEEPWOOD

Scandals

Regency drama, intrigue, mischief...
and marriage

VOLUME SIX

The Guardian's Dilemma by Gail Whitiker

In order to save his young stepsister from a fortune-
hunter, Oliver Brandon places her in a ladies' academy.
However, he realises that the schoolmistress may not be
as respectable as she appears...

❧

Lord Exmouth's Intentions by Anne Ashley

Vicar's daughter Robina Perceval has relished her season
in Town, but what of Daniel, Lord Exmouth?
A widower, with two daughters to raise, it would
appear that he's in search of a wife.

On sale 6th April 2007

Available at WHSmith, Tesco, ASDA,
and all good bookshops

A young woman disappears.
A husband is suspected of murder.
Stirring times for all the neighbourhood in

THE STEEPWOOD

Scandals

Volume 5 – March 2007
Counterfeit Earl by Anne Herries
The Captain's Return by Elizabeth Bailey

Volume 6 – April 2007
The Guardian's Dilemma by Gail Whitiker
Lord Exmouth's Intentions by Anne Ashley

Volume 7 – May 2007
Mr Rushford's Honour by Meg Alexander
An Unlikely Suitor by Nicola Cornick

Volume 8 – June 2007
An Inescapable Match by Sylvia Andrew
The Missing Marchioness by Paula Marshall

2 FREE

BOOKS AND A SURPRISE GIFT!

We would like to take this opportunity to thank you for reading this Mills & Boon® book by offering you the chance to take TWO more specially selected titles from the Historical Romance™ series absolutely FREE! We're also making this offer to introduce you to the benefits of the Mills & Boon® Reader Service™—

- ★ **FREE home delivery**
- ★ **FREE gifts and competitions**
- ★ **FREE monthly Newsletter**
- ★ **Exclusive Reader Service offers**
- ★ **Books available before they're in the shops**

Accepting these FREE books and gift places you under no obligation to buy, you may cancel at any time, even after receiving your free shipment. Simply complete your details below and return the entire page to the address below. You don't even need a stamp!

YES! Please send me 2 free Historical Romance books and a surprise gift. I understand that unless you hear from me, I will receive 4 superb new titles every month for just £3.69 each, postage and packing free. I am under no obligation to purchase any books and may cancel my subscription at any time. The free books and gift will be mine to keep in any case.

H7ZED

Ms/Mrs/Miss/Mr ....Initials ....

BLOCK CAPITALS PLEASE

Surname ....

Address ....

....

....Postcode......................................

Send this whole page to:
UK: FREEPOST CN81, Croydon, CR9 3WZ